VISIONS OF YOU

VISIONS
of You

Calypso Key
SERIES

VISIONS OF YOU

Calypso Key Series

ERIN BROCKUS

GREEN SAGE
PRESS

Chapter One

Gabe

WADS of gum stuck to the ceiling, but at least they looked solidly in place. Disgusting but not unexpected, given where I was. Turning my eyes from the gross, multicolored display, I held my breath, hoping the silence would last this time. The thin mattress was lumpy underneath my butt, and the cot was too short for my rangy frame. Not about to rest my head against the nasty pillow, I sat with my back against the cement wall. Staring up at the light-green ceiling and its multitude of cracks, I tried to ignore the gum.

"Six bottles of beer on the wall, six bottles of beer..." sang the guy in an off-key, warbling voice, and I resisted the urge to groan out loud, instead exhaling as I rubbed both hands over my very pronounced scruff. My rough fingers caught on the stubble—five o'clock was over twelve hours ago.

Before I'd made an idiot of myself and ended up here.

The drunk in the next cell over continued his song, and I took solace in the fact that the number of beers was nearing the end. And there was a certain poetic justice to being subjected to the man's irritating rendition—I was in jail, after all.

Not a place to enjoy oneself.

But I was counting down the minutes now, and my sister was on her way to get me out of here. A short time ago, Deputy Marvin Crutchfield had allowed me my one phone call, after explaining my bail amount had been set and I'd be free to go as soon as bond had been posted.

God, my first night back home in Calypso Key, and I spent it in a jail cell.

I almost snorted at the ridiculousness of it but caught myself in time—that would hurt my bruised ribs. One might even be cracked. Off-Key and I weren't the only two spending the night. Ben Coleridge was here too. At the opposite end of the cellblock as me. I guess the cops figured we needed to be kept far apart, even in jail.

But everyone was quiet, probably just waiting for that guy to finish his song and shut up. Like I was. As the drunk reached the proverbial final bottle of beer, I inhaled again. My lungs got tighter and tighter, then finally I expelled the held breath, relaxing in the blessed silence filling the Marathon City Jail.

"Ninety-nine bottles of beer on the wall, ninety-nine—"

A round of swearing, shouting, and hands clanging against bars greeted this encore performance, and I hissed a sigh through my teeth. Grimacing, I pressed my hand against my sore ribs.

"Jethro, if you don't shut your goddamn trap, I'm gonna strangle you through these bars."

That was Ben, and I wasn't surprised he knew the singer. No doubt he was more familiar with jail cells than I was. Which I probably should have remembered last night.

"You can't reach me," came the slightly slurred response. "You got arms like one of those dinosaurs—bronta, bronta, brontysaurus."

Someone else laughed. "T. rex has the little arms, you idiot."

Maia, hurry up.

I hadn't enjoyed making that phone call to my little sister. Eight years younger than me, she was twenty-eight and pregnant with her first child. But she'd always be my little sister. However, my only other choices had been our dad—hell no—or our brother, Evan. Who would have delighted in rubbing my face in this. So Maia it was.

The sound of a key turning in the metal door at the end of the cell block brought the conversation over dinosaurs and terrible songs to an end. Everyone paid attention as the heavy door swung open.

I smiled grimly.

Ask not for whom the bell tolls...

Heavy steps echoed through the cells as the person treaded along the center aisle. They stopped before my cell.

"Gabriel Markham?" Deputy Marvin Crutchfield asked, as if he hadn't personally escorted me to make my phone call less than an hour prior, and as if we hadn't gone to school together until we graduated.

I rubbed my tired eyes and turned an irritated stare to him. "No, I'm the tooth fairy, dumbass."

Marvin unclipped a ring of keys and rifled through them but didn't react to my words. Dressed in a tan button-down shirt and dark-brown slacks, a silver star-shaped badge was pinned to his breast. His clean-shaven face frowned at me as he inserted a large silver key and unlocked my cell. "Your bond has been posted, so you're free to go."

That was music to my ears, so I swung my legs off the

cot and pushed to my feet. I still wore work boots. I wasn't about to go shoeless in this place, and after the long night, my jeans and T-shirt were more than a little rumpled. I crossed the cell and pulled the door all the way open as Marvin backed up a step.

He was only five-foot-nine or so and had to crane his neck back to stare me in the eye. "Let's go. You first."

I nodded and stepped out of the cell, walking down the aisle as the singer started his tune again from the top. With Marvin there, no one challenged him.

When I walked by Ben Coleridge's cell, he stood just behind the locked door, hands on his hips. His light hair was disheveled, and his shirt was half untucked. I gave him a hard stare and he met it—with one eye anyway. Satisfaction filled me at the impressive shiner he sported on his right eye, which was completely swollen shut. A purple bruise adorned the left side of his mouth and dried blood covered his cracked lips.

I turned my head as I passed by, pinning him with my gaze until he dropped his eyes. Turning around, he walked to his cot. Facing forward again, I breathed a long sigh, relieved our stupid confrontation was over. Marvin unlocked the metal door and ushered me out of the cell block and into the local police precinct with its white walls and non-descript tile floor. At seven in the morning, the open room was mostly silent.

Maia stood stiffly across the room, both arms tightly crossed over her chest. Her dark hair was up in a messy bun, and her T-shirt was almost as rumpled as mine. She'd hurried to get here. Shame caused my stomach to plummet that she'd had to experience this. As she met my gaze, her eyes flickered up and down my body, presumably searching for injuries.

Marvin swooped over to a desk and picked up a bulging, sealed manila envelope and handed it to me. "Here are your personal belongings. Everything you had on you when we brought you in last night."

I accepted the envelope, feeling my wallet and keys inside. We continued across the room of desks to stop before my sister. She was tall and had the same dark hair and eyes I did—the Markham signature.

Marvin nodded at both of us. "We'll be in touch if Ben insists on filing assault charges. Personally, I think it's best for all of us if he just drops it, but he's not known for his calm, calculating mind, now is he?"

Marvin's last words had been directed straight at me.

"Look," I said, not in the mood to be conciliatory. "I'm not exactly proud of this. But if Ben wants another fight, I'll give it to him."

The deputy snorted. "Well, I'll see if I can talk him out of it. A night with Jethro singing his fool head off might have cooled him off a little."

I sighed. "Thanks, Marvin. Let me know."

We exchanged nods, then I crossed the aisle to stand before my sister. "Thanks for coming. Let's get out of here."

Her nod was slow, and she searched my face, her forehead deeply lined.

Yeah, I can't believe it either.

I pushed through the glass door into a beautiful Florida Keys morning and squeezed my sore, itchy eyes shut as the sun warmed my face. When I opened them, Maia had already marched ahead, her shoulders squared. She pointed her key fob at her late-model SUV and its lights beeped.

I slid into the passenger seat and belted in. "My car is at Salty's. You can drop me off there and I'll drive home."

Maia pushed the start button and whipped her head to

me. "Let me see if I got this straight. You went to Salty's last night and got drunk. Then you got in a bar fight with Ben Coleridge and were *arrested?*"

"Marvin gave you the scoop, huh?"

"Yeah," she replied in the same tight voice, backing out of the stall. "When I posted your bond, Gabe."

I rubbed my face. "It wasn't my finest moment. I'd had a couple of beers, but I wasn't drunk. Just in a piss-poor mood. Then Ben showed up and just made it worse. That guy has always had a talent for pushing my buttons."

The police station was off the main drag in Marathon and Maia headed back toward the highway. "You don't have a mark on your face. Did he even hit you?"

I prodded my midsection and grimaced. "Yeah. He got a couple good shots in my ribs. But I won the fight."

Maia barked a laugh. "Well, thank God! After all, that's the most important thing."

I couldn't help smiling, though I could hardly blame her for being pissed at me. "With any luck, Ben won't press charges, and this will all go away." None of the Coleridges were worth wasting time over, let alone a whole night in jail.

Nothing but turquoise water lay beneath us as we traversed Seven Mile Bridge. Early morning sunlight sparkled on the water, boats already zooming under the bridge.

"I sure hope so, Gabe. Did you just leave Hailey all alone last night?"

"No!" I whipped my head toward Maia, tightening my jaw. "Nona had already made up a room for her in the Big House, and she wanted to try it out last night. That was the only reason I went to Salty's in the first place." Nona was our grandmother and the only mother most of us had ever known.

Except for me. I still remembered.

"And how exactly are you planning on telling your eight-year-old daughter that Daddy spent the night in jail?"

"I'm not. Let's keep the whole thing between us, all right?"

"Between us?" Maia's eyes opened wide, and she laughed again. "You got in a bar fight at the local tavern! Everyone in both Calypso Key and Dove Key probably knows by now."

I breathed a heavy sigh as we pulled off Highway One and headed south. "Yeah, I know. Can you stay quiet for now? At least until I know what I'm facing?"

Tapping her index finger on the wheel, her face became calculating, and she shot me a quick glance. "Okay. I'll keep my mouth shut. For a price."

I groaned. "What?"

"The Barn. You move out as soon as we get back."

I scowled at her. "Seriously? You're uprooting me and your *niece* on our second day?"

Maia lifted a neat brow, humor glinting in her eyes now. "Maybe you should have thought about that before you entered the O.K. Corral last night."

I didn't reply and just stared at her. She gave me a hard look before turning back to the road, remaining silent too. Maia and I might be the oldest and youngest of our siblings, but we were cut from the same cloth. She wasn't going to give in. And she had bailed me out of jail.

"Fine," I said begrudgingly. "Your friend can have the Barn apartment. But I'm keeping the shop. I plan to make furniture for the resort."

Now that Maia had gotten her way, she inclined her head regally. "Agreed. This will be better anyway. You and Hailey will be closer to Wyatt and me, not to mention Dad and Evan. And with April in the Barn apartment, she'll be near the dive shop. I'll even help you move today, helpful sister that I am."

I grunted and crossed my arms.

She glanced at the dashboard clock and frowned as we drove over the short bridge that connected Big Pine Key to Dove Key. We continued down Calypso Causeway, the main street of the island. "April texted yesterday and said she'd be here early, so I'll need to duck out and get her settled in a guest cottage. Meanwhile, we need you and Hailey out ASAP so I can get her apartment cleaned today."

The sun's glare was killing my eyes, but my shades were in my car. Hopefully. "It's not her apartment. It's mine. I'm just letting her use it."

Maia broke into musical laughter. "Gabe—it's hers. And don't be a grumpy jerk to her about it, okay? It's not her fault you're an irresponsible idiot."

I glowered at my sister but couldn't deny the accusation. At least when a Coleridge was involved. But she just gave me an opening to shoot back. I glanced at her stomach. "Well, I'm not the only irresponsible one, am I? The only reason she's here as our new divemaster is because you and your boyfriend don't know how birth control works."

Maia's happy expression fell, which only made me feel even more like an asshole. But I was in too shitty a mood to be conciliatory. She pulled into the parking lot of a dingy local hangout known as Salty's. I breathed a relieved sigh at the sight of my Mercedes convertible sitting unharmed in one corner of the gravel lot.

"Wyatt isn't my boyfriend—he's my husband. Something else you're going to have to get used to."

"That would be easier if I'd been invited to the wedding."

"It was very spur of the moment! And I did invite you." She stopped next to my car.

Now it was my turn to snort. "Spur of the moment because it was a shotgun wedding. It wasn't exactly easy to rearrange my life so I could move down here with Hailey, you know."

Maia's expression softened as she reached out to take my hand. "I know it wasn't. Thanks, big brother. I'm glad you're here. We all are."

I turned my hand and interlaced my fingers with hers. I wasn't at all sure *I* was glad to be back home. But when Dad had called and said he needed my help, refusing wasn't an option. I had to find a way. "Thanks, little sister. And thanks for being here for me today."

As I crossed to my car, I waved goodbye to Maia and dug my keys out of the large manila envelope. Coffee and a shower would be my first order of business before I vacated the apartment I'd only moved into yesterday. Because of family.

Nothing was more important to me than family. Hailey might be at the top of that list, but Dad and Calypso Key weren't far behind. And Maia needed me too, even if she wouldn't admit it.

For better or for worse, I was back home again.

Chapter Two

April

I GLANCED in the rearview mirror, trying to memorize the wonder now falling behind me. Seven Mile Bridge spanned the distance between Marathon and Big Pine Key, soaring over the expanse of aquamarine water beneath. Nothing but seven solid miles of ocean and the occasional small island lay on either side of storied Highway One.

Amazing.

Though I was sad to leave the famous bridge behind, the end of the fabled structure couldn't squelch my excitement. I spared one last glance at the scene around me—a rare experience worth the hype.

My driver's window was down, and my elbow rested on the ledge as I enjoyed the warm breeze drifting in. I was still getting used to my two-year-old Honda CR-V. I'd sold my old car before leaving St. Croix—it was easier to just buy a new one than mess with the hassle of shipping it.

A flutter rippled through me as I exited the highway and turned south.

Toward my new home.

Maia had called a few days previously and told me to take my time traveling down the Keys, and to enjoy the sites and the diving. I'd stayed in Key Largo for two days to dive some of the famous wrecks there, finding them plenty advanced for anyone's taste. I'd been buddied up with a man who wasn't quite up to the challenging conditions, and I'd spent as much time watching out for him as enjoying the enormous shipwrecks. But that was all in a day's work for me and didn't detract from the experience.

I passed a large flashing sign alerting drivers to watch out for Key deer and slowed down. I craned my neck around eagerly but didn't see any of the tiny Lower Keys inhabitants. A smile rose on my face as I turned onto a road named Calypso Causeway, then crossed over a bridge to Dove Key. The smile wasn't just due to my new surroundings. It was also the realization that for the first time in a very long while, I was happy.

I had a whole new life to start.

I'd left everything behind in St. Croix, including my emotional baggage and bruised heart. I'd always looked on the bright side, and around a year ago realized that facet of me was being inexorably worn down. A new job as a divemaster at Calypso Key Resort was exactly what I needed.

Along with a self-induced sabbatical from men. I'd proven I was lousy at picking them, so romance was officially off the table for me.

And that was tremendously freeing.

Dove Key was a decently sized island and town, though it only had two main streets, intersecting at the single traffic light. As I passed a ramshackle tavern called Salty's, a long metal building stretched in the distance along a bluff to my left. A sign alongside the road pointed toward it, proclaiming the long structure the Conch Republic Brewpub.

But exploring could wait. I continued on Calypso Causeway and the buildings thinned out, a fringe of scrubby brush and mangroves replacing them eventually. I traveled over a short bridge connecting the island to its smaller, southern neighbor, Calypso Key. The paved road rose in a gentle climb, and I could barely glimpse a sizeable multi-story house, screened by trees and brush, along a sheer bluff to my left. I reached the crest of the hill and the remainder of the island spread out before me to the south. I continued slowly rolling down the asphalt road.

Most of the western half was undeveloped, a large expanse of marsh and mangrove wetlands. Along the eastern side of the key, a road branched off toward the house and several other nearby buildings. After passing a grassy meadow decorated by several flame trees, a long two-story building appeared on my left. Two large sliding doors were open, and I spied machinery inside as I drove by.

The road ended in two parking lots, a sand one facing east and a larger, neatly paved one on my right. Directly ahead lay an airy, one-story white building. Maia had sent a text with preliminary instructions, so I pulled into the sandlot and parked next to several other employee vehicles. Maia Markham and I had recently reconnected after meeting six years ago. When she'd offered me a position at her family's resort, the opportunity was too good to pass up. The position became even more enticing after she arranged living quarters for me too.

Excitement quickened my pulse as I turned off the engine and studied a protected canal with several buildings behind it. A red flag with a diagonal white stripe running through it flew from the top of the largest building. The entire area was neat and clean, which pleased me since I was staring at my new domain.

The dive operation.

Grabbing my phone out of my purse, I sent Maia a text, letting her know I'd arrived.

Then I studied the resort around me. A lawn of neat green grass lay behind the parking lot, surrounding the long structure housing the machinery. A sand path led from the buildings on the bluff and passed near the long building. More flame trees threw shade over the area and farther to the south, I spotted a row of palm trees.

The white building where the road ended was of considerable size. I assumed it was the lobby and other resort facilities. My text tone pinged, and I grabbed my phone.

> Maia: Welcome! I'll meet you in the lobby in a couple minutes.

After texting back a thumbs-up, I took a deep breath and exited the car.

Let's get this show going.

I crossed the parking lot and climbed a short flight of steps onto a covered porch. Twin doors painted a soft blue were propped open, and I entered a bright, breezy room cooled by ceiling fans. A long wooden counter lay directly across from me. It was staffed by a woman currently helping guests, and several blue couches and armchairs were spaced around the room. Soft music played from hidden speakers, and the lobby exuded a cozy, old-school tropical vibe. Several framed pictures drew my eye, and I crossed a weathered but clean wooden floor, the boards squeaking under my sandals.

Three color prints were prominently displayed, and I

immediately recognized Maia, who smiled at the camera, her brunette hair pulled into a ponytail. *Maia Markham-Taylor, Lead Divemaster* read a small placard beneath. I smiled at her new name—she had been married less than two months. In the picture next to Maia's, a man with somewhat lighter hair and a full, bushy beard smiled at me. Evan Markham was the general manager. A third, larger picture was centered above both of an older man. He had Maia's eyes and darker hair with a liberal amount of gray, but he carried an obvious resemblance to both siblings. The placard read Warren Markham, Owner.

The sound of footsteps trotting up the stairs reached me. "April! You're here!"

I spun around, my blond braid swishing to one side, and broke into a grin as Maia ran toward me. I held out my arms and we hugged. She was taller and nearly knocked me back.

"Sorry it took me so long, but I'm here at last."

Maia pulled back and patted my arms. "Don't worry about it. You couldn't have predicted an earthquake. Was everything okay when you left?"

My departure from St. Croix had been delayed several weeks due to damage caused by an earthquake. My former employer had been injured in the quake and I couldn't very well take off and leave them—him—in a lurch when he'd been unable to work.

Employer. That's a good one. But men are in the past. Especially ones in love with someone else.

I smiled at Maia. "Yes. The island is more or less recovered, and Alex is back to work. Half Moon Bay Resort needed some repairs, but they're back on their feet now. And I'm extremely excited to be here."

Maia's expression sharpened, but she didn't press the point. She knew about the torch I'd carried for Alex Monroe for an embarrassing number of years, a romance that had only been on my side. And once he'd met the woman who was now his wife, I'd done my best to bury my feelings and find someone else.

Which had been another disaster.

I turned my mind back to the woman in front of me. "Congratulations! On both the baby and the wedding."

She grinned. "Thanks. It hasn't been dull lately. Today's a little hectic—I'm helping my brother Gabe, and your apartment is being cleaned. We'll put you up in a guest cottage tonight, then you can move in tomorrow. Enjoy the experience. Beachfront views aren't part of the deal, I'm afraid."

"I can't believe you're letting me use an apartment! Thanks for hiring me, Maia." Even if mice infested my apartment, I wasn't about to complain, no matter how cramped or old it was.

We walked toward the parking lot so I could collect my suitcases. "I'm glad you're here," Maia said. "It'll be nice to have another woman around. I'm surrounded by men. There's way too much testosterone around here."

I assumed she meant her husband and family, and figured I'd get to know them all in time. I lugged my two suitcases out of the back of my SUV and Maia stared at them, both brows halfway up her forehead. "You only brought two bags?"

"My dive gear is in a duffel in the back seat, but I figured I'd leave it there for now."

"Yeah, take today off and just relax. You want to tag along on a dive tomorrow and get the lay of the land?"

"That sounds perfect."

She grabbed one of my suitcases and rolled it down a concrete path and around the lobby. We passed a casual open-air restaurant and pool area. Reggae beats thumped from a nearby bar. Maia pointed with her head at the airy restaurant, where several groups were eating lunch. "This is Dorado, our casual restaurant. Staff eat in the kitchen. Our fine dining restaurant, Orchid, is on the western side of the island and gets the great sunsets."

Everything was spotlessly clean and casually tropical, though not particularly modern or luxurious. We skirted a free-form resort pool and neared the palm trees I'd glimpsed earlier. A row of ten cinderblock cottages, all painted light blue, were spaced between the palms and sat on a white sand beach.

The Caribbean Sea washed gently on the shore and a soft breeze blew a lock of hair that had escaped my braid across my face. I tucked it behind my ear as Maia led me toward a cottage.

"This is beautiful!" I said, giving myself whiplash as I took in the area. "I had no idea you had such a big beach."

"We're very lucky. Beaches are rare in the Keys, let alone one this big. It stretches all along the southern part of the island. There are ten beach cottages, all one-bedroom units. You're in number eight."

She lifted my suitcase up a short flight of stairs onto a screened, covered porch and I followed. Producing a key from her pocket, Maia unlocked the front door, and we entered an open, very stuffy room. She picked up a remote from the coffee table and pointed it at a modular air conditioning unit on the wall. It whirred to life after she pushed a button. "It'll cool down quickly in here. Don't worry."

She left my suitcase next to a king-sized bed covered with a pale blue comforter. A blue sofa and love seat lay across the room.

Maia turned to me. "The bathroom is in the back, and

feel free to use anything you want from the minibar. I need to get back to my brother, so I'll leave you to relax this afternoon. There's a hammock on the porch, and I imagine you're ready to swing in the breeze a little."

We both laughed and I nodded. "I'll keep the unpacking to a minimum since I'll be moving tomorrow."

"I'll stop by later, okay? I'm sorry I'm not more available —we've had a little family drama this morning."

My smile fell, wondering about the comments regarding her brother. Was she referring to the one whose picture I saw? I knew she had more than one brother. "Nothing serious, I hope?"

Maia waved at me casually. "Not really, and nothing I'm going to bore you with when you've just arrived." She crossed the room and halted at the front door. "All of us are glad to have you, April. Welcome to Calypso Key!"

After a final hug, she exited and left me alone. I glanced around the room. Like the restaurant I'd glimpsed, it was clean and comfortable, though more on the modest side than luxurious. Though it was undoubtedly posher than what I'd be moving into tomorrow.

I smiled. "My *free* apartment. I'm damn lucky and I know it. I can't wait until tomorrow."

Digging a paperback out of my purse, I stepped onto the shady porch and climbed into the hammock. Settling in, I read as a warm tropical breeze gently blew me back and forth.

Chapter Three

Gabe

I GLANCED around the bedroom one final time to make sure I hadn't left anything. The bedroom I hadn't even slept in last night. My eye fell on the king-sized bed with its hand-carved teak headboard, and I shook my head. The bed was the best piece of furniture I'd ever made, but it was much too big and heavy to move into the new cottage. I'd installed it on my last visit home but had never used the damn thing. And now I never would.

"Hope you enjoy it, April," I muttered, scowling at the empty room before heading downstairs. The wooden staircase emptied into an open room, painted white with natural wooden floors and trim. I nodded to Lucinda, already at work cleaning with her full arsenal. Hailey and I always used this apartment when we visited, so I was more than a little pissed about having to vacate it. Housekeeping had only performed a cursory cleaning before I arrived yesterday with Hailey.

Apparently, the new divemaster warranted a more thorough approach.

The one good thing to come from our hasty move was that the physical labor eased my sore body, and I'd concluded I didn't have any cracked ribs after all. With a deep sigh, I exited through the back door and onto a cozy covered patio with a flagstone floor. It faced east and I loved to drink my morning coffee as I watched the pure blue Caribbean Sea. My new cottage also had a sunrise-facing patio, but this one was more like home to me. A soft meow interrupted my musings. I turned as a large gray-and-white tabby stood from where he snoozed on a couch.

I ambled over to him and scratched his ears. He head-butted my hand and purred, making me smile. Then, with resolve, I scooped up the cat in my arms and walked off the patio. "Hemingway, you're coming with me."

He was my cat, dammit.

I walked along the side of the two-story apartment, which was attached to a large shop. We referred to the combination building as the Barn. We'd never kept animals in it, though, just miscellaneous landscaping equipment for the resort.

And my woodworking tools. I had firmly put my foot down about that, and Maia agreed April likely wouldn't need anything in the shop. I was giving up enough.

A sand path led in front of the Barn, ascending at a comfortable slope to the bluff at the northeastern edge of the island. As I walked along it, my back pocket vibrated. I transferred Hemingway to one arm as I dug out my phone. The Caller ID indicated it was Marvin Crutchfield, so I figured I'd better answer it.

He got right to the point. "Ben Coleridge dropped the

charges. I think his hangover was bad enough that he just wanted to go home and forget what happened."

Relief flooded through me, tension draining from my bones. "So is this the end of the whole thing?"

"Yeah. You don't have any priors, so there's nothing pending. Try to stay out of bar fights, though, okay?"

I ran a hand through my stiff hair. With the rush to clear out of the Barn, I hadn't gotten either my shower or change of clothes yet. "I will. Ben just pissed me off last night."

"He pisses a lot of people off, Gabe. Doesn't mean you needed to beat the hell out of the man."

"I was in a bad mood and my fuse was shorter than normal. It won't happen again. Thanks, Marvin."

"You're welcome. And welcome home."

I ended the call and shook my head as I glanced around the peaceful island. A night in jail was not how I had expected my homecoming to go.

After crossing the grassy field studded with orange blossomed flame trees, I came upon a row of three cottages. The Big House where we'd all grown up soared in the distance, commanding an incredible view. The three cottages were identical, and all constructed of stone, cinderblocks, and timber. Solid bones that had withstood over a century of storms.

I angled toward the middle cottage, Hemingway purring happily in my arms. The front door was solid mahogany, and I frowned as the hinges screeched upon opening it. Voices drifted to me from the kitchen at the back of the cottage. I hardly spared a glance at the living room dominated by a stone fireplace in one corner and furnished with two couches and several armchairs—earlier creations of mine.

As I entered the bright, sunny kitchen, my daughter

broke into laughter, easing my grouchy mood and bringing a smile to my face. She sat at a bar stool snugged up to the counter, and my father stood on the other side, sliding a glass of lemonade toward her. Hailey was eight, a happy, loquacious child who wasn't afraid to strike up a conversation with anyone.

Basically, the opposite of me.

She had been nearly blonde for the first several years of her life, but her hair was darkening now and becoming more Markham-like, which pleased me. The less she looked like my ex-wife, the better.

She saw me in the entryway and squealed. "Hemingway!" Launching herself off the stool, she bounded across the tile floor and took the cat from me. He went happily enough, settling in her arms.

I lifted her and parked her back on her stool. "Yeah, figures you're only interested in the cat."

Hailey smiled up at me. "I'm glad to see you too, Dad. Does this mean Hemingway is moving into this cottage with us?"

"One hundred percent."

"I was surprised to hear you two are moving in here, instead of the Barn," Dad said, pouring two more glasses of lemonade from a pitcher. He slid one to me and I nodded my thanks. Dad and I were nearly the same height, with the same dark-brown hair and eyes. My whole life, everyone had exclaimed about our resemblance, and it became more obvious as I grew older. But that was comforting. In his early sixties, Dad remained fit and strong.

I took a long drink of the sweet, cold liquid. "Maia wants the Barn for her friend, and I'm being chivalrous."

Hailey finished her lemonade as she panned her eyes

around the room. "This cottage is brighter than the barn. I like it, though my room is pretty bare."

I leaned down to look her in the eye. "We'll decorate it together. However you want—this is your home now and I want you to be happy."

She smiled as she set her glass down. "I know. I love it here."

"And I couldn't be happier to have my favorite granddaughter around all the time," Dad said.

Hailey's face lit up. "I might not be your only granddaughter soon! When is Maia's baby due?"

"Not for a while yet," he replied. "August."

She frowned. "Six months, huh? Guess I'll have to wait."

I hadn't had a chance to talk to Maia's new husband yet, but it was high on my list. I'd heard of Wyatt Taylor—he'd been a friend of my brother Evan's. But he was family now, not to mention the father of my little sister's baby. I needed to get the measure of the man. Soon.

Dad raised both brows as he stared at Hailey. "I have some news that might interest you. Felicia is cooking at the Big House this week, and I know for a fact she made her pineapple coffee cake this morning after you left with your dad. You want to run up and have some?"

Hailey was already off her stool before he finished, dumping Hemingway unceremoniously on the floor. "I'm outta here. See you guys later!"

I laughed as I watched her run out the front door. Upon returning that morning, I'd run up to the Big House right away to make sure she was okay. Then breathed a huge sigh that she had no idea I hadn't been around last night. She sat in the kitchen eating French toast. I collected her and took her down to the Barn to inform her of our move but wasn't about to admit I'd been in jail.

Now, Dad leaned back against the counter and bounced his eyes all over me, his forehead creasing. "You look a little rough around the edges. I know you like the stubble-beard look, but that doesn't explain the rumpled clothes or blood-shot eyes. You all right?"

I rubbed my palms over my itchy eyes, then moved to the fridge. I couldn't keep this from him, though his question confirmed Maia had held up her end of the bargain. A six-pack of Conch Republic IPA sat inside the stocked fridge, and I removed two. I slid one can over to him. "Not exactly. You might want a beer for this, Dad."

Several minutes later, his forehead was even more lined as he stared at me. He snapped his open mouth shut. "Well, thank God Ben is dropping the charges."

"Yeah. It wasn't my finest moment. I just kind of snapped."

Dad stared at me hard. "Are you that unhappy about moving back here?"

I sighed. This was hard to explain. "No, and it's very important to me to get Hailey away from big city Miami. Even if it does mean uprooting her and putting her in a new school. But this isn't exactly a happy homecoming either. Evan shot glares at me yesterday, Maia's life is completely upside down, and I need to brainstorm about how to turn the resort around. *And* I've been kicked out of the Barn."

Hemingway meowed at my feet, and Dad and I both smiled.

I pointed to the cat. "He got kicked out too. I brought him with me."

The smile lingered on Dad's face. "I'm sure he'd rather be with the two of you."

"Hopefully. He's always considered the Barn his turf."

"It means the world to me that you moved back here," Dad said. "I haven't been doing a great job with the finances, and it's been hard to admit that."

"I'm glad you called me, Dad. I just need a good night's sleep," I said with a tired smile. "There's no way I'd sit by and let this place—or you—suffer without helping. We'll get things straightened out."

Dad came over and clapped my shoulder. "Give it some time, Son. You don't have to eat the elephant in one day."

THE NEXT MORNING, I dropped Hailey off at school personally. The bus would make a stop at Calypso Key, but I wanted to drive her on the first day. I needed to know she got there safe and sound. After returning, I strolled down the hill, at last freshly showered and wearing clean jeans and a work shirt. It was after 8:oo a.m. and my quarry should be at work by now.

After passing by the canal where our boats were tied up, I angled away toward a brick lane stretching between two one-story buildings. The dive shop lay on my right, and I passed Maia's butterfly bush, an explosion of lavender and dark-purple blooms on one corner. Across from the dive shop, the gear storage and compressor rooms butted up against the canal.

The door to the gear room was wide open and I stepped through the doorway. A man several inches shorter faced away at the end of the room, slinging a scuba buoyancy compensation device over one shoulder.

"Good morning," I said, leaning against the jamb.

He froze, then slowly turned around. When I saw

Wyatt's face, I recognized him from his days hanging around Evan, though now he was in his early thirties. His brown hair was short and neat, and he was clean-shaven. He wore the typical dive uniform of a resort staff T-shirt and board shorts.

He looked me straight in the eye. "Morning, Gabe. Welcome home. I trust you had a better night's sleep?"

I narrowed my eyes and took a big step forward.

Wyatt straightened but held his ground.

We stared at each other, neither giving way, though a pulse throbbed in his temple. I thought about closing the distance further, but after the disaster with Ben Coleridge, the last thing I needed was another pissing match. I was here to learn more about my new brother-in-law, nothing more. I nodded. "Much better, even though Maia changed my living arrangements."

A tiny smile raised the corners of his mouth. "She loves the idea of having you and Hailey next door, believe it or not."

I relaxed my stance but kept my face even. "That's good because we're not going anywhere. Congratulations on your marriage and impending fatherhood."

The air became charged between us once again.

And again, Wyatt met my hard stare without backing down. "Thank you. Maia and I didn't plan this, but we're both looking forward to the baby's arrival. I intend to be the best father possible... and the best husband."

I gave him a slow nod, accepting his statement and impressed that he refused to be intimidated. "I'm glad to hear that, Wyatt. Because if you're not, you're going to answer to me." Then I turned around and walked out of the gear room.

Yeah, I could be an asshole when I wanted to be, but I

wasn't about to buddy up to the guy who knocked up my little sister. He'd have to earn my respect.

I continued down the brick pathway but passed by the glass door leading into the dive shop. Maia had told me April would be getting her dive orientation this morning. But after having my home usurped, I wasn't in any rush to meet her. I stopped behind the building, where a covered patio overlooked a glade of gumbo limbo trees with picnic tables scattered beneath. The fish-cleaning station and shack sat at the end of the clearing, near the canal entrance. This early, no divers or anglers rested at the tables, and I had the place to myself.

I leaned against the white cinderblock wall of the dive shop, the concrete warming my skin through my shirt. I slid my foot up the wall and relaxed with one leg bent as I surveyed our dive operation. I hadn't been over the detailed financials of the resort yet, but I wasn't at all sure hiring an additional divemaster was a good idea. Maia might be out for only a matter of months, so what would happen to April then?

Above me, the dive flag on top of the building fluttered in the morning breeze, and I frowned.

Scuba diving has brought this family nothing but heartache. Doesn't look like that's changed, with Maia getting pregnant and me possibly needing to fire someone we just hired.

But those were problems for the future. Like Dad said, I didn't have to tackle everything at once.

Soft footsteps approached. A woman walked past the end of the building and angled over to stand at the patio railing, unaware of me. My breath stilled as she lifted both hands to gather a mane of thick, long hair, its color like a field of spun gold.

I knew without asking this was April.

She was average height, though that sheet of golden hair was anything but average. Board shorts and a T-shirt covered what looked like a perfect hourglass figure. Still facing away, she pulled her hair through an elastic band, then circled it into a bun at the nape of her neck. Muscles in her arms flexed with the motion. Her face was in half-silhouette, and I caught sight of a sharp cheekbone and snub nose. I swallowed over a suddenly dry throat, unable to look away.

Why the hell am I reacting like this? I might have to fire this woman next week. She might be stacked, but I don't mix business with pleasure. And after Kora, I'm sure as hell not getting involved with anyone again. Ever.

She stilled again and smiled as she studied the glade. Then she turned around and saw me. The smile fell, her full lips forming an O as her eyes opened wide.

Eyes the color of a perfect tropical sky. The kind of eyes a man could get lost in.

Good thing I'm not that kind of man.

Chapter Four

April

I TOOK A MEANDERING journey to the dive shop, wanting to explore during the calm of my first morning at Calypso Key Resort. As I wandered up the cement path after eating breakfast at Dorado restaurant, a sand trail veered off toward the canal. I followed it, figuring if it wasn't brick or cement, it was for employees. The path turned to brick as it led between the back of the dive shop and another building directly across.

A stunning butterfly bush with a profusion of lavender and dark-purple blooms stood at the corner of the dive shop. I'd never seen one that flowered in two colors, and it was obviously lovingly tended. Colorful butterflies danced in the morning air, and as I passed by, a sense of peace filled me. I continued along the brick path, laid in a herringbone pattern. On my left, I passed an open door. A rack of hanging wetsuits lay on the far side of a crowded room, and I could hear sounds emanating from inside.

But I wasn't quite ready to meet my coworkers yet. A

shady grove lay in front of me, drawing me toward it. Several sizeable white boats were tied up in the canal, and I studied the nearest. Empty white plastic tank holders lining the two side benches proclaimed this the resort's dive boat, and I was impressed by what I saw. I noted the name and smiled. *Shark Bait* was a solid forty feet long with a canvas canopy stretching over the front half. A ladder led up to a small, elevated bridge. Another boat lay behind it, Calypso Key's fishing charter.

My feet carried me toward the open end of the canal, and the adjacent grove of gumbo limbo trees lay ahead. Panning my gaze around the empty picnic tables, I could imagine the area full of waiting guests, eager for the day's adventures. But in the silent early morning, no one was there yet.

A covered patio lay to my right, and I eased forward to the rail. The morning sun was already warm, and I gathered my hair, circling it into a low bun.

Anticipation built within me, raising a smile on my lips.

Then the back of my neck tingled, and a shiver ran over my shoulders—a strong feeling I wasn't alone. Glancing to my right, I saw something out of the corner of my eye.

I nearly gasped as a man was revealed. He casually leaned against the dive shop wall behind me, one leg bent at the knee.

"Oh!" I said, my stomach flopping over. "I didn't see you there."

The stranger was very tall, I'd guess six-foot-three. He had dark hair, cut short, and his intense brown eyes gave absolutely nothing away. A trimmed scruff covered his jaw, but he didn't look sloppy.

In fact, he damn-near stopped my heart, and not just because he'd startled me.

He was dressed strangely for a diver in a button-down shirt and jeans. When he lowered his leg to stand on both feet, his work boot made a solid thump on the brick floor. Remaining silent as he eyed me intently, the man was over-the-top handsome.

A slow ripple moved from my neck farther down my body. Taking a firm imaginary grip, I got a hold of myself.

Sabbatical from men, remember?

And I sure wasn't interested in a guest, despite the gorgeous pair of bedroom eyes staring at me. However, I was still an employee. Though not leading dives today, I should be helpful.

I smiled at the stranger. "Hi, I'm April."

"I know who you are." He didn't smile back as his eyes held mine. His voice was deep yet smooth, like fine whisky.

I swallowed reflexively.

Again, I was surprised. How had word gotten around that I was here? Hopefully, he wasn't a creepy guest, though he wasn't friendly either.

Guess I'll find out.

"Can I help you get checked in at the dive shop?" I lifted my right arm to point toward the pathway.

His lips moved in what was almost—but not quite—a smirk. "I'm not a diver."

Then, without another word, he pushed away from the wall and strolled off the patio toward the guest cottages.

My mouth dropped open as I stood there watching him.

God, what an asshole!

Flustered heat spread over my face as I watched him walk away in jeans that looked like he was born wearing them. Wide, muscular shoulders tapered to trim hips.

I took a deep breath and muttered, "Why were you near

the dive shop if you're not a diver? And why do I care, anyway?"

No one but a small yellow bird replied. It landed on the deck railing and chirped at me.

At least you're friendly.

Surly guests weren't the best part of my job, but at least they were temporary. They all left eventually.

Hopefully, Hot Grumpy Guy was on his way out.

A noise distracted me, and I turned as a man around my age walked toward *Shark Bait.* Four BCDs were slung over his shoulders, and I trotted to catch him. "You want some help with that?"

He swung around and smiled. Several inches shorter than the surly yet glorious man who had just left, he had neat brown hair and warm, friendly eyes. He lowered his right shoulder and the two BCDs slipped off. "Sure. Are you April?"

I bent down and picked one up in each hand, carrying them by the handle in the back of the vest. "I am. Looking forward to diving."

"I'm Wyatt. Nice to meet you."

I grinned. "Maia's husband! Congratulations."

He smiled, and there was something shy in it that endeared him to me. As if he still couldn't believe the changes in his life. "Thanks. It's a pretty exciting time around here."

Wyatt beckoned to me, and we boarded the dive boat. He gave me a quick tour, and my first impression of *Shark Bait* was confirmed when I looked closer. It was spotless and well-maintained. Calypso Key Resort ran a tight operation.

"Is Maia down here somewhere?" I asked him.

"Yeah. She's in the dive shop. Corbin, our instructor,

and I are leading the two dive groups today, and she's leading a snorkeling group. Go ahead and check in with her. Corbin will be along any minute to help me." Wyatt gave me a sunny smile. "You'll be helping soon enough. Enjoy the break while you can."

I laughed in return and hopped back onto the brick pathway. The glass door into the dive shop lay in the middle of the one-story building. I opened it and entered an air-conditioned room filled with the sharp scent of neoprene, a scent I instantly recognized.

I was home.

The open area was filled with wetsuits, and displays of fins, regulators, and BCDs lined the walls. Resort T-shirts and rash guards hung from circular racks. A long glass counter lay on the other side of the room, and Maia and a man stood behind it, studying a piece of paper attached to a clipboard. They both looked up when I entered, and Maia grinned.

"Good morning!"

"Beautiful morning," I replied as I strolled over. I had a momentary flashback to my encounter with Hot Grumpy Guy but pushed it away. I probably wouldn't even see him again. A beautiful black-and-white cat lay on the floor next to the counter. He rose and sauntered over to me, rubbing against my legs as I crouched to pet his head.

"That's Santiago," Maia said. "He's our shop kitty."

I smiled. "Every dive shop needs one. He looks like a sweetie." After one final scratch, I stood and stopped before the counter.

The man next to Maia straightened and I recognized the general manager from his picture I'd seen yesterday. He was lighter-complected than Maia, with light-brown hair and blue eyes, coupled with a muscular, tall frame.

He reached out his hand and gave me a friendly smile. "Hi. I'm Evan. We're glad to have you on board."

I shook and his hand was warm, his shake firm but not overbearing. His eyes were soft, and he immediately put me at ease. "Nice to meet you, Evan. I'm excited to be here."

"So are we. The divemaster who's been filling in got another position, so yesterday was his last day. We'll just have you tag along and get the lay of the land today."

Maia tapped the paper on the clipboard. "We were just checking the schedule. Wyatt's got the smaller group today, so why don't you join him? He can go over procedures and how we do things."

"That sounds perfect. I met him just now."

Maia's face exploded into a giant smile, and I broke into laughter.

Evan rolled his eyes. "Yeah, don't get the two lovebirds started. It's embarrassing being around them."

"Oh shut up," Maia said and elbowed him. "You only notice because we all spend so much time together."

I knew Maia was from a large family but didn't know all the particulars. "You both live here on the island?"

Evan nodded. "Maia and Wyatt are in one of the family cottages up on the bluff. I live in the Big House with Dad and our grandmother, Nona."

"Dad's mother," Maia added.

"You have other siblings, though, don't you?"

Maia nodded. "Our sister Stella lives in Key West. And our brother Gabe just moved back here with his daughter Hailey. I'm sure you'll meet them soon."

Evan smirked. "As long as he's not cooped up somewhere else."

Maia shot him a dirty look but didn't elaborate. She turned back to me. "Gabe left a successful real-estate career to raise Hailey here. Dad wants to step away from some of the business responsibilities and Gabe's going to take over for him."

"Wow," I said, picturing a slightly different version of the pair before me. Gabe sounded like a dedicated family man, and I could picture him with Evan's warm, empathetic nature. "You guys have quite the family business. I'm sure your brother will be as successful as the two of you have been."

"He's not off to the best start," Evan muttered and stifled a laugh. Then he straightened abruptly as Maia made a sudden movement with her lower leg. I was pretty sure she kicked him.

If they didn't want to elaborate, I wasn't going to push. Instead, I mentally counted on my fingers. "Wait. Didn't you tell me you had three brothers, Maia?"

The two siblings stiffened, and the smiles fell off their faces. Maia swallowed and gave Evan a quick side-eye. "Yeah, but Hunter doesn't live here. He works in private security in South Beach."

"I need to head to the lobby and check over arrivals and departures for today," Evan said, but his voice was tight. He gave me a quick smile. "Welcome aboard, April. See you later."

I watched him move toward the door. He walked with a slight limp, but it didn't seem to slow him down any.

I turned back to my friend, wondering about the sudden change in atmosphere. "Sorry. Did I say something wrong?"

Maia sighed and waved a hand absently. "No, you're fine. Evan and Hunter don't get along. It's kind of a sore subject."

"Oh. I won't bring it up again."

She shook her head and smiled as she walked around

the counter. "Enough family drama! It's a beautiful day. Let's get ready to dive, or snorkel in my case."

She put an arm around my shoulders, which was easy since she was several inches taller, and we moved across the tile floor. I glanced at her slightly bulging abdomen. "Do you miss diving?"

"Definitely. The snorkel tours have been really popular, so that makes up for it. But I'm looking forward to getting back under the water once the baby's born."

I nodded as we stepped onto the brick pathway, wondering how I'd feel in her shoes. Diving was contraindicated during pregnancy. Then I pushed the thoughts away.

I'm thirty-two with no man in sight. Not sure that situation is anything I'll ever need to worry about.

"By the way," Maia said. "Your apartment is all ready to go. I'll show it to you after we get back from the morning trip. You'll love it—private and near here too, so you won't have too far of a walk."

"That sounds amazing. Thanks so much."

She smiled, and there was something slightly smug in it. "I wouldn't have it any other way. Where's your dive gear?"

I stopped next to the covered patio. "It's on the porch of the cottage I spent last night in. I'll run back and grab it and meet you on the boat, all right?"

She flashed me an okay signal. "Do you feel all right leading dives tomorrow?"

I nodded. I'd been leading dives for six years and didn't need to know sites intimately to do a good job. "No problem. You and Wyatt can get me oriented today, and starting tomorrow, I can get specifics on whatever sites we're diving right before we jump in. I'm a quick learner."

Maia gave me a smile. "I think you'll love the diving here. We're a special place in the Keys."

Chapter Five

April

MAIA and I ate lunch in the employee area inside the Dorado restaurant kitchen. Two long tables were reserved for employees to eat whatever meal fell within their shifts, and the on-duty chefs were available to make entrees to order. We both dug into our chef's salads.

She had been right about the diving. The previous reef dives I'd done during my trip down the Keys had been shallow near shore. But a deep trench lay just offshore of Calypso Key, making for much more dramatic topography. I had loved both dive offerings that morning and couldn't wait to get started leading dives.

After we finished eating, we walked up the cement walk, then angled toward another sand pathway that ran parallel to it, but nearer the canal and dive shop. I hadn't noticed this path before, but looking over my shoulder saw it was an extension of the one I'd used that morning to get to the dive shop.

Maia noticed my examination. "This is the private path

that leads from the Big House and family cottages to the dive shop. You'll be using it too."

The path rose gradually, and a long building appeared ahead of me on the right side. A stone foundation anchored the structure, and its walls were made from tan-painted cinderblocks. Light brown timber trusses provided a pleasing contrast under the roof.

"That looks like it was built to last," I said.

Maia laughed softly. "Almost everything here has stood for over a century. The first buildings were demolished during a bad hurricane. Afterward, my great-great-grandfather pulled up his bootstraps and built everything to withstand almost any storm, including the Big House. That's your new home." She pointed at the two-story building ahead. Two large barn doors were slightly open on the left side of the structure, and a wooden door and covered porch lay on the right side. "We call it the Barn. Most of it is a large shop, but that's a two-bedroom apartment there on the right."

A flutter ran through me. My apartment in St. Croix had been a tiny one-bedroom, and this looked like paradise in comparison. We climbed three stairs onto a small, covered porch and Maia pulled a key from her back pocket. She unlocked the door before handing me the key, then stood aside to let me enter first.

As I stepped over the threshold, I was met with a blast of cool air and the scent of lemon cleaner. An expansive open-concept room lay before me, containing a couch and love seat along with two armchairs. A flat-screen TV stood on a low table against one wall. A kitchen with a table and chairs took up the other half of the area. The walls were white plaster, and the furniture was sturdy and well-built. Timber beams supported a white ceiling, and a giant stone fireplace took up one corner of the room. Wood was neatly stacked in a cubby next to it. My feet were rooted to the wood floor—I could hardly believe my luck.

Fully furnished and included in my salary!

Maia pointed to a closed door on the right. "That's the powder room. You might enjoy the fireplace—winter nights can get chilly sometimes. Two bedrooms with attached baths are upstairs. You'll recognize the master when you see it. The whole apartment was remodeled about ten years ago, so it's pretty up to date. There's ductless air-conditioning throughout."

My two suitcases were lined up near the front door, but Maia waved me toward the kitchen. Our footsteps echoed as we walked across a weathered but spotless floor. The wide wooden planks almost glowed in the light.

A glass-paned door lay between the table and kitchen counter, its curtain drawn. Maia opened it and we stepped outside. A delighted smile formed on my face as I took in a sizeable, covered patio, complete with a seating area and a small patio dining set.

"This is amazing! Thank you so much." I turned to give her a hug and she burst into laughter.

"You're welcome. You deserve a nice place. Plus, I think this apartment needs a feminine touch. Feel free to dress it up however you want."

I was already picturing some potted flowers and artwork on the walls. But I couldn't keep my gaze from the view in front of me and I walked across the flagstone patio to rest my hands on the wooden rail. The blue Caribbean Sea stretched out as far as the eye could see. I glanced to my left, where Calypso Key continued its gentle rise. Three stone and wood cottages were visible in the distance, with a much larger house behind them.

I pointed. "That's where all you Markhams live?"

"Yep. Wyatt and I are in the farthest cottage, with Gabe and Hailey in the middle one. The nearest one is empty. And of course, the Big House is in the background."

I shook my head, wonder filling me as I swept my gaze over the ocean again. To my right, the canal with the dive buildings was visible in the distance. "I'm going to love it here."

"I sure hope so." We hugged again, then Maia patted my shoulders. "I'll let you get settled in. Feel free to eat any meals you want at Dorado, but of course there's a full kitchen here if you'd rather make your own. See you tomorrow at seven?"

"I'll be there."

Instead of reentering the apartment, Maia walked off the patio to the north, rejoining the sand path as it wound up the hill. I opened the door and went back inside, leaving my sandals near the door. The room was silent, and as I looked around, I understood what Maia meant about it needing a feminine touch.

Though no personal touches graced the room, it had a masculine aura to it. "Well, that's nothing some colorful throw pillows and a painting or two won't solve."

A door I hadn't noticed lay across the room next to the staircase. I padded over, unlocked it, and peeked into the large adjoining shop area. I wrinkled my nose at the scent of machinery and fresh lumber.

I had been expecting dirt floors and rusty equipment, but the huge room was spotless. The brown-speckled epoxy floor stretched throughout, and nearest to me lay a plethora of mysterious equipment—saws, lathes, and vices. Pallets of lumber were stacked up nearby and a long workbench area stretched for fifteen feet along the back wall. Corkboard was attached to the wall over it, and an assortment of chisels and knives hung from pegs.

Woodworking?

The area looked sterile and pristine, so I had no way of knowing if it got regular use by a fastidious craftsman or was just cleaned by housekeeping. Lawnmowers, edgers, and several large tractors took up most of the rest of the structure, silent behind the slightly open doors.

I didn't feel any need to investigate the shop, so I closed the door and relocked it. With the upstairs beckoning, I climbed the wooden staircase. Expecting a multitude of creaks, I was surprised to find the risers warm and smooth under my bare feet, as well as silent except for one squeaky stair near the top of the flight. The wooden floors continued on the second story, where a short hall lay with open doors on either end. I headed left at random and pushed open the door to enter a decent-sized room with a queen-sized bed. A bathroom was visible on one end. Wondering if this was the master, I turned around and headed to the other end of the hall.

A shiver tickled down my spine at what I discovered. This room was much larger. The stone fireplace from downstairs continued through this room, anchoring one entire corner of it. Two armchairs and a fluffy gray rug lay in front.

I slowly turned my head in the other direction and my jaw hit the floor. The beautiful king-sized bed was covered in a white-striped comforter. The bedding was tucked into a solid mahogany frame, beautiful in its craftsmanship.

But the headboard was exquisite.

I crossed the floor in a daze to run my hand across the warm teak surface. The artisan had taken advantage of the natural contours and shade variations of the wood to create a headboard that was irregular, and yet completely harmonious and pleasing to the eye. The top was a live wood edge, with coves and crevices that reminded me of a coral reef wall. Several different colored pieces of teak had been joined to create striations of color, and all of it was sanded to soft, velvety smooth perfection. I could hardly stop stroking it.

Finally, I rose and crossed the floor to glance at a fully modern bathroom, with two sinks and a large walk-in shower. A window was open, white curtains fluttering in the soft breeze.

I turned around and slumped against the doorjamb, my legs wobbly. The apartment was more beautiful than any place I'd ever lived. My eye was drawn back to that incredible headboard and bed, and I felt a deep connection with everything around me.

I stepped forward and stood in the middle of the silent, yet welcoming room, and tears sprang to my eyes.

My life had truly started over.

Chapter Six

Gabe

I STARED at the columns of numbers on the spreadsheet, making sure to keep my breathing even and my face expressionless. Dad watched me closely. We sat behind a massive wooden desk inside his office. As a kid, I'd loved this room, with its fishing books and mounted trophy fish Dad had caught over the years. But sitting side by side, with me in his usual chair and him in a simple metal folding one, was new. And uncomfortable. I paid the decorations no mind, my eyes fixated on the red figure in the bottom right corner of the spreadsheet. Month after month.

Calypso Key Resort was bleeding money.

I inhaled a long breath and tried to relax my stiff shoulders.

Dad sighed. "We used to have a healthy savings account, but I've been dipping into it for a while now to balance that negative bottom-line number. I'm sorry, Gabe. I know the news isn't good. I've been in charge of this resort for over thirty years, and it's time for me to take a step back."

That made me smile. I relaxed in the big leather chair as I turned my eye to the stunning thirteen-foot blue marlin mounted on the wall. I squeezed his knee. "You're hardly ready to go out to pasture yet. But we need to get you out on the fishing boat more. That's why I'm here."

Why didn't you tell me about this two years ago when you started running in the red?

But I didn't need to ask the question out loud. I already knew the answer—because he thought it was temporary. Then he desperately hoped it was temporary. Until he couldn't deny it anymore.

And here I was.

I was partners with a friend I'd met while getting my MBA at the University of Miami. One of our projects was a successful thirty-story commercial tower in downtown Miami, and divesting myself of the day-to-day operations was what had delayed my moving back home. I was still an equal partner in the business but no longer took a regular salary.

I didn't have any doubts I could get Calypso Key back on its feet again, but some of the changes might be painful. "Do Evan and Maia know about this?"

"Not the specifics."

I rubbed a hand over my scruff, my eyes returning to those red numbers. "We need to get together and make some decisions. Evan especially needs to be brought fully up to date, whether he enjoys it or not." Evan hated dealing with money, and I had more of a natural inclination for finance. But I wasn't going to keep the general manager of the resort in the dark.

"I agree," Dad said, crossing an ankle over his opposite knee. "But I don't like the idea of worrying Maia. She's got enough going on."

I nodded. "Let's keep her out of it for now. I don't want her to stress out over whether April has a permanent position or not. We can inform her after we get some plans made."

I wasn't pleased by the powerful, visceral attraction I'd experienced when I met April yesterday, and that had made me gruffer than I should have been. That hair, those eyes.

Those lips.

When she'd turned around and spoken to me, it only got worse. She was sweet, upbeat, and helpful... everything I was not. Tied up in an irresistible, unrelenting, legs-forever package.

But hurting employees' feelings was the least of my concerns right now. Keeping them employed was.

Warm, dry laughter came from the doorway. Dad and I looked up in unison, which only made Nona laugh harder. My grandmother's long, snow-white hair was plated into its usual braid, and she wore a white button-down shirt with an elaborate turquoise and silver necklace tucked under the collar. Smiling, her gaze bounced between the two of us before settling on me.

"Oh, Gabriel, it is so good to have you back home. Seeing the two of you together like this just made my day. You are *so* alike!"

I sat back in my chair and glanced at Dad, grateful for her interruption. Sometimes I wished she took a little less interest in our personal lives, but Nona would fight to the death for us, and we'd do the same for her.

Dad clapped me on the shoulder. "Well, Mom, at least Gabe got the brains you so helpfully passed down to me."

A reluctant smile rose on my lips as I shook my head.

Nona pointed to me. "That's better! You two looked so serious when I arrived. I won't keep you—don't worry. But I expect to see you and Hailey at supper regularly, Gabriel. Don't break an old woman's heart."

"Never," I said softly. "We'll be up tonight."

"I'll let the chef know," she replied, inclining her head. "You two enjoy your numbers."

She disappeared from the doorway, which brought Dad and me back to the reason we were there. I sighed as I lifted my phone off the blotter. "I'll text Evan and ask him to meet us for lunch by the pool. That work for you?"

Dad nodded. "Of course." Then he stood and folded his chair, placing it against the wall. "I've got a couple of things to do. See you soon."

After he left, I swiveled the big chair back to his computer terminal. The red numbers were still there, and I began turning over possible solutions.

An hour later, Dad, Evan, and I sat around a circular glass table on the expansive slate patio behind the Big House. A rectangular inground pool sparkled in front of me, but at least the umbrella was up, giving us plenty of shade from the noontime sun. Tall shrubs screened the pool area from curious eyes and also hid the adjacent manicured lawn area. A chef from Dorado rotated each week to cook meals in the Big House, and we were finishing up our lunches of blackened fish sandwiches.

We'd made small talk during the meal, pointedly not discussing why we were here. Instead, I filled them in on Hailey's successful first day of school. She'd had no problem assimilating into her classroom and had been eager to ride the bus this morning. I tried not to feel a pang at that.

Evan tossed his napkin on his plate and sat back in the chair. "Looks like we're done eating. I'm assuming this meeting has something to do with finances? Unless you just couldn't wait to see me again?"

He smiled at me, which was good because we'd had a few tense conversations since I returned. As much as I tried to stay away from the operations side of the resort, Evan thought I was stepping on his toes. And him gleefully poking me about my night in jail didn't help my irritation any. I just wanted to put the whole thing behind me.

"Gabe and I spent some time this morning going over the numbers, and he wanted you brought into the conversation," Dad said.

Evan's smile disappeared. "Oh? The Great Oz has spoken. I'm honored."

My temper frayed. "Cut the crap, Evan. You've done a great job managing this place, and I'm no threat to you."

My brother and I stared at each other, neither backing down.

Dad scowled. "Both of you—knock it off! Evan, you're the manager of the resort. Gabe is now the CFO. There's plenty of work to go around, I assure you."

Evan pressed his lips together, then nodded, accepting my compliment as he broke eye contact. "I take it we're not doing well?"

"No, we're not," I said. "The resort's been losing money most months for several years, and the reserve fund is almost gone."

Evan stilled, then slowly turned his head to stare at Dad. "You said it wasn't that bad."

"I didn't want to worry anyone unnecessarily, and it's not like we're going to go under at any moment."

We will if I don't do something...

Evan shifted his gaze to me. "So what's the big plan to plug the leak?"

I shrugged uncomfortably. "An immediate hiring freeze, to start. And no unnecessary expenses. You or I will authorize any expenditures over five hundred dollars. I'll comb over the budget and make cuts where I can."

"That sounds doable," Evan said, taking a sip of iced tea.

"I doubt it will be enough," I said. "But I need to think about the next steps some more."

Evan set his glass down with a thump. "Are we going to have to lay people off?"

"Maybe. I hope not."

Evan rubbed his forehead as he looked between Dad and me. "Does Maia know about this? We just hired April."

Dad shook his head. "No. I don't want to worry her right now. We can tell her about the hiring and expenditure freezes, but let's keep any potential staff cuts between us three for now."

"With all the turmoil going on in the dive operation—Wyatt and Maia—and now April onboarding, I've been spending a lot of my time in the dive shop," Evan said. "I'll be honest, Dad. It's getting to be too much."

"I know, Son. I spoke to Maia about becoming dive operations manager, but that was before she became pregnant. Who knows what she'll want to do after the baby's born?"

"Ask Wyatt to take over some of the day-to-day stuff," I said to my brother. "He's been here long enough to figure it out. Or don't you trust him?"

Evan shot me a dubious look. "I trust him, and he's family now. But he's only been here a few months too, you know. He's pretty green."

I paused, thinking it over. But there was really no other option. "I can take over the dive op."

I hadn't lied when I told April I wasn't a diver. It had been over a decade since my last dive, but I'd help out if I needed to. I'd practically grown up in the dive shop and on the boat and had no doubt it would come back to me quickly.

All those bad memories will come back too...

Evan and I shared a long look, nonverbal communication passing between us, then I nodded. Evan had gone above and beyond, especially with dive operations. Especially that. "I'm here to help, Evan. Let me."

His eyes softened, and a tiny smile stretched his lips. "That would really lighten my load. I'm glad to have you around, big brother."

Chapter Seven

April

I PUSHED through the glass door into the dive shop, a blissful sigh as a blast of cool air hit me. I had just finished my first dives as Calypso Key's newest guide and was on cloud nine about my new home. Maia stood in front of a display of fins with an older man. He was tall and handsome with salt-and-pepper hair. He looked familiar, but I was sure I hadn't seen him before.

The pair looked up at my entry and both smiled. The man straightened and held out his hand. "Hi, April. I'm Warren, Maia's dad." His voice was deep and rich, and the thought that I should know him niggled my mind again.

Then it came to me. The photo in the lobby!

Pleased to solve the mystery, I shook and smiled back. "Pleasure to meet you, Mr. Markham. Thank you very much for hiring me. My apartment is incredible."

"Oh, don't start with that! Call me Warren, please. And you're welcome on both accounts."

I laughed, liking him already. "You got it, Warren."

"How did your first dives go?" he asked.

"Fantastic! I love it here already. That trench really makes for some spectacular dives. Wyatt gave me pointers before each dive, so everyone in my group seemed happy."

Maia laughed. "She's being modest, Dad. April had them eating out of her hand."

I shrugged but was pleased with the compliment. "The job isn't too hard on days like this."

I hooked a thumb toward the long building on the other side of the brick path behind me. "I got the tanks all changed over and the empties are lined up next to the air compressor."

"Perfect. Wyatt and I will fill them. Why don't you take the rest of the afternoon off and finish unpacking? You can start full days tomorrow."

"You sure? I don't mind staying to help."

Warren nodded, and that sense came over me again. That I'd met him before.

"Take the afternoon off because tomorrow is an early start," he said. "We're going to have a staff meeting here at the dive shop at six forty-five a.m. That's why I'm talking to Maia. Her brother Gabe is going to take over as the dive operations manager, so we'll have a quick pow-wow about it."

At last, I'd get to meet the mysterious Gabe! I looked forward to it. Every Markham I'd met was warm and friendly, which made a fun job even more enjoyable. Maia was smiling and didn't look upset about the change.

"I'll be here," I said. "See you guys later."

I left via the front entrance, which faced toward the beach cottages. I casually cast my gaze about, telling myself I wasn't looking for Hot Grumpy Guy. I hadn't seen him again since our encounter the previous morning, so maybe he'd left the resort. I didn't know whether to feel disappointed or relieved. Just because I didn't want a relationship didn't mean I couldn't enjoy looking.

And Hot Grumpy Guy was most definitely enjoyable to watch.

An hour later, I opened my patio door and stepped outside, a cold bottle of beer in my hand. Maia had fully stocked the kitchen with initial supplies, and I sent a silent thanks to her as I tipped up the bottle of Queen Conch, a local craft beer from Conch Republic, the brewpub I'd passed on my way here.

A meow came from my right, and I swallowed quickly.

"You're back again, huh?" I asked the gray tabby cat lying on the couch in a sliver of sunshine. He stretched and flexed his claws, purring. When I'd come out that morning to enjoy my coffee and watch the sunrise, he'd been lying on a nearby armchair. He was friendly and sat in my lap until I had to get up. When I set him on the floor, he'd ambled toward the shop.

Now he was back.

I sat next to him and ran a hand over his shiny gray fur. His pattern was striking. In addition to the standard tabby M on his forehead, he was white on his legs and belly, while darker gray stripes whorled dramatically in swooshes and circles on his sides.

After I sat on the couch, the cat climbed onto my lap and began kneading his front paws into my thighs. His claws pricked slightly, but I didn't mind. "You're welcome anytime, buddy. You probably have a name. You're obviously well cared for."

I stroked my finger down a white front leg, then paused as something odd caught my eye. Both of the cat's front feet had an extra toe, almost like a thumb to the inside of each paw. I'd never seen an oddity like that before, but it didn't appear to hamper his movement at all. As I stroked the cat's back, he stretched out his front legs and lay sphinx-like along my thighs.

I took another sip of beer as my eyes slowly traveled across the bluff in front of me. I'd wandered to the edge this morning to find a sheer drop of about twenty feet. The waves lapped gently against the cliff, but I had no doubt the ocean was capable of much more forceful smashes. The bluff rose continuously to my left until it leveled out at the Markham cottages and Big House visible in the distance. The drop there was more dramatic, vaulting to more than a hundred feet.

As I looked toward the Markham residences, I got another surprise. A girl strolled along the bluff toward me. She was a safe distance from the edge and ambled with a free, easy walk that brought a smile to my face. Glancing up and seeing me, she broke into a wide grin and skipped toward me. The girl had long, golden-brown hair with a nice wave to it and was very pretty. Her chin tapered to a point and her dark-brown eyes glimmered as she smiled at me. It dawned on me this must be the niece Maia had mentioned.

The girl slowed to a walk as she stepped onto my patio. She looked around eight or nine years old. "Hi, I'm Hailey. You must be April." She spoke confidently with no hint of shyness, and I couldn't help it as my smile widened further.

"I am. Nice to meet you."

"You, too." She sat in a matching blue-and-white-striped armchair across from me and swung her legs back and forth. "I just moved here too. With my dad. Of course, I've been here lots, but now it's home."

"This is a beautiful island. I think we're both lucky."

"Definitely." She studied the patio we sat on. "Do you

like the Barn apartment? It's where my dad and I used to stay when we visited, but now we live in a cottage next to Maia and her new husband."

That was a surprise. Maia hadn't said anything about my apartment being used by family. "I love it, but I hope you two didn't move out on my account."

Hailey shrugged, her hair bouncing. "The new cottage is really nice. I like it better because it's closer to the Big House. I think my dad likes your apartment, though." Then she cocked her head and glanced at my lap. "There you are, Hemingway!"

I laughed. "Is that his name?"

Hailey nodded. "He likes to hang around the Barn. Dad and I took him up to our cottage, but I'm not sure he wants to stay there." She lifted her eyes to mine and smiled. "We can share him!"

"I already told him he's welcome to come and go as he pleases. How did he get the name Hemingway?"

Her smile froze and puzzlement filled her eyes. "Because he's a Hemingway cat, of course."

I laughed. There was nothing condescending or snotty in her tone. My question genuinely puzzled her. "I don't know what a Hemingway cat is."

Her smile returned as she pointed to his front paws. "He has six toes on his front feet."

"I noticed that! I didn't realize that was a thing."

Hailey nodded sagely. "Oh, yes. He's descended from one of Ernest Hemingway's six-toed cats. We have three of them. Santiago lives at the dive shop, and Pilar in the Big House. She's strictly an indoor cat. I let her out one time and Nona wasn't happy with me."

I'd interacted with black-and-white Santiago in the dive shop but had never counted his toes. I'd take her word for it that he had six of them. Hemingway hopped off my lap and moved to a sunny spot on the flagstone floor. He sat and licked his paw, then washed his face with it.

"Where did you live before you came here?" I asked the girl, already liking her immensely.

"Miami. Dad said he didn't want me growing up in *that den of thieves*"—she made a fierce face and deepened her voice to utter the phrase before returning to her normal, breezy tone—"but I don't know what he was talking about. We lived in a big apartment at the top of a high-rise, and it was really nice."

I smiled. I couldn't imagine having this kind of poise and confidence at her age. She obviously knew she was loved, and as a child of divorced parents myself, that was of paramount importance. Though I had no idea where her mother was or why she wasn't in Hailey's life. "So it's just you and your dad?"

Her smile faded slightly, and her eyes clouded. I mentally kicked myself.

"Yeah. My parents divorced a few years ago. My mom left and didn't contact us for over a year. Then she told my dad she settled in California and wanted to have me with her. I overheard his part of the conversation, though he doesn't know that." She giggled, then deepened her voice again. "If you think you're taking *my* daughter away from her home and across the country, you better think again. Hailey stays with me. If you fight me on this, Kora, I'll come after you with everything I've got." Hailey lifted her shoulders, her equanimity restored. "I miss my mom sometimes, but plenty of people here love me, so I think I'm better off. My dad isn't afraid to put his foot down when he needs to."

Her declaration astonished me and how matter-of-fact she was about it. How utterly confident she was of her father's love and secure that he'd do anything for her. It made me even more curious to meet Gabe. He sounded like an amazing father.

I gave her a soft smile. "I'm sorry you had to go through that. But it sounds like you have a terrific family at Calypso Key."

"I do, and I love it here. I'm going to learn to dive when I'm twelve."

"Then you've got one up on me. I didn't learn until my early twenties."

"Are you a divemaster, or an instructor?"

"I've been a divemaster for six years. I was in the same class as your aunt."

"Oh! That's so cool. And now you're working together! I can't wait to meet Aunt Maia's baby."

My head spun at the rapid subjects a young mind was capable of flitting through, but I thoroughly enjoyed her company. I was getting ready to ask her about school when a shout reached us.

"Hailey! Where are you?"

A man's deep voice echoed around us, tight with fear. Hailey and I whipped our heads toward the hill where the shout had come from, and Hemingway stopped washing his face. A man trotted down the sand path, cupped both hands around his mouth, and called Hailey's name again.

"Uh-oh," she said quietly. "I might be in trouble." She stood and waved. "I'm here, Dad!"

The man skidded to a stop and ratcheted his head toward her call. Then he broke into a jog, running across the short grass, straight toward the patio.

As he neared, I had to tighten my jaw to keep my mouth from dropping open.

It can't be!

Hailey's father stopped at the edge of the flagstone patio, dressed in a plaid button-down shirt and gray cargo shorts. There was no denying that tall frame, or the broad, muscular shoulders. Neatly manicured scruff covered his firm jaw.

Hot Grumpy Guy stood on my patio.

This man was Gabe?

The panicked expression in his brown eyes relaxed at locating Hailey, but his chest heaved. "You can't just run off without telling me!"

Her mouth pursed, a contrite expression washing over her face. "I'm sorry. I was only going for a short walk when I saw April, and we got to talking. I didn't mean to worry you."

Gabe wrenched his gaze away and met my eyes. His expression hardened, as if it was my fault he hadn't known where Hailey was. My pulse raced, though I couldn't decide if it was from attraction or irritation.

Then he slid his eyes back to Hailey and spoke softly. "Head on back to the Big House, angel. Lunch is ready. We'll talk more later."

She nodded, then glanced at me, demure now. "It was nice to meet you, April."

"You too, Hailey." The way Gabe had glared at me convinced me my reaction was irritation. Most definitely not attraction. Despite his dark, smoldering eyes. "Come back anytime. I enjoyed our chat."

A small smile crossed her lovely face, and she trotted past her father and toward the sand path. Hemingway sat in the sunbeam watching.

Gabe and I stared at each other. As I got over the shock of discovering who he was, a hot ball of anger formed in my stomach at how he'd treated me. From the beginning. "So you're Gabe, huh? Guess I wasn't worth the effort of an introduction yesterday?"

A red flush crept up his neck as he drew himself upright to his full glorious height. "I'm sorry. It's been a rough few days. Yes, I'm Gabriel Markham."

"April Desmond. But you know that already, don't you?"

A muscle in his cheek moved as he ground his teeth. I don't know why I was so pleased to get a reaction out of him.

Or maybe I did know.

Maybe because I wanted him to feel embarrassed and inadequate like he'd made me feel. Then I recalled what Hailey had said about my apartment. Was he hostile because I'd displaced him and his daughter?

Or was he just an asshole?

"Hailey told me she and you stayed here when you visited. I hope I didn't kick you two out."

Several expressions flitted across his face, surprise, calculation, even a brief flash of anger. Then he covered all of them, his face becoming completely neutral when he answered. "Not at all. We're closer to my family, and you're closer to the dive shop. This works for everyone."

His voice had that deep, rich timbre I remembered. With a flash, I realized why Warren had looked so familiar. I was staring at a younger version of him right now. A version who had just made it crystal clear he was family, and I was an employee.

Anger widened my eyes. "Well, don't let me keep you from lunch."

With a stiff nod, he turned around and took a step. Then I nearly jumped when he whirled back around and strode across the deck of my patio. Stopping in front of

Hemingway, he bent down and swooped up the cat. Hemingway settled in his folded arms as Gabe glared at me. "This is my cat. He comes with me."

Then he spun around again and stalked back the way he'd come.

I stared at his retreating form, once again unable to dismiss his towering, muscular build. The way his shoulders moved with every stride. How could he be the man I'd been told of?

This sullen, dismissive, and cantankerous jerk.

Oh yeah. And the new dive manager.

"Now he's my boss. Great."

My head flopped back against the couch as I took a long pull of beer. I was stuck with Gabe whether I liked it or not. Dammit, I was here for a new start—to be the positive, happy person I'd once been.

You're not going to stop me, Gabe.

Clearly, he wasn't *all* bad. He'd certainly done a stellar job with his daughter, and Maia spoke fondly of him. Maybe I was going about this wrong. Instead of trying to get under his skin, maybe I needed to provide a ray of sunshine instead of a challenge. That was my natural inclination anyway. But something about Gabe got under my skin.

I stared at the ocean, my eyes unfocused. "A spoonful of sugar instead of vinegar? I guess it couldn't hurt."

Chapter Eight

Gabe

HEMINGWAY PURRED in my arms as I stomped up the hill, either oblivious to my mood or trying to calm me down. I snorted and scratched him behind one ear.

Probably the latter.

I forced myself to slow my stride, to lengthen each breath.

After my first meeting with April, I'd convinced myself my reaction to her—the raw, crushing attraction—was due to the effects of my night in jail. And because of that, I'd be able to treat her with more courtesy the next time.

"Yeah, look how that went," I muttered under my breath.

Earlier, I'd walked into my cottage and found no sign of Hailey. No one at the Big House had seen her either. Panic became a real, slithering creature inside me as I imagined every awful possibility. I tore down the hill, and when I'd seen her safe with April, my relief had been so great I'd just lashed out. At both of them, but mostly at April.

That first day, our new divemaster obviously hadn't known who I was, and being caught out like that had only made me more defensive. And she hadn't backed down one inch—the challenge in her gorgeous blue eyes had been unmistakable.

Goddamn if that wasn't hotter than hell.

I knew I was big and intimidating, and yeah, I could be grouchy too. A woman who would stand up to me was my kryptonite. But that didn't matter—I couldn't be a complete dick every time we interacted. She'd quit.

And I just realized I didn't want that.

Tomorrow, I'd make a concerted effort to start over with her.

By the time I reached the cottage, my mood was somewhat improved. I opened the front door and Hailey was stretched out on the couch, leafing through a tourist magazine we kept around for the guests. She put it aside when I shut the door. I set Hemingway on the wooden floor.

"He followed you back, huh?" she asked, and that made my flush come back. I was too embarrassed to admit I'd acted like a petulant child and stomped off with him, so I just nodded. Hailey folded upright as I sat down next to her, and I drew her into my arms, holding her tight.

"I'm sorry I snapped at you," I whispered against her soft hair.

"I didn't mean to run off like that. I should have left a note. I was just wandering over the grass when I saw April. Then I got distracted."

"It's okay, angel. You know you're the most important thing in my life, right?"

She snuggled tighter. "I know, Daddy."

I smiled. She called me that less and less as she got

older, and I treasured the word every time she said it. "What's our rule about where to go in the resort?"

"I can go to any of the public areas as long as staff are there, but I have to stay away from the guest bungalows."

"Good girl." I closed my eyes and kissed the top of her head.

"Do you want me to stay away from April and the Barn?"

My eyes snapped open. "I don't know her well enough to answer that."

"She was really nice, and she's a friend of Maia's."

I was well aware of what an outgoing, gregarious child Hailey was, which was why I wanted her far away from the guest quarters. I couldn't vet those people, and none of them were going to be alone with my daughter. But staff was different.

I hadn't exactly covered myself in glory either time April and I had met, and if Hailey were her child instead of mine, April probably wouldn't want her anywhere near me. And Maia would never allow anyone on the resort she wouldn't vouch for. "April's fine, as long as she doesn't mind your visits." I poked Hailey several times in the side, earning myself a fit of giggles. "But I don't want you buttering her up so you can move back into the Barn and leave old Dad here by myself."

"That will never happen! We're a team, right?"

"Always. What do you say we head to Marathon and look for some stuff to decorate your room?"

She bolted upright, staring at me. "Now?"

"Why not? You have a pressing engagement?"

Her grin warmed my soul.

"Of course not! But I didn't think you'd have time."

My smile faded and I held her gaze. "I will never be too

busy for you. Never." Then I pushed to my feet and lifted her into my arms. "Come on. Let's go decorate your room."

THE NEXT MORNING, I walked down the path from my cottage as the sun peeked above the horizon. I'd left Nona with Hailey to ensure she got on the school bus safely, since I'd be in the dive staff meeting when the bus came. Our shopping trip to Marathon had been a success, and we'd come home with a bedding set, table lamp, and several framed prints in a matching seahorse motif. I'd washed the sheets and put them on before bed, and my daughter fell asleep a very happy girl.

If only my troubles could be solved so easily.

My eye automatically drifted toward the Barn as I passed by, and the front door of what I had yet to consider April's apartment. Then my gaze narrowed. Several potted flowers were placed around the entry and a colorful mat lay on the wooden landing. The place definitely looked homier and more welcoming.

And April was probably still inside. I wondered what she might be doing right now. Was she in the shower? Naked with beads of water running down—

"Stop it!" I hissed and almost slapped myself.

I turned my gaze firmly to the dive flag fluttering in the distance. It wasn't even six thirty yet. I wanted to get to the dive shop early and prepare for the meeting. My big plan for the day was to scour the schedule and see if we could trim any expenses for both the dive operation and the fishing charter.

When I reached the dive shop, the front door was unlocked, and the lights were on. I entered and headed toward a hallway behind the counter. The scuba classroom lay on one side, with the employee shower/locker room across. A combination break/meeting room as well as an office—soon-to-be my office—lay farther down.

At the end of the hall, light filtered out of the meeting room, and I headed that way. Evan stood behind a table at the front of the room. Two additional rectangular tables faced it, and whiteboards hung on all four walls. Two windows faced the beach to let in plenty of natural light.

"For a guy looking to lighten his load, you're sure here early." I leaned against the edge of the table facing Evan.

Several stacks of paper were neatly arranged before him, along with a pink box from Sweet Dreams, a new bakery on Dove Key. Evan smiled, but his eyes were blood-shot. "It's a busy day today." He dropped his gaze, then met mine firmly. "And my leg was killing me last night. I must have walked five to ten miles yesterday."

I kept my face expressionless since he didn't want pity from me. I was one of the few people Evan felt safe enough to admit his physical problems, and I didn't want to jeopardize that. "Can you stay off your feet more today?"

He shook his head. "I took some ibuprofen, so I should feel better soon. And Dr. Nelson says exercise is good for me. Besides, I'm already dealing with the first crisis of the day—no rest for the weary and all that."

"What's up?"

"Miguel is sick. He's not coming in today." Miguel Cervantes had been the captain of *Shark Bait* for over five years and was as dependable as people got.

"He must really be feeling shitty to call in. Who's your backup?"

Evan laughed, but there was little humor in it. "We've

got two. One is in New York visiting his grandkids and the other one is currently driving a charter in the Bahamas."

"How about Dad?"

"His captain's license expired three months ago, so he's out. Which brings me to backup number four. You, I hope."

I groaned. "Aw shit, Evan! I don't want to do it!"

This time his laugh was more genuine. "You're the one who offered to take over the dive operation and help out. Do you still have an active Coast Guard captain's license?"

I'd had my own boat in Miami, which I sold prior to moving. Wanting to stay current in regulations and safety, I'd gone through the Coast Guard course. If Hailey was going to be on my boat, I wanted it as safe as possible.

"Yeah," I said grudgingly.

The certification had been a luxury for me in Miami, but *Shark Bait* was a Coast Guard-inspected vessel and required a certified captain or we'd have to cancel the charter. I scowled. "How many people are scheduled?"

"Seventeen. Wyatt's got six divers, April has five, and Maia's got six snorkelers."

"Super. I can't wait."

Evan rolled his eyes. "You should be proud of Maia. Her idea to add snorkel groups has brought in extra money we weren't getting before."

I stared at him, not ready to jump for joy just yet. I loved driving boats and being on the water, but being a dive boat captain was damn hard work. And not what had been on my agenda. I folded my arms across my chest. "Can't you see my enthusiasm?"

Evan grinned and opened the pink box. He slid it toward me, and the delicious scent of baked pastries drifted toward me. "Here. Have something sweet. Maybe it will rub off on you."

I thought about pointing out the stupidity of going to Dove Key to buy donuts when we had our own pastry chef a hundred yards away, but if Evan wanted to spend his own money, that was his choice. If he turned it in as an expense, though, I'd string him up by his balls. Straightening to inspect the offerings, I selected an apple fritter. I took a huge bite and had to admit it was pretty damn good. I came around the counter to stand next to him.

"I thought it would be nice to have treats for the meeting," Evan said.

I swallowed and prepared for the shitty day ahead. "All right. Save me a maple bar and I'll forgive you. Let's get this show on the road. People will start showing up any second."

Chapter Nine

April

I LED my group at fifty feet along a sheer wall. Craning my head around, I looked for Spencer. The diver had drifted down a good ten feet, and I rapped my tank with my metal pointer, getting his attention. Grasping my inflator hose, I tapped the inflate button and nodded at him. I could see the lightbulb go off before he added more air and rose to my depth.

After applauding him for understanding what to do, I turned around to lead again. Spencer had been my project for the morning. Middle-aged and overweight, scuba diving had been a lifelong dream he'd finally realized and was celebrating with a solo trip to Calypso Key.

Some divemasters hated working with new divers. I loved it, even though it occasionally gave me some new gray hairs. Spencer had been a pleasure to work with, enthusiastic and wanting to learn anything and everything about diving.

I angled us up and over the lip of the wall onto a flat

patch reef, then checked my compass to set a course back to the boat. My dive pattern was a large triangle from the boat to where we spent most of the dive on the wall, then back to the boat.

I stilled as a school of midnight parrotfish came to investigate us, and I made sure to get all five of my divers' attention. The fish were each over three feet long and a brilliant combination of mottled blue and black. Their mouths ended in a large beak they used to gnaw on corals. Spencer's eyes were like saucers behind his mask as several swam right by him.

As we traveled back to the boat, I checked my compass several times. I knew we were close when I recognized the underwater landmarks I'd memorized upon entering the water. Satisfaction filled me as I looked up at the bottom of *Shark Bait* when we reached the forty-five-minute mark.

Right on time.

I was fully confident in my skills, but it could still be unnerving to lead groups in an unfamiliar area. Early in my career, I'd had a few blunders finding my way, but now had a system worked out and new sites didn't faze me in the slightest. I gestured for Spencer to join another couple who were also low on air, while I finished the sixty-minute dive with the other two.

After our safety stop, the three of us surfaced and headed to the stern of the boat. Two metal ladders reached out of the water, and the divers each headed toward one. They removed their fins and handed them up where Gabe stood at one ladder and Maia at the other.

While they helped my final two divers to their spots, I swam up to Maia's ladder. I placed my face in the water and pulled my fins off to hand them to her. Except when I raised my right arm, Gabe stood at the top of the ladder, not her. Our eyes met as he took the fins from me.

When I'd showed up for the staff meeting this morning, I hadn't been surprised to see Gabe at the front of the room with Evan. But I'd been shocked to hear he was our boat captain for the day. He hadn't seemed overly thrilled about it either, and his official boat briefing for the new guests on board had been terse and direct.

On the way to the dive site, everyone on board was quieter than the previous day, picking up on his mood. I'd sighed inwardly, already dreading my morning with Captain Growly. Then I recalled my intention to be nicer to him. I went to work on the guests first, talking to them and bantering back and forth as we prepared for the dive.

I was polite and friendly to Gabe, and my ploy must have worked. Over the course of the morning spent with two dives and an hour-long surface interval between them, he gradually thawed. Both toward the guests and me.

I got the feeling I'd surprised him this morning. During the surface interval, I'd huddled with Maia and Wyatt to get pointers on the site we chose for the second dive. Then I'd led the briefing about it, even though this was my first time at the site. Gabe had watched me closely. His sunglasses rested on top of his head, and for once his eyes didn't hold disdain or resentment.

They were filled with interest.

And maybe a little respect too.

Now, as I climbed the ladder, he swept both my fins under one arm and grabbed my tank valve with the other, helping me back onto the boat. I dripped salt water all over the stern platform as I nodded to him. "Thanks."

"You're welcome. I'll help you back to your seat." My spot on the boat was the last tank holder in front of the stern, so it was only a few steps. But if Gabe was feeling helpful, I wasn't going to argue.

"I watched your group's bubbles on both dives," he said as I slid my tank into the holder and unbuckled my BCD. "You guys were easy to follow—your pattern was very clear."

I grinned up at him. "Surprised I didn't get lost?"

His eyes softened, and maybe, *maybe*, a tiny hint of a smile graced his lips. "Not necessarily surprised. But... impressed, let's say."

Our gazes held as something fluttered through my abdomen. Something that had nothing to do with sabbaticals from men. Especially bosses. "Thank you. All in a day's work."

Wyatt moved to one ladder, raised it from the water, and tied it off. Gabe did likewise with the other, then made ticking motions with his index finger as he counted off the people on board. Satisfied, he climbed a ladder to the wheelhouse and started the engine. Staff kept our personal belongings in the wheelhouse, and I'd been self-conscious earlier when I'd had to strip off my staff rash guard and board shorts, exposing my bikini. I'd stuffed my clothes into the bag before hurrying to the deck to tug on my wetsuit. But Gabe had been a gentleman, or not interested, and carefully studied the boat console instead.

Now, I removed my wetsuit and added it to the pile already growing in between the stern benches. Guest divers were either relaxing under the shady canopy or stretched out enjoying the breeze and sun on the fiberglass bow.

As Gabe drove us back to the island, I climbed the ladder and moved around him. I rooted through my bag and pulled out my towel to wipe my face. I wrapped it around my waist, then turned to him.

I caught his eyes quickly darting away from my breasts, and that fluttering rolled through me again.

Sabbatical, sabbatical...

"How long have you been driving boats?" I asked, my knees soft to absorb the motion of the vessel streaking over the waves.

His rimless sunglasses were over his eyes now, and he kept his gaze on the water as he answered. One hand loosely gripped the wheel. "I've been driving boats since I was a kid, but I've had my captain's license for five years or so. This is the first time I've driven *Shark Bait* in an official capacity."

I couldn't resist a smile. He'd found the dive sites easily and followed our instructions exactly on where to stop to drop our groups in the water. "I guess this is our day for impressing each other."

He darted his eyes to mine, and this time a smile definitely appeared on his face. He was even more gorgeous with the sunglasses on. The brown shades accentuated his dark looks. Maybe there was a chance he was becoming Hot Not-So-Grumpy Guy. "Maybe I need to fill in for Miguel more."

I arched a brow and leaned toward him slightly. "Someone's got to give the guy a day off. Maybe that's why he's sick."

His smile broadened, showing a set of straight white teeth, and the air became charged between us.

"April!" Maia shouted from the deck below, and I jumped. "Are you going to chat with my brother all day or help us?"

Heat rocketed across my cheeks, and Gabe's smile faltered. Blinking, I turned my head to where Maia stood on the deck with her hands on her hips. "Be right there!" Then

I turned back to Gabe. "Do you realize we've gone an entire morning without antagonizing each other?"

He had faced forward again, but his eyes shifted to me momentarily. "Don't go jinxing it. We're not back at the dock yet. Besides, I like a woman who's not afraid to stand up for herself."

"Oh, I don't lie down for just anyone, don't worry." I couldn't believe the words had come out of my mouth. Good thing I was already blushing.

Gabe slowly turned his head to me, his eyes becoming molten behind his sunglasses. "Noted. You'd better go help Maia before she gets any more pissed off."

Afraid of what might come out of my mouth next, I swallowed hard and pulled on my board shorts. I avoided eye contact with him as I tossed my towel next to the bag. Then I moved to the ladder, grateful to put some distance between us. Away from the very charged air between us.

Chapter Ten

April

MIGUEL RETURNED to work the following day, and the next two weeks passed quickly. Gabe moved into Evan's old office in the dive shop but wasn't there often, at least when I was around. As I stepped onto the boat for the morning trip, my eye fell on the wheelhouse, even though I knew he wouldn't be there.

I'll see him soon enough. Probably tomorrow.

He'd driven *Shark Bait* several times when Miguel was off, and fortunately, his irritated, surly countenance diminished the more he drove. In fact, there were times he bordered on being *nice* to me. He'd even brought me a coffee the other day.

Miguel drove us out of the canal, and I turned my mind fully to the morning ahead. Maia, Wyatt, and I had meshed as a team and got along well together.

I was settling down in my new home and looking for ways to get to know people. I'd come across a post advertising a group of women who met monthly to discuss books and drink wine. They sounded like my kind of people, and I was quickly reading the current book before the meeting in a few days. As much as I liked Maia, I wanted other friends too.

After the second dive, I was breaking down equipment when Maia came over to me. "What are you doing for lunch?"

"Going to Dorado, like normal. You want to join me?"

"I can do better than that. Why don't you join me for lunch up at the Big House? You haven't been up there yet, so I can give you a quick tour. We've got time before you need to be back for the afternoon trip."

"Thanks. That sounds great."

As we walked around the dive shop, I glanced toward the beach, recalling the lights I'd seen the previous evening. "Was there a special occasion last night on the beach?"

Maia smiled. "No. That was our weekly beach barbeque. It runs from six to eight, and staff are welcome to any leftovers. Feel free to show up near the end and dig in. It's a great meal."

My stomach growled just thinking about it. "Sounds fantastic. You guys treat employees well here. Especially me!"

She pulled me into a quick side hug. "You might be getting a little more special treatment, but we have a great reputation for a reason. We try to keep it that way."

The Barn was on the way, so I stopped to change into dry clothes. Since I was being invited to a home with its own name, I went with a white sleeveless blouse and skirt. I twisted my hair in a clip, then Maia and I continued up the sand path. My eye lingered when she pointed out the cottage next to hers that belonged to Gabe and Hailey.

We went around a bend and the family home came into view. I blew out a low whistle. "I guess it's aptly named."

Maia laughed. "Yeah. It's got six bedrooms and baths. But I've got four siblings, so that came in handy. People on Dove Key like to call it Markham Manor, and we pretend we don't know that."

The home was three stories high and rectangular. The foundation and lower walls were made of stone, which transitioned to cinderblock. Timber accented the top portion of the structure and the eaves under the roof. The Barn and family cottages were similar. "When was this built?"

"Late 1800s. We've been on Calypso Key a long time."

I nodded, recalling her saying the buildings had been reconstructed after a hurricane destroyed the originals.

Maia opened a glass-paneled door and we stepped into a massive kitchen, cool air blowing over us. A long wooden table stretched out before us with the kitchen proper on the other side of the room. I inhaled a lungful of delicious scents. A dark-skinned man in a white chef's coat stood over the gas six-burner stove. He turned around when we entered.

Maia waved to him. "This is Anselm, a chef at Dorado. What's for lunch?"

"I have pasta primavera or a Cuban sandwich today."

Maia grinned at me. "Take your pick. They're both great."

I ordered the Cuban, feeling slightly stunned as Maia and I took two seats across from each other at the table for eight. I faced the door and glimpsed sunlight sparkling off a pool behind the house. "Are we eating alone?"

"Probably," Maia said. "Lunch is pretty unscheduled. People just show up when they have time."

My Cuban sandwich was divine. Spicy and juicy. "I

only have a little brother. It must be wonderful to have so much family around."

A shadow crossed her face for a moment, then she smiled. "It is. We're close, and Gabe coming home is just what we needed. Prodigal son returning and all that."

I couldn't help being curious. "Why did he move home?"

"My dad's ready to turn over some of the financial side of things, and Gabe is the one in the family with the business mind. And he wants to raise Hailey here."

"I met her. She's a hoot."

"Isn't she great? This move will be good for both of them. Especially Gabe." Maia took a sip of water and shook her head. "He got divorced a few years ago and he hasn't been the same."

I told myself knowing more about my new boss would be a good thing. My curiosity had nothing to do with the fact that our eyes met anytime either of us walked into a room. Gabe and I had kept our flirting quiet, and I hadn't said anything to Maia about how hot her brother was. "Not an amicable split, I take it?"

Maia whipped her head back and forth. "No. Kora up and walked out on them. She really did a number on Gabe. He told me he's never getting married again."

That was comforting. Even if sparks were starting to fly between us, at least I didn't need to worry about a serious relationship on either side.

She took a bite of a French fry. "He needs to open up again. Gabe has always been serious and conscientious. But after Kora... He's *grim*. And he was never like that before. My God—he ended up in jail, for crying out loud!"

I was drinking my water and sputtered, almost dropping it. "*What?*"

Maia shot me a rueful look. "Yeah. That family drama I told you about on your first day? Gabe got into a bar fight and spent the night in jail. I had to bail him out. Nothing came of it, but the incident just highlighted how much he needed a life shift. Moving back home will be good for him. It already has been. He was super grouchy that morning he first drove *Shark Bait*, but his mood has been lighter every time since."

That gave me a fuzzy feeling, but it faded at the thought that the man I'd been flirting with had been in jail. And was my boss. Maybe sabbaticals weren't such a bad idea.

Crisp steps entered the room behind me, and I turned as a tiny older woman walked into the room. She wore jeans and a western-style shirt with snaps up the front.

Maia made the introductions. "April, I'd like you to meet my grandmother."

The woman crossed the floor and folded her arms over the back of the chair next to me. "Very nice to meet you, and welcome to Calypso Key. Please call me Nona—everyone else does."

I smiled at her friendly, yet no-nonsense introduction. "Same to you, Nona. And I've felt very welcome here. This house is magnificent."

She waved a gnarled hand. "More of an empty old mausoleum now."

"Nona!" Maia burst into laughter.

"This big house is meant to be filled with laughter and people, child. Now that you've moved out, I only have your father and Evan for company."

"Gabe and Hailey are just down the path!"

Maia had told me that her grandmother stepped into a mother role for the family. I smiled at Nona. "And the new arrival is coming in less than five months."

Nona pointed a finger at Maia. "I'm counting the days, you know."

Maia sighed as she brushed her hand over her noticeable abdomen. "I've put away my bikinis for the time being."

"Nonsense!" Nona rapped her knuckles on the wooden table. "The world has moved on from hiding pregnancies, thank God. Flash that stomach!"

Maia shuddered, and we both burst into laughter. She grinned at Nona. "I'm not as brave as you. I'll keep my stomach covered, thank you very much."

Across from me, the door we'd entered through opened. Gabe stepped inside, breathing hard. He was dressed in running shorts and shoes.

And no shirt.

Sweat glistened across his sculpted pecs. The perfect amount of dark hair covered his chest, leading downward to smooth skin that showed every shadow of his six-pack. He still held the doorknob with one hand and froze in place.

I inhaled sharply, unable to help myself. All thoughts of manly sabbaticals fled, drowned out by pheromones. My eyes took in the rippling muscles as his abs contracted and his shoulders tensed.

Oh. My. God.

Next to me, Nona snapped upright. "Gabriel Michael Markham! What are you doing walking into the kitchen half naked? Good God, people are trying to eat."

If I'd suddenly forgotten about my food, it sure as hell wasn't because of disgust. A bead of sweat ran down the center of Gabe's chest, and I couldn't help wondering what it would taste like.

His eyes were huge as he stared at his grandmother. Then he saw me sitting there and they got even bigger. "I didn't think anyone would be in here! I just came to get a drink of water."

The temperature had become a hundred degrees hotter, but it had nothing to do with the warm air drifting in through the open door. My pulse pounded as our eyes locked, and a hungry look entered his. I had the ridiculous urge to vault across the tabletop and into his arms. Gabe and I stared at each other, both breathing hard as we were caught in some spell between the two of us.

I wrenched my eyes away when Nona spoke. "Of course people are here—it's lunchtime!" she snapped. "And we've got company, so show some manners. Make yourself presentable and come back, young man."

A heated flush turned his handsome face scarlet. This was the first time I'd ever seen Gabe anything but fully composed or snarly. The sight of Hot Grumpy Guy getting dressed down by his grandma was almost too much to keep inside and broke the swell of desire running through me. I bit the inside of my cheek and held in my laughter.

Maia curled her lip as she twisted around in her chair. "Gross. You're dripping sweat all over the floor, Gabe."

He raised both hands, palms out toward us. "I'm sorry, okay? I'll just leave now." And after one giant step backward, he shut the door with a hard thump, and we were alone again.

I held it in for a long moment, until I was sure he'd had a chance to make his escape, then burst into laughter. Praying I wasn't insulting Nona. I didn't want to be her next victim.

But she joined me, cackling as Maia buried her face in her hands. All three of us shared a good, long laugh.

"Oh, my!" the old woman said, wiping her eyes and

fanning herself. "My grandson is quite the fine specimen, isn't he?"

"Nona!" Maia said, lifting her head and trying to rein in her laughter. "Eww! Besides, you just embarrassed the hell out of him. He probably thinks you hate him now."

"Oh, he does not. My Gabriel knows me better than that." Nona patted me on the shoulder and gave me a knowing look. "Never let a fine-looking man think he's God's gift, dear. Only trouble can come from that."

Still laughing, I placed my hand on top of hers. "Nona, I don't think we need to worry about that with Gabe. You just put him in his place pretty well." I placed my napkin on the table. "Thanks for lunch. And the entertainment. But I'd better get back to work now."

As I strolled back down the hill, I examined Gabe's cottage, but there was no sign of him. I grinned, having the feeling he wouldn't be making an appearance for a while yet.

Chapter Eleven

Gabe

"WHAT'S THIS LOAN ABOUT?" I asked. Dad and I were back in his office, once again with me in his chair and him sitting in the metal folding chair. I'd been going over the profit and loss statements and other financial reports.

The loan caught my eye immediately, and I was not happy about it.

"I took it out two years ago when we hit a rough patch. It's provided most of the extra cash flow since."

I tried not to stiffen. "You mean what was in the savings account?"

"Yes. I just kept thinking things would turn around. But they haven't."

I made a quick calculation comparing the principal and interest that were listed on the statement, and it was way too much. "Maybe we can refinance. The interest rate is way above market."

"That was the best they would give me." Dad hesitated for a moment, then his shoulders dropped. "I'm sorry,

Gabe. I didn't want to be known as the Markham who brought down the resort, so I grasped at any straw I could. And maybe I was a little too proud too. Is it too late to save us?"

I don't know yet.

I smiled reassuringly at him and clasped his shoulder. "Of course not. And you won't have that legacy. You've always put family and the resort first. We'll get this figured out. I promise."

His smile was full of trust and the role reversal hit me like a punch to the stomach. Why hadn't he asked me for help before things got this bad?

I'd spent several weeks since that ludicrous incident in the kitchen trimming and cutting expenses where I could, including driving *Shark Bait* twice a week to fill in for Miguel. I kept telling myself it was to save money. But I couldn't stop thinking about that moment in the kitchen.

Not the one where Nona had tried to make an idiot out of me. Hell, I'd gone in there the previous day in the same attire, and she'd handed me a glass of water personally. I don't know what she had been up to, but my grandmother rarely did things without purpose.

No, the moment that had been running through my mind like a movie was when April and I had locked gazes. Desire had flared in her eyes and my body responded immediately. There was no mistaking her reaction to me. And that memory kept me from being completely mortified about my grandma shooing me out of my own house like a misbehaving boy.

When I saw April the following day, I completely ignored the incident, instead flirting with her lightly. She'd taken the hint and not brought it up either. She had been astonishingly fast at learning on the job and was already a favorite with guests. Her smile and upbeat attitude even dragged a smile out of me once or twice.

Since my divorce, I hadn't lived like a priest, but my encounters with women had been fleeting and... unsatisfying. I didn't believe in love—not after Kora. But I wasn't into casual flings either. All I knew was the effect April had on me was something new.

I had yet to decide whether it was good or bad.

Dad stirred and brought me back to the present. I had an idea and now was a good time to float it. "*Reel Deal* isn't chartered every day, and I think we're missing an opportunity there."

He nodded. "Sam, our fishing guide, splits his time here and at Sunset Siesta. He likes the variety of working for two resorts. A year or so ago, I mentioned more hours to him, but he wasn't very receptive. I can't imagine you want to hire another guide."

I twitched the corner of my mouth. "Why hire one when the best guide in the Lower Keys is sitting right next to me? You've been wanting to get out on the water more, so why not kill two birds with one stone?"

Dad's face went slack as he rubbed his clean-shaven chin. "I could certainly get a line in the water while I was leading charters. That's an interesting idea, Gabe."

I swept my gaze over the mounted fish on the walls. "I guarantee guests would be thrilled to be guided by Warren Markham himself. I can ask Evan to make flyers like he did for the snorkeling trips. I bet we fill up in no time, and that will give us more income."

Excitement flickered in Dad's eyes as he pushed to his feet. "I'd better go through my fishing gear in the shed. Make sure it's in good repair."

I kept a straight face. Dad's fishing shed was so spotless

you could eat off the floor, every piece of equipment lovingly tended.

Dad stilled and looked down at me. "I knew bringing you home was the right thing to do. You've always had a head for figures."

"Thanks. I'm glad we're back here too."

As he left, my eyes drifted back to the report on my terminal, and I shook my head.

I just hope I can come up with enough.

The good news was I'd managed to trim expenses enough to prevent any layoffs in the immediate future. April's tanned face flashed into my mind, then more than her face. Given the nature of her job, I'd had an eyeful of her spectacular body. She wore a mixture of one-piece swimsuits and bikinis under her wetsuit, but they were utilitarian. Then again, with a figure like hers, she didn't need to draw attention to it.

At least she's a pleasant distraction from trying to dig this place out of the hole.

I glanced at my watch, not surprised that I'd been in Dad's office for several hours. I needed to talk to Felicia, the chef in charge of the beach barbeque tomorrow night, and make sure she made the changes I'd requested. But that could wait.

I needed a break.

It was late afternoon, and the sun was dropping to my right as I strolled down the hill. I'd left Hailey at the Big House, working on a jigsaw puzzle with Nona. I angled over to the double doors of the Barn and slid them open enough to permit my entry. We never bothered to lock the main doors.

The cavernous space with its tall ceiling kept the heat at bay, though I still turned on a floor fan after crossing the room to my work area. Four eighteen-inch pieces of mahogany lay on top of my workbench, the legs of my current project. Only one still needed to be shaped, and I turned on my power planer in the corner. I lost myself to the soothing, familiar motions of sliding the piece of wood over the blade, shaping the surface until the warm structure in my hands told me it was done.

I held the wood up and inspected it, pleased with the four tapering sides of the leg, which came to a blunt end. After placing it on my workbench next to the other three, I lined them up to ensure they were all the same size.

A deep satisfaction filled me at their perfect form.

I attached a new sheet of rough paper to my hand sander and moved to the large rectangular piece of mahogany, resting on two sawhorses in the corner.

The door to the apartment opened and April ducked her head out. She met my gaze and her eyes opened wide.

"Oh!" she said, stepping out. She wore a light-green tank top that showed a hint of cleavage and black shorts. "Are you the mysterious wood artisan?"

I ignored the way my heart turned over at the sight of her. She carried Hemingway in her arms, stroking him with one hand as she padded over the floor barefoot.

"Stop," I called out, and she halted immediately, her brows raised.

I pointed to her feet. "Go put some shoes on. I keep this place clean, but it's not safe for bare feet. I don't want you to get hurt."

Her brow smoothed, and she raised one side of her mouth. "Excellent advice. Can I put the cat down first, or does he need shoes too?"

I burst into a grin, and April blinked several times, her eyes slightly glazed for a moment.

"If you can get that cat to do your bidding, more power to you," I said. "He sure doesn't do mine."

She bent over gracefully and deposited Hemingway on the floor, giving me a very nice view of her lacy white bra in the process. Then she spun around and reentered the apartment. She returned moments later wearing flip-flops. "These were the handiest to put on. Are they acceptable, or do I need steel-toed work boots?"

I glanced down at my boots, then eyed her flip-flops and tried not to smile. "I'll let it slide this time. But trust me, dropping a two-by-four on bare toes is no fun."

Hemingway sauntered over and sat next to me. April crossed the floor and picked him up again. Her hair was wet from a recent shower, and a heady, exotic scent wafted toward me. I filled my lungs, resisting the urge to bury my face in that thick, golden mane. Hemingway stretched out in her arms and laid his head on her breast.

Lucky cat.

"I'll keep that in mind," April said. "Your cat has become a regular. I don't feed him or anything, but he comes by at least once a day. He seems to like it here."

Her eyes were a clear, light blue, and my first impression still held. I could get lost in them. A smattering of freckles dotted her nose and cheeks. Very kissable freckles. "Maybe it's not the Barn he likes."

She gave me a smile that made my pulse take off. "How did you end up with three six-toed cats, anyway?"

I picked up my sander and moved to the formed piece of wood on the sawhorses. With an even, firm stroke, I slid it down the smooth surface. "Have you noticed that black-and-white picture in the dive shop?"

She cocked her head to the side. "The one of the two

men? I've seen it. One of them looked familiar, but I couldn't place him—the guy with the beard."

I glanced up as I made another pass over the surface. "The guy with the beard is Ernest Hemingway."

"No shit!" She laughed and it made me grin again. April brought a lot of smiles to my face.

"The other man is my great-grandfather, Charles Markham. He was friends with Hemingway and used to drive to Key West every Friday afternoon. He'd park at Hemingway's home. They'd walk down Duval Street together to Sloppy Joe's—among other places—and start drinking. Charles would inevitably get hammered enough that he spent the night there, then drove home on Saturday. In 1936, Hemingway gave my great-grandfather one of his six-toed cats for Christmas. And we've kept at least one ever since."

A delighted smile covered April's face, making my breath catch in my throat. She held the cat up in front of her face, so they looked eye to eye. "How about that! You're famous."

"The oldest cat always takes the name Hemingway. When he or she dies, we bury them in a pet cemetery near the Big House. Then a new cat takes the name."

She resettled the cat in her arms, then lifted him toward me momentarily. "What was his name originally?"

"Anselmo."

She scrunched up her nose. "That's an unusual name for a cat."

I eased out a deep breath as I resisted the urge to kiss the tip of her nose. "*For Whom the Bell Tolls*."

Her mouth dropped open and her eyes became huge. "Santiago at the dive shop! That was the character from *Old Man and the Sea!*"

I couldn't resist another smile as our gazes held. "Give the pretty lady a gold star."

April's eyes changed. That frisson ran between us again, the electric current. Eventually, she dropped them, and I ran my sander in a long sweep again.

"How old is Hemingway?"

I had to stop and think. "Around eight. He's the patriarch. Santiago and Pilar are both his."

"And who was the lucky lady?"

I ran my hand over the wood, enjoying the smooth warmth of it. Trying not to think about other things that were smooth and warm. "The Hemingway House in Key West lets us borrow a cat when we're ready to breed one of ours. Then we give them the kittens after we take one or two. That keeps the bloodlines fresh." I raised my eyes to hers again. "Then, like responsible pet owners, we have our cat fixed. Pilar is going to continue the line."

A mischievous smile stretched her lips. "So poor Hemingway found his true love, then got his balls cut off?"

My grin matched hers. "He's not the first guy that's happened to."

She laughed and shook her head.

"And he was still Anselmo back then," I added. "He became Hemingway a couple of years ago."

Her lovely smile lingered as she studied the wood. "What are you making?"

"A coffee table for a guest bungalow."

She bent over and ran her hand over the reddish mahogany surface. I'd varied different shades of wood planks to give the tabletop a striking appearance. Her fingers were long and shapely, yet I'd seen her strength firsthand.

What would those fingers feel like stroking me? Stroking all of me?

I swallowed hard.

"It's beautiful," she purred. When she looked up, her eyes held admiration and respect. Which was a hell of a lot better than the animosity of when we'd first met.

"Thanks. I went to college for a business degree, but I love working with my hands. I've made furniture for years."

Her eyes darted to my hands, and a hungry look came into them. An expression that sent a rush of heat straight to my core. Before I could think about it, I set the sander down and took a step toward her, closing the distance between us. Earlier today, I'd thought of several reasons why getting involved with her would be a bad idea. But hell if I could think of a single one right now. All I wanted was to kiss her. To run my hands through that golden hair. We locked eyes as I leaned toward her.

Then my watch alarm beeped.

I straightened with an inward groan and silenced the noise.

"Fun time over?" April's voice was breathy.

I thought of several answers to that, but the moment was over. "Yeah. That's my reminder to meet with Felicia about the barbeque tomorrow night."

"Maia told me they're a weekly occurrence."

Our gazes met again as I nodded. "You should stop by. It's usually over by eight p.m. There should be plenty of food, but the crowd will be gone by then."

The air grew charged between us once more. She got the message I was sending.

"I'll be there."

Chapter Twelve

April

I TOWELED dry and pulled on a dressy black tank top and knee-length skirt, keeping one eye on the clock. I had led a night dive, and to save time afterward, had showered inside the dive shop. But it was still after 8:00 p.m. If I wanted to get to the barbeque, I needed to hurry.

Especially if I wanted to catch Gabe.

A nervous little ripple ran through me at the thought. Over the previous weeks, the angry, withdrawn man I'd met had become casual, even easygoing. Unless someone did something he thought was a safety risk. Then Hot Grumpy Guy came back in full force. There was no point in denying Operation Sabbatical was in serious jeopardy. Gabe had driven *Shark Bait* today, and the friendly sibling teasing between him and Maia had made me smile all morning.

And after our conversation yesterday in his wood shop, I was even more eager to see him. His smile had made me weak. It made my insides melt. And he'd been about to kiss me. Until his watch alarm went off, anyway.

I brushed out my damp hair, then frowned in the mirror. "I don't have time to do anything with this." Digging into my bag, I pulled out a clip, twisted my hair into a coil, then clipped it at the back of my head. I didn't have any makeup with me and generally didn't wear any. I shrugged at my reflection. "I'm going for dinner and maybe some conversation. It's not like it's a date. He might have left by now anyway."

Not a date.

I kept repeating that as I made sure the shop was locked up. Then I headed toward the beach. The western corner past the last bungalow was alight with party lights, criss-crossing over a dozen picnic tables. The breeze wafted a rich, delicious scent toward me, and I took a deep breath. Soft sounds of an acoustic ensemble band drifted into the night.

As I entered the area, I swept my gaze around, but the place was nearly deserted. No guests sat at picnic tables, which had already been wiped clean. A small area before the stage had been cleared to make room for dancing. Foot-prints in the sand said people had been dancing there earlier, but now the area was empty of revelers.

And Gabe wasn't around, either.

A willowy woman, her white apron contrasting her dark skin vividly, stood behind a line of covered metal pans.

"Am I too late to get something to eat, Felicia?"

"Evenin', April," she said in a soft Caribbean accent, smiling as she stepped forward. "There's plenty left, and it's still nice and warm."

She dished me up a plate of grilled chicken along with rice and beans and homemade coleslaw, and I made my way over to the bar and sat at the counter. I kicked off my flip-flops. After another glance around the nearly empty area, I tried not to be disappointed that I'd missed Gabe. "Can I get an IPA, Charli?"

The woman behind the counter nodded and wiped out a pint glass. Charli had been a bartender at the resort for ten years and was one of the first employees I'd met. Her blond hair was slightly too platinum to be natural. Her tan arms were well muscled, and she could turn on a hard edge to deal with troublemakers when needed. But otherwise, she was friendly and affable, a perfect fit for the job.

As she tilted the glass under the tap, I couldn't help asking, "Was Gabe here earlier?"

"Yeah. He left to make sure Hailey was settled in for the night. I was surprised—he usually doesn't show up to these things. But now that he's here for good, I guess he wants to interact with guests more."

I nodded and scooped rice and beans into my mouth, trying to decide if he'd been looking for me.

Well, if he was, I missed him.

"Night dive tonight?" she asked, sliding the ice-cold beer toward me.

"Yeah. It was a fun one. Two enormous tarpons followed us and used our lights to hunt. The divers loved it."

Charli's eyes got huge, and she shuddered. "You and I have different ideas of fun, then."

I laughed and we traded small talk as I ate. After finishing, I couldn't resist seeing if Felicia had any desserts left. I clapped my hands when she presented me with a slice of cherry cheesecake.

I had just sat back down when Charli returned, and our conversation transitioned to a Saturday outdoor movie night held on Driftwood Beach, near Conch Republic Brewpub. Leaning casually on the bar, she was telling me the lineup when the overhead party lights threw a shadow over me. Someone sat down on my right.

Charli straightened with a grin. "You're back!"

My heart lurched, then took off at a dead run as Gabe nodded. He wore a soft blue button-down shirt and dressy shorts, his beard trimmed to stubbly perfection. His eyes met mine for a long beat before turning back to the bartender. "Officially off duty now."

She reached under the counter and pulled out a glass tumbler. "I know what that means. The only question is whether you want Macallan or Glenlivet?"

Gabe leaned forward and pressed his hands against the counter. "Do you have any of the 18 Double Cask down here?"

Charli rolled her eyes. "It's a barbeque, Gabe! The eighteen-year-old stuff is kept nice and safe behind the main bar." She pointed toward Dorado. "The Glenlivet I've got is a 12. But you're in luck because I brought one bottle of the Macallan 15. Just in case you might want some."

He sat back again and rested an elbow on the counter, looking impossibly gorgeous. "True. The really good stuff is to be saved for special occasions only. Macallan, please." He turned to me and smiled.

My mouth went dry.

Charli poured a healthy shot into the glass and pushed it toward him before retreating to the other end of the bar.

"No ice?" I asked.

Gabe lifted the glass with its amber fluid and took a sip, rolling it around in his mouth before swallowing. I tried not to imagine what it would feel like to be that whisky right now. "Never with ice. Distorts the purity of the drink."

I lifted my pint glass. "To purity. I'll stick to my beer."

A slow smile rose on his face as he turned to me. "I can appreciate all kinds of fine things. Beer included."

Our eyes locked. There it was again.

That live current running between us.

I took a deep breath and lifted the last bite of cheesecake, placing it in my mouth. Gabe's eyes followed every movement, remaining on my lips. "I take it you got dinner?"

I nodded. "Felicia fixed me up. It was delicious."

His eyes rose to mine at that last word. The small three-person band broke into an upbeat, funky version of the '70s hit "Boogie Shoes", making me smile as I tapped my foot on the barstool. I loved to dance, though it had been a very long time since I had. Ignoring the music, Gabe took another long, loving sip of his whisky. I watched his throat move as he swallowed.

Then he pushed the glass away, half empty, and turned fully on his stool to face me. "You want to dance?"

My mouth dropped open. Those were the *last* words I'd expected to hear from him, especially involving a song with a definite beat like "Boogie Shoes". But Gabe's eyes held a definite challenge, like he realized he'd surprised me and was waiting for my reaction.

I leaned toward him. "I thought you'd never ask."

He clasped my right hand within his left and led me to the small, cleared area of sand near the band. His hand was rough—the hands of a carpenter, not a businessman. The powdery white sand was warm and soft beneath my bare feet, while Gabe kept his gray Sperry Top-Siders on. As we stopped, I expected to settle across from each other, both of us dancing with our own individual motion.

That's not what happened.

Gabe raised my right hand, held firmly in his left, and slid his right to the back of my waist. With gentle pressure, he guided us in a steady rhythm, stepping softly over the sand as he moved us in a basic swing dance.

Expertly.

To say I was stunned would be the biggest understatement ever.

But I was no stranger to dance myself, and easily fell into the matching steps, moving effortlessly with him. His eyes took on a new glimmer as he recognized it. I lost myself to the fun, upbeat music, a wide smile rising on my face. Gabe was more serious—of course—but an answering smile was beginning to tug at his lips.

He leaned in. "I'm going to dip you."

After I nodded, he swooped me over backward, his right arm supporting me. He folded over me, our faces inches apart, and he held me motionless for a long moment, just staring at me until he raised me back up.

I swallowed, a deep thrumming running through my body now as we continued moving, circling, and swaying with each other. My blood pulsed in rhythm with the music, singing through my veins.

He arched a brow. "How about a spin?"

"Only one?"

He broke into a wide smile as he removed his hand from my waist. Raising my clasped hand with his left, I twirled underneath. The differences in our heights made the maneuver effortless, like we were made to do this. Instead of stopping after one rotation, I continued, spinning to look at the center of his chest and orient myself with each round. It wasn't easy because the sand was uneven, but I held my balance. After four rotations, I stopped.

Standing completely still, I faced him, arching a brow of my own.

Gabe burst into deep laughter, a sound that was carefree and unreserved. It was so unlike him, and I couldn't get enough. He pulled me tight, and we moved back into our former rhythm, twirling and stepping in tandem. Our motions were effortless. He only had to hint with his hand, and I knew what he wanted. I shot him a level stare and he immediately dipped me, our lips an inch apart. With a smile that melted my insides, he stood me back up. We moved again in a different swing dance pattern but still completely in sync with each other.

I didn't care that the man I danced with was my boss. And an owner of the resort. All I cared about was that he made my body soar.

Finally, the song ended with a flourish, and both of us nodded at the band. Then we broke into wide grins as we turned back to each other. He still held my left hand, his right pressed against the small of my back. Not my upper shoulder, the correct position for formal dancing.

And I was sure Gabe knew that.

Before either of us could say anything, the band started into a slow, atmospheric instrumental rendition of "Fields of Gold". The song was sumptuous and melodic, inviting motion.

We instantly swayed to the music, not needing to discuss it. No fancy steps this time, Gabe tightened his hold on me, bringing his arm closer so my hand rested against his shoulder. His eyes were dark in the dim light.

"The divemaster has some serious dance moves," he said softly.

I smiled and tilted my head, emphasizing the length of my neck. A long, hot roll ran through me as he lowered his eyes to watch.

"I took years of dance classes growing up. What about you?"

That smile rose again. The smile I'd seen more in the last two days than in the last two weeks. "My dad made me take dancing lessons as a kid. I hated it. But after I went to college, I discovered it impressed women, so I guess he wasn't totally full of it."

I grinned as we danced together, circling to the sensuous, emotional music. "Why did he make you take dance lessons?"

Gabe briefly clenched his eyes shut. "Since I was the eldest son, he thought I should make a practice of dancing with all the blue-haired old ladies at the resort. You wouldn't believe the fights we used to get into about it."

"I can imagine. Though, the last time I looked, my hair's not blue."

"No, it's certainly not."

He removed his hand from my waist and reached behind my head. Removing my hair clip, Gabe shoved it in his pocket before fanning his fingers through my still-damp strands. The scent of my shampoo filled the air around us. His right hand still clasped my left, and he leaned over and took a deep breath. He was gentle, his motions slow and sumptuous. "Your hair is much too glorious to be pinned up like that. And it fits the song too."

After running his fingers through my mane one final time, he placed his hand between my shoulder blades, over my hair, and softly stroked the strands with his thumb. The world faded away as we danced in a slow circle. I became oblivious to everyone around us.

Unaware of everything but the man holding me in his arms.

Gabe's eyes were like liquid fire. He held me captive with them. "This song is appropriate for us. The very first time I saw you, your hair reminded me of spun gold. I pictured a wide field of it."

"I wondered if you'd been born in the jeans you were wearing. They looked like they were a part of you. You took my breath away, Gabe." My voice came out softer, huskier than normal.

In one smooth motion, he removed his hand from my upper back and softly grasped my jaw, stretching his thumb along my jawline. Holding my face still, he lowered his head and kissed me.

The pure confidence of his move made my legs weaken. His hold on my jaw was light—I could pull away if I wanted to. Which was the *last* thing I was thinking about. As our mouths melded together, his lips were soft and yet firm at the same time.

I let go of his hand and linked my arms around his neck. At the same time, he slid his hand up to softly cup the side of my face. Neither of us deepened the kiss. Though the beach was nearly deserted, certainly some people could be watching us.

And I didn't care.

A soft, yearning moan escaped from my lungs and his hand tightened on my cheek. With one final brush of lips, I pulled away to rest my head against his chest. Gabe wrapped his arms around me, lifting one to press my head to his chest. His heart pounded under my ear. Though outwardly he appeared calm, the rapid pulse I heard—and felt—said otherwise.

He was a man of contradictions.

I took another deep inhale, catching his scent for the

first time. Pure male. "A few minutes ago was the first time I've ever heard you laugh."

Gabe's swaying feet paused in their rhythm for a moment before continuing. "I don't laugh much."

I pulled my head back to meet his eyes. "I liked it, Gabe."

He stroked a finger down my cheek. "So did I."

The song ended, and the performers announced they were done for the night.

I blinked, feeling like I had been brought down to earth after soaring in the clouds. Suddenly, I could feel the sand under my feet, and the lights strung overhead were too bright. Charli wiped the counter with a rag, and Felicia cleaned the grill, both studiously not looking at us. Like it was any other night.

Except it was anything but.

"It's getting late, and we both have to start early tomorrow," Gabe said softly. "Let me walk you home."

His words brought a pang of disappointment, even though I recognized the sense of them. I smiled as we headed toward the concrete path. "Protecting me from marauding six-toed cats?"

He clasped my hand and swung it softly as we walked. "Calypso Key's pretty safe, but that doesn't matter. This is who I am."

I recalled his face that day when he hadn't known where Hailey had wandered off to. And his relief when he'd seen her with me. Safe. Yes, Gabe was protective. I squeezed his hand. "Thanks."

As we walked up the hill, we angled to the sand path. Too soon, I stood at my front door. Butterflies flitted everywhere inside me. I wasn't ready to ask him inside yet.

As I raised my head to tell him that, Gabe gripped my face in both hands and kissed me.

Hard.

Opening his lips, he plunged his tongue into my mouth.

The butterflies inside me turned to molten, liquid heat as our tongues circled.

With a deep, wrenching noise in his throat, Gabe stepped forward and pushed me against the front door, pinning me with his chest. My lungs couldn't fill—he left me breathless. The remnants of whisky in his mouth tasted smoky and exotic. He slid one hand down and around to grab my ass, pushing me tight against him.

I couldn't exactly miss what was pressed between us. It was impossible not to notice.

Then he broke the kiss and took a deliberate step backward, resting his hands on my hips. Mine draped loosely around his neck. Both our chests heaved, and he gave me a crooked smile. "I've wanted to do that for a while now. It was killing me to hold back down at the beach."

My lips were still parted. My mind was whirling, my heart racing, and I didn't know what to say. I needed to keep some perspective here.

I was horrible with men.

I couldn't let myself get swept away, even though every cell of my body wanted him to possess me at that moment. And wanted to possess him. And yet I was afraid to ask him inside. I licked my lips, which felt swollen with need.

Oh, this man was dangerous!

I took a deep breath to reply—whatever might come out —when Gabe placed a single finger over my lips.

"Thanks for the dance," he said, his voice soft and velvety. "I'll see you tomorrow."

With a slow wink, he turned around and strolled back

to the path. I followed him with my eyes, unable to move. Still hardly able to breathe. When he was twenty feet away, he turned his shoulders toward me and nodded, a silent, respectful gesture as he strode into the night. I hadn't known what to say, how to express what I needed.

Yet Gabe had known anyway.

Chapter Thirteen

Gabe

AS I STROLLED up the hill, the raging throbbing in my groin gradually subsided. Then I realized I was stroking my bottom lip with my thumb. Over and over.

I snorted.

I couldn't blame April for that stunned, shell-shocked look on her face after we'd kissed at her door. I felt the same way. But I'd gone too far. There was no doubt in my mind that the flaring desire we'd shared had been mutual. But something had changed for her there at the end, and I pulled back.

I was an asshole, but not *that* much of an asshole.

Since my divorce, I'd been very cautious around women. Always in control. I hadn't been with many women since Kora, but the forced abstinence didn't explain why I was so goddamn attracted to April. Or why I acted the way I did around her.

Had I wanted to show off when I'd asked her to dance? Maybe impress her a little? Yeah, I had. And I'd liked seeing her reaction. It had been so long since a woman had made me feel good about myself, I'd forgotten what it was like.

But I sure hadn't expected her to match me step for step. That had been a massive surprise—the way we'd melded together seamlessly. I couldn't help wondering what other ways we'd move perfectly together.

If she hadn't pulled away, who knows where we would have ended up. I wasn't upset that April had taken a step back. If—or when—we got physical, I wanted her to be one hundred percent sure. I wanted her so hot for me she couldn't help herself.

Like I was starting to feel about her.

I still wasn't interested in a serious relationship, but having a girlfriend again? That might be in the cards. If April wanted it, anyway. Maia had said something about her leaving St. Croix due to a bad relationship. Maybe she wasn't interested in something serious any more than I was.

I was only certain of one thing. I wanted to see her again.

I opened the front door of my cottage and stepped into the dim living room. Nona sat in an armchair, the lamp next to it throwing a halo of light on the paperback she was reading. When I closed the door, she shut her book and looked up with a smile.

"Hailey give you any problems?" I asked quietly as I sat on the couch across from her.

"Of course not. I told her a story about your grandfather and me, and she settled right in."

I smiled. "Must have been one of the G-rated ones, then."

Nona narrowed her eyes but didn't rise to the bait. Instead, she asked, "Did you get a chance to talk to Felicia? You were gone for a while."

I considered my answer. I'd asked Nona to watch Hailey so I could have a conversation with the chef. But I was a lousy liar. And we Markham kids had all learned to our detriment that Nona had an unerring sense for the truth. "I did, then I ran into April down there. We talked for a few minutes." I resisted the urge to rub my lip again.

Nona's expression turned sly. "Did you now? That sounds promising."

Nona was forever trying to fix her grandchildren up. It was a mystery to us why she'd left Dad alone since Mom passed, but he was still single and content with it. "If you say so. It was just conversation, Nona."

She scooted to the edge of her chair and peered at me. "Not considering what I saw when you barged into the kitchen."

I sighed, knowing there was no getting out of this. "And what would that be?"

"You and April were about to rip each other's clothes off, right there at the table! Who knows what might have happened if I hadn't stepped in?"

I couldn't resist a smile. "So that's why you were so hell-bent on making me look like an idiot?"

"You didn't need my help for that, Gabriel."

My smile widened.

Nona clasped her hands in her lap. "Maia and Evan both have a high opinion of April. And I enjoyed meeting her too. You have my blessing."

"Well, thank God that's settled! Now I can sleep tonight."

She laughed and shook a finger at me. "It might have only been a conversation, but it was a beginning."

It was a hell of a lot more than that.

My smile faded, and her gaze sharpened. "Of course,

you've been driving the dive boat rather frequently, haven't you? I'm sure that's just a coincidence."

"I'm here to trim expenses, Nona. Driving is a part of that." I wasn't sure why I was hesitant to tell her about my interaction with April, other than the obvious reluctance to give her any more ammunition to use against me. Except I'd kissed April in front of several employees. It was bound to go around the resort grapevine like wildfire. But that didn't mean I wanted to tell my grandmother about it.

Her smug smile told me she wasn't buying my denials. "And if it causes you to spend your mornings with a beautiful woman in her swimsuit, I'm sure you keep your eyes averted."

"She wears a wetsuit most of the time."

Nona dropped the teasing tone, eyeing me seriously. "Just because you had an awful experience with Kora doesn't mean you should write off love altogether. You're too fine of a man to be alone, Gabriel."

I sighed. "I have no interest in a permanent relationship, but there's a pretty huge gulf between that and alone. I might be ready to investigate the space between."

I stood and held a hand out to Nona, helping her to her feet. "Come on. I'll walk you home."

"Home is all of two hundred yards away."

"Why do women keep arguing when I try to be chivalrous? Doesn't anyone appreciate a nice gesture anymore?"

A smug smile came over my grandmother's face as she looped her arm through mine. "Oh? Did you walk another woman home tonight?"

Shit!

I opened the door, and we walked into the warm night. "Yes, I walked April to her door."

Nona patted my bicep. "Trust me, Grandson. Women

appreciate a gallant gesture. *Especially* ones from tall, dark, and handsome men. Kora was an idiot."

"At last, we agree on something."

"I just hate seeing you angry and bitter. I think April could be good for you."

We walked up the sandy path, crickets chirping around us. "We haven't even gone out! I'm not having this conversation, Nona."

"Fine, I'll stop. I don't want you getting angry at me."

We stopped at one of the side entrances of the Big House. "I could never be mad at you." I wrapped her tiny form in my arms and held her tight.

"I love you, Gabriel."

"Love you too, Nona. Thanks for watching Hailey."

She patted my arms and smiled. "Go on now. I know you don't like to leave her alone for even a few minutes. And you've seen the old lady home safe and sound. Go back to your daughter."

AFTER AN EARLY BREAKFAST with Hailey at the Big House, I left her to wait for the school bus. Being part of a founding family could be a pain in the ass, but it had its benefits too. Like being picked up for school from the front porch.

I ambled down the path toward the dive shop. The morning was alive with sparrows flitting and singing in the flame trees. As I neared the Barn, I looked closely, but April wasn't on her back patio. I was curious whether a night's sleep might erase that unsure expression I'd seen last evening. I hoped so.

After unlocking the front door of the shop, I headed

down the hall to the final room on the right, formerly Evan's office, and now mine. I wasn't driving today, but I liked the atmosphere here and found it a good place to work.

I was combing over budget line items, looking for more ways to trim costs, when the bell over the front door rang. Fast footsteps trotted down the hall. I looked up as Maia burst into my office.

She skidded to a stop in my doorway, her belly leading the way. "Oh. My. God!"

I blinked. "Uh, good morning?"

Her eyes were huge. "Gabe! I just ran into Felicia. She said you tried to suck April's face off last night!"

I winced and screwed one eye shut. "Close the door, for God's sake!"

She turned around and shut the door, then slid into one of the chairs in front of my desk. I raised a brow as she drummed both heels on the floor.

"So is it true?"

"Maia, no one sucked anyone's face off, I assure you. When April arrives, you'll find everything right where it's supposed to be."

Her face split into a giant grin. "Oh, that is *so* not a denial!"

I flopped back in my chair. "Yes. We kissed. We were dancing, and it just happened." *Boy, did it happen.*

I'd have had an easier time not breathing than stopping myself from kissing her.

Maia gasped, the sound loud in the quiet room. "Oh my God! You danced? *And* kissed?" Then her face became still, and she narrowed one eye at me. "Is that all that happened, Gabe?"

"Yes, Maia. That is all that happened. Happy?"

She actually squealed. "Yes! I can't wait to talk to April this morning."

I dropped my gaze to the desktop. "Take it easy on her, okay? Things got a little... weird at the end."

"Weird how?"

"I think the entire thing caught us both by surprise. And when I left her, she looked... confused. Like she didn't know how to feel about what happened."

"How did you feel about it?"

I stared at her, deadpan. "I'm not discussing my love life with my little sister."

"You will when your love life involves a good friend of mine."

I sighed again. "Fair enough."

Maia's smile returned. "I'm happy for you, Gabe. April's great. She's funny and sweet and upbeat. Actually, she's the direct opposite of you."

"Gee, thanks."

"But be careful, Gabe. She's had some bad relationships. That's probably what the vibe you got last night was. When she first got here, she told me she wasn't going near a man for a long time."

I raised my brows. "Maybe I changed her mind."

Maia didn't smile back. "I mean it, Gabe. I've heard you talk about how you never want to be seriously involved again. Don't break her heart. She deserves better."

"I'm not planning to. Maia, we haven't even been out on a date! She might not even be interested."

Maia's grin returned. "After dancing *and* kissing? With my big brother? Oh, trust me. She's interested. I'd say you need to ask a girl out on a date."

After she left, I rubbed my face with both hands, then

stared at the empty room. "Why did I think it was a good idea to move back to a place where nothing is private?"

Chapter Fourteen

April

THE MORNING SUN threw my shadow before me as I strolled along the beach. The warm Caribbean Sea washed over my feet, soothing me. I hadn't been back to the resort beach since the day I'd arrived and stayed in a guest bungalow. After waking, I'd decided to leave my apartment for some ocean therapy. To try to make sense of what had happened.

How had I gone from wanting nothing to do with men to damn near jumping Gabe's bones last night? What about my sabbatical?

Do I really want a sabbatical?

That was the real question. I wanted Gabe in my bed, and there was no denying it. What I didn't want was the strife and angst that had accompanied my past relationships.

At least I don't need to worry about him not returning my interest.

And truth be told, that was a definite salve to my

wounded ego. Proof that a gorgeous, successful man could find me attractive. Maybe I wasn't cursed after all.

I wandered down the shoreline, eventually crossing under the now-unlit party lights Gabe and I had danced beneath. A cement path continued northward, past the watersports hut with its locked-up kayaks and paddleboards, and I stepped onto it. The path wound around Orchid, Calypso Key's fine dining restaurant. It was only open for dinner and now sat dark and still. A handful of garden cottages lay to my right, a more affordable option for guests than the oceanfront variety.

Gabe turned me into someone I hardly recognized—bold, confident. I liked that. I liked the mixture of barely restrained passion and protective chivalry he displayed. But I needed to know more about him, especially why he'd spent the night in jail. That was one of the strangest things about this situation. Despite him being potentially dangerous, I felt safe with him.

Or was that just my raging hormones talking?

Eventually, the path petered out near the mangrove wetland area, which was kept untouched and natural. A majestic blue heron flew past, not ten feet in front of me. Two kayaks sat under a makeshift shelter, sleeker and more expensive-looking than the ones guests used. A glance at my watch told me I needed to get something to eat and head to work.

I went back to my apartment for a quick breakfast, then headed to the dive shop. It was already open, which wasn't surprising, since it was now 7:00 a.m. Someone had made coffee and I filled my travel mug, trading small talk with Miguel. When I turned around to leave, Gabe strode into the room.

My palms became damp at the sight of him, and I gripped my mug tighter.

He gave me a smile and held my eyes as he said, "Morning, guys."

Miguel returned the greeting, but I couldn't get any words out. With the boat captain there, we couldn't say much anyway. I just nodded and stepped forward. As we passed, Gabe's hand softly brushed mine. Turning my wrist, I pressed my fingers against his wrist, a smile rising on my face.

Wyatt's and Maia's voices came from the gear room, so I headed toward the compressor room next door to load tanks. I pushed a cart inside and had loaded half a dozen tanks when a voice called out behind me.

"Hey."

I froze at Gabe's words, then slowly raised myself upright. "Hi."

He softly shut the door and closed the distance between us. I hadn't put my hair up yet and he gently slid a lock behind my right ear. "You doing okay?"

His lips were so full, and I vividly recalled the taste of them. I nodded again. "Yes." I tried not to wince at my inability to form more than one-word sentences around this man.

"I'm sorry if I came on too strong last night. I didn't mean to make you uncomfortable."

I smiled and relaxed, leaning into his hand as he cupped my face. "I was a little... stunned. More at myself than you." With a deep breath, I squared my shoulders and looked him in the eye. "Gabe, I have a pretty bad history with relationships. Either I choose men who want nothing to do with me, or the guy I think *is* into me dumps me with no warning. It's like there's no in between."

"I don't think anyone gets to our age without some baggage. And I hope you realize after last night that I'm very attracted to you."

I smiled again. "Same here. This is what I need you to understand. I don't want a serious relationship at this point in my life."

The corner of his mouth twitched. "Neither do I. Sounds like we're perfect for each other."

That made me laugh, and the tight knot in my gut unfurled. "Maybe."

My smile faded as he moved his hand, trailing a finger down my neck and across my collarbone. Shivers tickled down my chest.

"Only one way to find out," he said softly. "You want to go out with me?"

"I would. Very much. What do you have in mind?"

He lifted one shoulder. "On Saturday night, Hailey is sleeping over at a new friend's house. I'm kind of an old-school guy. How about dinner and a movie?"

"A classic! Can't go wrong with that. Saturday works for me."

"There's a Cineplex on Big Pine Key. I'm sure we could find something there to watch."

My conversation with Charli came back to me, and I inhaled sharply. "I know! There's an outdoor movie series near Conch Republic. And this week, they're showing a rom-com I've been wanting to see. How about that?"

Gabe took a step back, a deep frown stretching his mouth. "Do I look like a rom-com kind of guy?"

I grinned. "Well, no, you don't." I stepped forward and skimmed my hands over his chest, feeling the taut muscles under his shirt. The muscles I'd seen with my own eyes, yet this was the first time I'd touched them. I wanted more.

"But you do look like a man who wants to make his woman happy."

His frown grew marginally less. "Rom-com, huh?"

"It'll be fun. We can bring a blanket and hang out on the beach."

"Can I pick dinner?"

"Of course. Fair's fair. Are you in or out?"

He stared at me for a long beat, evaluating. "In."

Then I tilted my head back and traced my finger over his stubbly beard. The skin around my mouth tingled at the memory of how it had rubbed last night. *Who am I when he's around?* "Besides, I'm a woman who likes to make her man happy. I might be willing to do something to please you."

Gabe's frown disappeared, intense interest flaring in his eyes. "Now that's intriguing. Anything?"

"Well, if your idea involves whips and chains, we might need to negotiate."

A slow, sexy grin reached across his lips, and I took another step closer, my feet moving without any help from my brain.

"Nothing like that, I assure you."

"Then take some time and think about it," I whispered, brushing along the sharp line where his beard met his neck. "You don't have to answer now."

Gabe lowered his head, and our mouths were close enough that his breath caressed my lips. "I don't need any more time." His voice was deep and throaty. "I know exactly what I want."

My finger stilled. "Really? What?"

He took one step closer and grasped my waist with both hands. "I've got a special bottle of thirty-year-old Macallan. I've never opened it—been saving it. I want to pour that whisky over every inch of your body and lick it off."

My knees buckled.

Gabe gripped my waist to keep me from falling as I leaned a palm against his chest.

A sexy grin stretched his mouth. "I think the lady likes the idea."

"The lady definitely likes the idea."

"Then I'll pick you up at six on Saturday."

"Okay." I stared at him, feeling like my lungs could hardly function. "I'd better get back to work."

He nodded, but instead of stepping back, he leaned down and kissed me. I closed my eyes, losing myself to the softness of his lips. There was none of the frantic passion of our goodnight kiss, but this one was still warm, welcoming, and delicious.

A promise of things to come.

As he broke the kiss, Gabe pressed something into my hand. Then he turned around and walked out the door. I opened my hand to look and smiled. The clip he'd removed from my hair last night lay snug in my palm.

THE FIRST DIVE site we visited was the *Benson*, a freighter that had naturally sunk. Storms over the years had pushed it farther to sea, gradually moving the ship deeper. Located twenty minutes from Calypso Key, the wreck was a popular dive. I'd done it many times now, enough to be familiar with it and to view it with the respect it deserved. The ship sloped along the sandy bottom, with the stern at the deepest point, 150 feet down—well below recreational limits where we would take divers.

The Florida Keys were famous for their wreck dives, which made the *Benson* a regularly scheduled trip, though it had never fallen on the days Gabe drove the boat. The shallowest part of the *Benson's* elevated bridge lay forty feet below the surface, making the site unsuitable for snorkeling. So, after the dive, we made a quick trip back to the resort to pick up Maia and her group of snorkelers for the second site.

When we were underway again, I smiled at Maia and Wyatt rubbing noses near the covered bow area. I approached and dried my hair with a towel. "Reunited at last, huh? It was a terribly long couple of hours, I'm sure."

Maia stuck her tongue out at me, and I laughed. I'd liked Wyatt since my first day, and he was a good husband, always attentive to her. He refused to let her do any heavy work now that her pregnancy was more pronounced.

Wyatt kissed her quickly on the lips. "I'll get to work swapping tanks."

"I'd better join you," I said and had taken a step forward when Maia grasped my arm.

"Hold up a second. I want to chat a little."

"Sure," I said as we sat on the side bench. "Everything all right with you?"

She smiled and slid a hand over her belly. "Picture-perfect. I'm monitoring my blood pressure regularly and everything's going by the book. Between Wyatt and my dad, I'm not sure a pregnancy has ever been watched so closely."

Maia's pregnancy had been a surprise. After she first found out, I'd helped her to sort out her feelings about it. "I'm glad you're more optimistic about things now. More settled."

"Being married, with Wyatt by my side, made a big difference. Now I'm looking forward to her arrival."

I inhaled sharply, my lips stretching back into a grin. "Her? You found out the sex?"

Maia nodded and slid a hand over her abdomen again. "At my last ultrasound. Now we just need to figure out a name."

"Oh, how exciting! I'm sure everything will go great."

"I'm finally starting to believe that, even though you've been hammering it into my head for months now. I'm glad you moved up here. I miss having a woman to talk to."

I reached out and squeezed her hand. Maia's mother—and Gabe's mother—had died giving birth to her. Maia had told me it was due to eclampsia, a high blood pressure emergency.

"I'm glad I'm here too."

She sent me a shifty side-eye. "Yeah, I heard."

My stomach dropped. "About what?"

She laughed and draped an arm around my shoulders. "April, the resort grapevine is faster than the speed of light. And when the owner's son is seen dancing and making out in *public*, that's way too tasty to keep to yourself. Good thing it was late. That might keep the gossip from getting around Dove Key."

Flaming heat rushed over my face. Maia knew about my man failures and was sympathetic. But I didn't know if that sympathy would extend to her beloved older brother. "I think we both forgot where we were. Are you mad at me?"

"That it was Gabe?"

I nodded.

She made a dismissive noise. "He's thirty-six years old. He can take care of himself. Though I'm a little surprised at you, considering your stance on men when you first got here."

"Me too. We're going out Saturday."

"Ha!" she shouted triumphantly, and I jumped. That made her laugh. "Sorry. But this morning, I gave him the third degree and told him he needed to ask you out. Obviously, he did."

"*I want to pour it over every inch of your body and lick it off.*"

After a deep inhale, I blinked several times and turned my attention back to my friend. "Yeah, we're doing dinner and a movie at Driftwood Beach."

Maia's brow furrowed. "Driftwood Beach? I thought they were showing a rom-com this weekend."

"They are."

She stared at me, then her chest started shaking. She rushed a hand to her mouth but couldn't hold in the guffaws. "Oh my God! You convinced my brother—Gabe!—to go to a romantic comedy? Girl, he must be seriously ga-ga over you. If I asked him to do that, he'd smack me in the head and tell me to piss off."

"I might have some charms he can't see in you."

She shuddered, still laughing. "Well, I hope so, but have fun. Who knows? The movie is a comedy. Maybe he'll even laugh once or twice."

Chapter Fifteen

Gabe

I GLANCED QUICKLY at my jaw in the rearview mirror, verifying the sharp line on my cheek and across my neck. The evening was warm with hardly a breeze. I'd planned on putting the top down on my car, but April wore her hair down and I didn't want her to worry about it blowing everywhere.

She wore a dark red sleeveless button-down shirt matched with a white skirt and sandals. And makeup—the first time I'd ever seen her wear any. She knew how to apply it too, and I was pleased she wasn't one of those women who slathered it everywhere. Instead, I couldn't really tell what she'd done, except she was even more gorgeous than normal.

And that was saying something.

We passed over the causeway between Calypso Key and Dove Key. Halting at the stoplight, I smirked at Salty's Tavern across the street. I turned right onto Main Street. A large sign stood at the side of the road, pointing the way to Conch Republic Brewpub at the end of the street.

April ducked her head to read the sign. "Are we going to the brewpub?"

"No," I said and made a left turn a short distance later. "I'm taking you to a little hole-in-the-wall place called Rousseau's. It doesn't look like much, but it's one of the best restaurants in the Lower Keys."

She smiled at me, and my heart flopped over. Something about this woman captivated me—more than physical attraction. For the first time in forever, I wanted to make a good impression. To have her think highly of me. Before picking her up, I had spent an embarrassing amount of time in my closet before deciding on a dark-orange button-down shirt and khakis.

The narrow lane ran between a pizza parlor and an ice cream shop, then I turned into the small sand parking lot of Rousseau's. The building was a light-green, single-story cottage with white trim. April exited the car before I had a chance to open the door for her. So I settled for pressing my hand against the small of her back as we climbed the short flight of stairs, stepping onto a covered porch that ran the length of the building.

With my head, I pointed to the left end of the porch where the bathrooms were. "I need to use the men's room before we go in. Wait for me?"

"Of course."

She leaned against the railing as I headed down the wooden floor. When I came out a few minutes later, she was standing upright and talking to someone on the other side of her who was leaning down on the rail. My eyes narrowed as I took in her stiff shoulders.

Then the person straightened upright.

It was Ben Coleridge.

Anger exploded in my gut, and I strode toward them, my footsteps echoing loudly.

Ben looked up and widened his eyes when he saw me.

"Get out of here, Coleridge." I tried to keep my voice low, but my words still came out menacing. I placed an arm around April's shoulders.

Ben raised a hand. "Sorry. I didn't know she was with you, all right?"

"What you don't know could fill up a swimming pool."

Ben's eyes flashed. I removed my arm from April's shoulders, balancing on the balls of my feet and preparing to move quickly if I needed to.

Then the anger left his eyes and a small smile appeared. "Relax, man. I was just leaving. I don't think we need a repeat performance, do we?"

I relaxed slightly, relieved he wasn't picking a fight. "No, we don't. Goodbye, Ben."

He nodded to April. "Nice to meet you. See you around."

She stood at my side, stiff as a board now. "Thanks. Uh, you, too."

Then Ben trotted down the stairs, headed toward his truck I hadn't noticed before.

I placed my hand between her shoulder blades, feeling them relax as I rubbed. "Sorry about that. Are you all right?"

"Fine. He wasn't bothering me or anything." She shot me a curious glance, but Ben Coleridge was the last person I wanted to talk about.

"Let's go inside." Shaking off the encounter, I opened the door for her. We stopped before the hostess's podium.

She recognized me and smiled, inclining her head. "Good evening. Your table is all ready. Please follow me."

Since the place didn't take reservations, I'd called Henry Rousseau yesterday to ensure a quiet table. The hostess led us through the small dining room and onto a screened, covered porch. She seated us at an end table for two with a view over the mangroves, the ocean visible beyond.

I pulled out April's chair for her and smiled at the hostess. "Thanks very much."

We ordered a bottle of white wine and our glasses clinked softly over the crickets chirping. But April's forehead still had some lines on it that weren't usually there.

She swirled the wine in her glass, then looked at me from under her lashes. "Can I ask you something?"

"Of course."

"Was that guy at the entrance the one you got in the fight with?"

Dammit.

I smiled. Reassuringly, I hope. "You know about that, huh?"

She stared evenly at me. "Maia told me."

"Yeah, that was Ben Coleridge." I shifted in my seat and sighed. But I understood why she needed to clear the air about this. "I'm not a violent guy, April. I don't normally go around getting in bar fights, and I've never been in jail before. I have no intention of it happening again. That night wasn't one of my finer moments."

The side of her mouth twitched, amusement glinting in her eye. "I'm glad to hear that. I was a bit alarmed when Maia mentioned it."

My pulse sped up.

There it was again. That desire for her to have a positive opinion, even when I was an idiot. "Yet you're still here with me."

"I'm capable of making up my own mind. Though I was relieved when Maia said jail was out of character for you."

I sat back in my chair and took a drink of wine. "Very, though that wasn't the first time I've thrown a punch at a guy. The Markhams and Coleridges go way back. And it's not a friendly relationship."

"The Keys version of the Hatfields and McCoys?"

I grinned. "Something like that. They have a resort on the western side of Dove Key called Sunset Siesta. It's more of a... lower budget option than Calypso Key, so there's always been a rivalry between us. And the bad blood goes back longer than that. I'm sorry if I upset you. When I came out of the men's room, you looked stiff and uncomfortable. I don't want anyone making you feel like that. And when I saw Ben, I wasn't about to stand by."

"He came out the door and saw me, then came over to say hello. I was only uncomfortable because I didn't want some rando talking to me when I was out with you."

I reached out and took her hand. "I like the sound of that. You being with me, I mean."

"So do I."

We both ordered fresh catch specials, and I could tell Henry himself was in the kitchen tonight because of how good they were. "Did you grow up near the ocean?"

April laughed, raising her napkin to dab her mouth. "No, I'm from Ohio! I never even saw the ocean until two friends and I went to Fort Lauderdale for spring break our senior year. They went out and partied while I stayed back at the hotel and the beach. Once I got my first taste of the ocean, I was hooked. I got certified to dive right away and moved to St. Thomas a year later and worked various jobs there for several years. I came back to Key Largo for my divemaster course, which is where I met Maia."

"But you didn't stay in the Keys afterward?"

She shook her head. "I liked the Virgin Islands a lot. St. Croix is quieter and less touristy than St. Thomas, and the diving's better. I was there for six years." She finished her entrée and pushed the plate away. "You were in real estate in Miami?'

I nodded. "My partner Jake and I have several projects, but our most successful one is an office tower in downtown Miami. I'm still a full partner in the company, but I resigned from day-to-day operations."

Jake called me a few days ago and offered to buy me out completely, which let me know the business was doing very well indeed. But I wasn't interested. I liked the idea of having an income separate from the resort. Plus, I wasn't drawing any type of salary right now, trying to keep resort expenses as low as possible. I had a healthy savings account and was using it to provide for myself and Hailey. Quarterly profit allocations from the Miami business would provide any extra income we'd need.

April finished off the last of her wine and stared at me, a gleam in her eye. "Here's what I want to know. Why is a guy whose family owns a tropical resort—and is the manager of the dive operation—not a diver himself?"

If I answered that question fully, we'd miss the movie. It was a *long* story, and not one I enjoyed telling. "I used to dive but gave it up years ago. Maybe I'll take it up again."

That last sentence left my mouth without thought, and I was somewhat shocked to discover it was true. I loved driving the boat and had felt an envious pang a time or two as I watched the dive groups descend.

"Well, if you want a refresher, I know a pretty good divemaster who could help you."

I smiled back at her. "I'll certainly keep that in mind."

I'd worked with April enough to recognize her skill and talent, but I wasn't about to let her see me dive for the first time in over a decade. I was trying to impress the woman, not make her laugh at me. If I took a refresher course, it would be from Corbin. I didn't care if he saw me flopping and fumbling. April could see me dive after I'd gotten the hang of it again.

Am I really considering this?

Then again, why shouldn't I be? Just because Evan couldn't dive anymore didn't mean I had to give it up forever. He certainly wouldn't hold it against me, so what caused my hesitation?

Because I was responsible...

I didn't want to go down that thought path tonight. Especially when that bottle of Macallan 30 and two crystal tumblers were waiting for us back in my cottage—which brought on more enjoyable thoughts.

Much more enjoyable thoughts.

Warmth rolled through me that had nothing to do with the balmy evening. I couldn't wait to get my hands on April. Her skin was sun-kissed and soft, yet she was strong too. Her arms rippled anytime she moved them. I tried not to squirm in my chair.

It was completely dark when we left the restaurant, and Conch Republic was only a short drive away. I parked in the parking lot at the farthest end from the facility.

"Why did you park so far away?" she asked as we exited my car.

I popped the trunk and pulled out two blankets. Folding them over my arm, I pointed opposite the brewpub. "The staircase down to the beach is just ahead."

I firmly held April's hand as we descended the wooden staircase. It zigzagged down the bluff, ending at a broad stretch of white sand. A huge pile of driftwood at the south end gave the beach its name, but tonight's event was at the opposite, northern end. A large inflatable screen was tethered to the sand and people were scattered around the beach. Some sat in camp chairs, while others sprawled on blankets. The only light came from cell phone flashlights and the slide show cycling on the big screen.

Despite not being a rom-com fan, I had to admit the setting was pretty fantastic for a movie. The ocean splashed softly against the sand, and the sky was full of winking stars. After selecting an out-of-the-way place with no one near, I dragged over a driftwood log. Tossing one blanket on the sand, I sat down on it and leaned against the wood before lifting my hand to April. "Here. You can settle against me."

She lowered gracefully onto the blanket next to me. Scooting closer, she rested her back against my chest and stretched her legs out next to mine. I tossed the second blanket over the top of us before resting my hands on her stomach underneath it.

Tilting her face up, April gave me a smile. "This is nice and snug."

"Very." I brushed my lips over hers, feeling her smile widen. I was grateful for the darkness and the anonymity it brought.

The movie started right on time but didn't hold much interest for me. April thoroughly enjoyed it, however, which at least made it tolerable. I loved listening to her laugh. After half an hour, she shifted position, rising up a bit, and I moved one hand across her chest to grasp her shoulder.

However, as the movie progressed, it became more and more difficult to ignore the solid, attractive warmth resting against me. And the effect she was having on me. Underneath the blanket covering us, I slowly stroked my fingers down the velvety skin of her chest, keeping them on her bare skin next to the V-neck of her shirt. One of her hands was entwined with my other one. She squeezed it, encouraging me.

When I reached her shoulder again, I slipped my hand under her shirt and bra strap. Slowly lowering it again, I could feel her chest moving against my hand as her breathing deepened. I stroked up and down under her bra strap, drawing ever closer, yet not slipping under the cup of her bra.

Finally, she arched her back, lifting her breast into my fingers. With a smile, I closed my hand around it, stroking the very taut peak with my thumb. I glanced down at her. April's eyes were closed, her lips half parted.

I bent my head and kissed her ear. "Oh, the things I'm going to do to you."

A smile stretched her lips. "I'm starting to think you planned all this."

She jumped as I flicked my tongue in her ear. "This movie was your idea, not mine. You'd better pay attention to it."

April opened her eyes and watched the screen as I continued stroking my fingers across her breast. The pressure in my groin was becoming painful and I had to shift slightly. As I did, I removed my hand from her bra and slid it beneath the hem of her shirt. I fanned my fingers over her flat abdomen, then drew all four slowly from one side to the other.

I pressed my cheek against hers. "Hold still, now."

Both of us were looking at the screen, though at this point, she wasn't paying any more attention than I was. The movement of my hand was invisible under the blanket as I slid it under the waist of her skirt.

April closed her eyes, and I stopped my hand. She'd liked it the other night when I'd been commanding. "Keep your eyes open."

I whispered the words against her ear, and she snapped her eyes open. Her chest moved up and down with the force of her breathing.

Moving my hand downward again, I brushed my fingers over soft lace. "What color are your panties?"

"Black."

That image made me grunt in the back of my throat. I eased my hand under the lace and slowly stroked her, pleased at how ready she was. April gasped and pressed her back hard against me.

She closed her eyes again, but this time I let her be, stroking and circling with my fingers. I started slowly, concentrating on what I was doing in order to ignore the throbbing in my pants. My motion gradually increased, faster and faster. She turned her head, pressing her face into my neck as she breathed in quiet, gasping gulps.

Then her entire body went rigid, and she pushed her hips hard against my hand. She inhaled deeply through her nose and held the breath for what seemed like minutes. I closed my eyes and trapped her face between my head and shoulder, gripping her with my hand.

Finally, she relaxed, her body melting like butter against me. I withdrew my hand and rested it over her clothes and on top of her stomach. I turned my eyes back to the screen, with no idea whatsoever of what was going on in the movie.

Then April shifted sideways, resettling against me as she opened my pants. She thrust her hand inside, and now it was my turn to hold a deep breath as she began moving her hand up and down.

I held completely still and closed my eyes, the incredible pleasure washing through me in pulses. I tried to keep it together, but she was making me crazy. She had been for weeks. I grabbed her wrist, stopping her motion. "Stop. Not yet." I turned my head and kissed her hair, leaving my lips against the soft strands. "Not until I'm deep inside you."

She laughed softly in the darkness. "That hardly seems fair."

I lifted my head, staring at her liquid eyes. "It will be. We haven't even gotten started yet."

April sat up, and the blanket fell after I hastily zipped my pants. She leaned close. "Then what are we waiting for? Let's get out of here."

Chapter Sixteen

April

AS WE DROVE BACK, Gabe turned off Calypso Causeway and headed toward the Big House. But instead of stopping in front of the mammoth garage, he took a side road that led south. My body was a live wire, still thrumming with what had happened at the movie. When he stopped in front of his cottage, a thrill ran through me. What would happen next?

I was preparing to open my door when he placed a restraining hand on my arm. "I'll be right back."

Before I could question him, Gabe was out of the car and heading toward his front door with large, purposeful strides. He didn't fully enter his cottage, only grabbed something just inside the door. Then he was striding back with something cradled in his right arm.

As he sat in the driver's seat, he placed a glass bottle and two crystal tumblers in my lap. Macallan 30 was printed on the bottle.

I turned a smile to him, even as my insides liquefied. "I wasn't sure you were serious about this part."

After turning on the engine, Gabe stilled. Only his head moved as he turned to stare at me. "I've never been more serious in my life." His gaze narrowed. "Are you okay with this? We are moving a little fast here..."

My smile faded, pulsing desire taking over as that sense of being safe overtook me again. Of being confident with this man. "I'm sure. We're not teenagers, and it's not like we just met."

"Let's go to the Barn."

He parked in front of my door and took the whisky and glasses back. "Wait there."

I watched as he exited the door and hurried around the front to open my door. A grin spread across my face as he held out his hand to help me out. "You are quite the gentleman, aren't you?"

Once I stood upright, Gabe yanked me forward. I fell against his chest as he grabbed a handful of my hair with his free hand. He kissed me hard, raking his mouth over mine. I was so turned on I could hardly breathe.

Finally, he pulled back, his lips swollen. "I'm only a gentleman about some things."

Without another word, he spun around and led me by the hand into my apartment. We sat on the couch, and he placed the whisky and glasses on the coffee table before us. With one twist, he broke the seal on the bottle and poured two fingers of the rich amber fluid in each tumbler.

"I wasn't sure you were going to offer me a glass," I said. "You seemed ready for the main event out there."

He handed me the whisky, then stroked his fingers through my hair. "I want you badly, April. But like you said, we're not teenagers. I know how to do this right for you."

One of my brows flew up. "Just for me?"

A smile stretched his lips before he whisked them over mine. "Believe me. I'll enjoy every minute of this."

I swirled the liquid in my glass. "I should probably inform you I'm not much of a whisky drinker," I said, shooting him a side-eye.

Gabe smiled and lifted his glass. "Don't worry, there's nothing to it. Just take a big drink and let it roll around in your mouth. That way you get the different flavors."

We drank at the same time. At first, the Macallan was pure fire. I blinked several times and fought not to cough. But as I followed his instructions, different notes in the drink started to appear. Smokiness, a rich peat taste, and then a long, smooth finish after I swallowed.

Gabe's eyes were closed, and a blissful expression came over his face as his throat worked. As he ran his tongue over his lips, heat rolled through me that wasn't related to the alcohol.

I took a second, smaller sip, enjoying the flavor. Though I wasn't ready to say I was an aficionado yet, and that made me feel somewhat guilty. The bottle probably cost hundreds of dollars. "How much does a bottle of thirty-year-old whisky cost, anyway?"

Gabe slowly opened his eyes and took a deep sniff of the liquid in his glass. "Depends. This one was about five thousand dollars."

I almost dropped my glass. Only a last-second, panicked grip saved it. With my heart pounding, I stared at him. "Oh my God! You can't waste it by pouring it out."

A smile rose on his face that did nothing to calm my frantic heart. "I have no intention of wasting a drop." After taking another drink, he swallowed and leaned in. This time his kiss was slow and sensual.

I could taste the whisky on his tongue and the idea of what he wanted to do with it turned me on so much I could hardly stand it. Deep, regular pulses radiated from my core. After the wine at dinner, my head was filled with a pleasant buzzing.

But not all of it was due to the alcohol. I'd never met a more intoxicating man.

Gabe gently traced his hand up the back of my neck, watching as he ran the strands of my hair over his fingers. "Is the rug still on the floor upstairs in the bedroom? In front of the fireplace?"

"Yes." Another quiver rippled through me that he was so much more familiar with this room—this entire apartment—than I was.

He downed the rest of his glass in a single shot and placed it on the coffee table with a solid clunk. Grabbing the bottle by its neck, he stood and held out his hand. "Then what are we waiting for?"

My room was nearly dark when we entered. Gabe crossed the floor to stand before the massive stone fireplace. I hadn't done much with this part of the room, and two cream-colored pillar candles stood on each end of the mantle. Gabe's face came alive in flickering light as he struck a match and lit them both.

At the base of the four-foot-wide fireplace, a thick, fluffy, gray-and-white rug lay on the wooden floor. Two wingback chairs sat on the far side of it. Kicking my sandals off, I stepped onto the rug, scrunching my toes in the soft surface.

Turning back, he set the whisky bottle on the floor next to the rug and stopped in front of me. He raised both hands to fan my hair out, staring at me intently, as if he were studying every plane of my face. "Do you have any idea how beautiful you are?"

His eyes held me, even though his words made me uncomfortable. "I've never thought of myself that way."

Softly whisking his mouth over mine, he whispered, "You should. You should hear it every day until you believe it."

He lifted my shirt off and unhooked my bra with one hand. After he tossed it aside, I lifted the hem of his shirt. He was too tall for me to get it off, so he ripped it over his head. Our mouths came together again in a slow, delicious kiss. I skimmed my tongue over his lips, and he responded with a deep growl. He cupped my breasts with both hands, his thumbs moving over their hard peaks.

At the same time, we both rushed to remove the rest of our clothing and stood before each other naked. I slowly traced my hands over his chest, the soft hair brushing underneath my fingers. I still had trouble believing a man this magnificent wanted me. And Gabe was magnificent, every inch of him.

Our faces remained inches apart as his hands roamed over my body, never stopping. As if he were familiarizing himself with the territory. Becoming acquainted so he could investigate further soon.

I reached up and kissed him, thrusting my tongue into his mouth. His mouth was hot, wet, and smoky. I'd never done anything like what had happened at the movie. I liked it. Gabe made me feel confident—more than I had ever been.

I wanted more.

He took a step back. "Lie down on the rug. On your stomach." His voice was commanding, but there was nothing threatening in it. Nothing that made me uneasy.

Quite the opposite. And my arousal was only heightened when I dropped my eyes to see the effect I was having on him.

A very pronounced effect.

The warm, soft material caressed my breasts as I stretched out on top of it. Already, a deep rolling wave ran through me. From head to feet, then back up again. I closed my eyes and heard the soft sound of the whisky bottle being unscrewed.

Gabe swept my hair off my back, gently placing it to one side of my head. Then the liquid dripped onto my skin in a line from my shoulders, down my back, and over my ass. It was fiery hot and freezing cold at the same time. I gasped, shivering as it trickled into areas that took on a new heat of their own.

The air above my shoulders became warm as Gabe leaned over and blew gently across them. Then the base of my neck got wetter. The whisky trickled over my ribs as he ran his mouth down my spine. I shuddered and twitched, more turned on than I'd ever been in my life. I grabbed a handful of the rug, moaning softly. "Oh God, Gabe. That feels... incredible."

He made a deep, appreciative rumbling noise in his chest as he ran his tongue back up. He repeated the maneuver on each hip, gently licking up the whisky as the rug around me became wet and fragrant with its smoky scent.

"Turn over."

I flipped onto my back, hardly able to control my rapid breathing.

Gabe sat next to me on his knees. His eyes were smoky and mysterious as he held the Macallan bottle in his right hand. Agonizingly slowly, he poured a thin ribbon from the hollow of my neck down to my navel. Then he stopped over my sex, circling his hand as he continued to pour. I tightened every muscle in my body to keep from arching as the fire spread into every crevice. I didn't want to displace a single drop.

He met my eyes as he set the bottle down again. Settling over me on his hands and knees, he straddled me, then lowered and sucked a mouthful from the hollow of my neck.

With a deep moan, I tilted my head back, ruffling both hands through his short hair. Gabe moved downward, drinking and sucking until he stopped at my breasts. I cried out when he took one hard peak in his mouth. He stroked the other with one hand.

"Gabe. I'm not sure how much of this I can take."

He smiled and glanced up at me. "I haven't even started yet."

That made me groan louder, and he must have gotten my hint because he lowered farther. He drank the whisky from my abdomen, sucking it out of my navel. Then he moved his tongue in slow circles around my belly.

By now I was panting and couldn't keep from squirming.

Glancing at me, he pinned me with his eyes as he moved lower. Placing both hands between my thighs, he pressed my legs apart and settled between them. The movement sent whisky into new places, and I inhaled sharply. I was on fire, partly because of him and partly because of the Macallan.

He wrapped both hands around the outsides of my hips. Using the same confident, deliberate motion as when he'd first kissed me, Gabe lowered and took a long, sweeping taste of whisky.

And me.

I grabbed two handfuls of the thick rug, holding tight as I arched my back, nearly rising completely off the floor. Gabe gripped my hips tighter, moving with me.

Moving his tongue relentlessly.

Drawing me even closer, a tight, hot pressure building and building.

Until it swept over me, a thousand times stronger than at the movie.

Stronger than any climax I'd ever known.

Sounds tore from my throat I had no control over. It went on eternally yet ended too soon.

I had one arm thrown over my eyes, though I had no recollection of letting go of the rug. Gabe crawled back up my body. I took hold of his shaft, and the air rushed from his lungs.

"Flip over," I said. "My turn." I pushed hard against his shoulders, and he complied by rolling onto his back.

With a gleeful smile, I grabbed the whisky bottle and poured it over his groin. Gabe hissed through his teeth.

My grin widened. "Stings, doesn't it?"

His only reply was a strangled moan.

I set the bottle down on the floor and moved on top of him. The whisky had settled in between the ridges of his six-pack, and I licked it off eagerly, sucking it into my mouth. Meeting his eyes, I drew my tongue in a long line across his abdomen.

Who am I?

I didn't care, though. This was the most exciting thing I'd ever done, and it wasn't over yet. Scooting lower, I bent down and took him in my mouth. The luxurious, smoky taste of the whisky competed with his velvety soft skin.

A deep, wrenching moan tore from his throat. I smiled and made a humming noise that made him groan more.

I was considering grabbing the bottle again when he abruptly sat up. He ran his hands under my arms and lifted me. "Come here. I can't wait."

I laughed softly as he pushed me onto my back, but he remained serious. After crawling to his pants, he took a condom out of his wallet. He placed the wrapper in his mouth, ripped it open with one hand, and rolled it on. Watching him was intensely arousing. Meeting my eyes, he stretched out on top of me and gave me a hard, bruising kiss.

I parted my legs, and he reached between us. "No more waiting. I need to be inside you. Now."

As he entered me in a slow, steady motion, we groaned in unison. Our mouths came together in a wet, hard meeting of flesh. After pulling back, he pounded into me. I slid my hands to his ass, urging him on. He responded with another rough thrust.

We were raw passion and power coming together for the first time.

I was on a razor's edge between pain and pleasure, and it was divine. I ran my hands over his back, surprised to find it slick with sweat. The smoky scent of fine scotch whisky enveloped us, and Gabe's breathing got deeper and rougher. He made a growling noise I'd never heard from him before.

I shifted position, opening wider.

"Oh my God, yes," he said against my lips and thrust even faster. Harder. He filled every possible portion of me. Fiery, liquid heat pulsed through me, rising again.

Finally, he wrenched his mouth from mine and buried his face next to my neck. He froze all over, calling out into the flickering candlelight.

I closed my eyes and met him measure for measure.

Chapter Seventeen

Gabe

AFTER I AWOKE, I only needed a moment to recognize where I was. Dim light filtered through the blinds, casting my old bedroom in shadows. Reaching over my head, I stroked my hand across the headboard.

Then I broke into a wide, smug grin.

I might not have been happy about leaving the bed behind, but I'd returned in style. I constructed the solid-wood bed six months ago but had never slept in it.

Well, that sure changed.

I glanced to my left, but the other side of the bed was empty, the covers flipped back. "Damn, she gets up early."

Then again, April had to work today. I knew that because I wrote her schedule. The only thing on my agenda was picking up Hailey at 8:00 a.m. at her friend's. Her sleepover was the only reason I'd been able to spend the night.

My grin fell. *We need to talk about that. How this is going to work.*

The physical part had worked spectacularly. I'd never experienced anything close to what we'd shared on that rug.

After we'd finished, I'd had an overpowering urge to sleep with April in the bed. To hold her in my arms. I'd risen to my feet and held my hand out to her. "Come on. The bed will be more comfortable."

We crawled in together, and April had fit herself around me, resting her head on my chest.

"I wasn't planning on having a man in my bed, you know," she said quietly.

I wasn't ready for the mood to turn serious. "Well, you're safe on that front. Because it's my bed, not yours."

My ploy worked because April grinned as she rose, resting on her elbow with her head in her palm. "Did you make this? It's the most beautiful bed I've ever seen!"

"Yeah, Hailey and I spent a month here last summer. I made it then."

"Why didn't you take it with you when you moved to the cottage?"

I knocked on the headboard. It made a solid thump. "That's one-hundred percent teak. It weighs a ton. I pretty much attached it to the wall permanently. And the rest of the bed is solid mahogany."

April stared at me, a line between her brows. "I feel bad that I displaced the two of you. I didn't know."

I ran my fingers through her silky hair. I could get used to this. "Don't feel bad. It was all Maia's fault. She demanded I move out as a condition of bailing me out of jail —so you could have the Barn."

April sucked in her bottom lip, her face carefully blank. Then her shoulders started shaking and she broke into laughter. "God, no wonder you were so grouchy when I first met you."

That made me laugh too, and it wasn't lost on me that I'd laughed more with this woman in a week than I probably had in a year. "Fair warning—I don't have the sunniest personality on the best of days."

She snuggled closer and pressed her naked body against mine. "Maybe I can lend some of my optimism to you."

I stroked my fingers down her back, then rested them on one soft cheek. "Right now, it's not your optimism I'm interested in."

I leaned in and kissed her. Once again, intense desire flamed over me—the need to know all her secret places, what made her cry out, and what she didn't like. Maybe it was because we'd just been talking about Maia, but my sister's warning about April being treated badly by men ran through my head.

I wasn't known for being a tender lover. But that second time—for April—I had been. And in the silent room, we'd both discovered something neither of us had been looking for. Peace. Acceptance.

Now I stood from the bed and grabbed my wallet, which was on the nightstand. I padded across the room and pulled on my underwear and shorts. The bottle of Macallan still stood on the floor. I lifted it to eye level. It was a quarter full. I capped it and placed it on the mantle before glancing around the room for my shirt.

I couldn't find it anywhere. I didn't remember taking it off downstairs, but last night I'd been so turned on it easily could have slipped my mind. I descended the stairs, automatically stepping on the side of the squeaky one to keep it quiet.

As I reached the floor, my gaze dropped to the couch where we'd sat. No shirt. Then a thump from across the room drew my attention. April stood in the kitchen, facing away as she poured coffee from a glass carafe into a mug.

And she was wearing my shirt.

I stumbled to a halt, frozen in place. The oxygen was sucked from the air as I stared at her. I'd seen plenty of women dressed in my shirts before, but this was different. *Felt* different. Right now, she was the sexiest thing I'd ever seen. The dark-orange shirt hung to mid-thigh on her.

Why the hell does April affect me like this?

I couldn't answer that, and it made me nervous. I didn't like the feeling of not being fully in control of myself. Plus, she probably didn't want me jumping her bones first thing in the morning. After twice last night. And I had only brought two condoms.

I took a deep breath, willing my molten core to calm the hell down. April finished pouring her coffee and placed the carafe back in the coffee pot. She turned around and saw me, her eyes going wide. "Oh! You're awake."

That's the understatement of the year.

But I kept a tight rein on myself and forced my feet to move forward, sending an appreciative glance up and down her body. "I was looking for my shirt. Apparently, it's been claimed."

She broke into a grin, sending my pulse further skyward. "I wanted to wear it. It smells like you. Coffee?"

I blinked several times, as if she'd asked me if I was from another planet. "Uh, yes. Thanks."

Another mug sat on the counter, and she filled it for me. "Cream or sugar?"

"No. I drink it black."

I took a long sip, trying to keep my eyes off her. She stepped forward and ran her hands over my bare chest, which didn't help the situation.

"I suppose you want your shirt back. I could give it to you now."

"No. Keep it. I like seeing you in it." Her lips looked swollen in the morning light.

"You want to watch the sun rise on the patio?" she asked.

I jerked my head in agreement.

We sat side by side on the couch. Hemingway was curled up on one of the chairs and raised his head. He yawned at us.

At least he distracted me. "Damn cat spends more time here than he does with Hailey and me."

April laughed. "Maybe you're not the only male claiming me."

"So I'm competing with a cat?"

The smile faded from her face, and she eyed me intently. "After last night, I don't think you're competing with anyone."

I couldn't help the warmth spreading inside me at her statement. "We're pretty incredible together."

She nodded, and her throat moved as she swallowed a drink of coffee. "And that brings me to something I need to say. Just because I'm not looking for a deep, serious relationship doesn't mean I'm okay sharing you with anyone else."

I reached out and smoothed her hair. "You don't need to worry about that. My divorce pretty much ruined me on ever falling in love again, but I don't sleep around."

"Neither do I."

I crossed my legs, resting my ankle on the opposite knee. "So, it sounds like we have a pact. We have an exclusive but non-serious relationship?"

Her smile returned, and my lips answered it without me controlling them. "We do. Exclusive but no falling in love."

"Agreed," I said. "I have something I need to be clear on too. Hailey."

"What about her?"

"She likes you, so I'm sure she won't have a problem with us being together. But it's important to me that I set an example for her. I'd rather not have her see us together in the morning when she wakes up."

"I can understand that. You don't want her to know we spent the night together?"

I sighed, though I was pleased April wasn't upset. "She's had a rough couple of years, and I just want her to be a kid for as long as she can. I've talked to her a little about sex, but hopefully, she won't figure out the specifics until she's at least thirty."

April tipped her head back and laughed. "You're going to be a nightmare for her boyfriends."

I grinned. "That's the only part of her teen years I'm looking forward to."

"You do have plenty of sharp objects in the shop if any of them get out of line."

Leaning forward, I pressed a kiss to her soft lips. "I like you a lot."

"I like you too."

I drank the last of my coffee and set my cup on the table. "I'd better head up to the cottage so you can get to work. I've heard your boss can be a prick."

She tipped her head back and forth. "He makes a lousy first impression, but once you get to know him, he's not so bad."

I laughed, enjoying our banter.

April reached a hand to my jaw and stroked the stubble. "I like hearing your laugh, Gabe."

"Hailey's been the only person who could make me laugh. Guess I'd better add you to that list."

"Better add me to a bunch of lists, mister."

After another long, leisurely kiss, I stood and strolled off the porch. Hemingway followed me back to the cottage, apparently feeling breakfast outweighed morning sunshine with April. I glanced down at him as he shimmied through the door with me.

"I'm not sure you're right about that, big guy."

LATER THAT AFTERNOON, my swim trunks dripped water on the flagstone patio as I sat at a table behind the Big House. Hailey and I had spent over an hour in the pool together, diving for objects and playing catch. I'd had enough and was drying out while doing a little work, but not my daughter. She was throwing a softball into a small floating target and making the shot a respectable number of times.

Hailey was a lot more interesting to watch than resort profit and loss statements, so I sat back and stretched my legs out. She screwed an eye shut and tossed the ball at the target. It hit the top and careened off, heading toward the house.

"Oh, shoot!"

"Stay there, angel. I'll get it." I was gathering myself to stand when the patio door opened, and Evan stepped out.

He saw the small ball rolling toward him and put two and two together. "I got it!"

He cleanly fielded the ball with one hand and stepped to the edge of the pool. The goal floated three quarters of the way down and on the opposite side. Evan brought the ball up to the side of his face with both hands, wound up, and launched it at the target.

It swished into the net with hardly a sound.

Hailey's jaw dropped open as she spun around to stare at her uncle. "Do that again!"

Evan grinned. "Lucky shot. Maybe we can play in a while. I want to talk to your dad."

As he strolled across the patio toward me, Hailey went back to the ball, mimicking Evan's motions as she tried to toss it into the target.

"Still have your aim, I see," I said as he sat across from me.

Evan's brows flew up. "I certainly hope I can still hit a target that big!"

Several beers sat on ice inside a bucket at my elbow. I opened one and slid it over to him, taking a second for myself.

Evan nodded at my laptop. "Are you working instead of lavishing attention on your daughter?"

I flicked the fabric of my wet shorts. "I just finished lavishing attention on her. Unlike Hailey, I'm not half fish. I needed to dry out."

"The resort's doing better now, right?"

I took a drink and nodded. "Yeah, we're not losing money anymore. But we're not really making a profit either. Have you heard anything on your project?"

Evan had come to me with a great idea. Years ago, Calypso Key had stopped measuring which guests were first-timers or returners, and he thought we should start doing it again. I agreed and told him to get right on the project. Tracking how many guests returned was vital.

"I got the report back from the data processor yesterday. Our return guest rate is fifteen percent."

I almost dropped my beer. "Shit! That's much worse than I thought."

"Yeah. Me too. After I started thinking about it, though, I realized I haven't seen too many familiar faces in the last few years."

"We need to send every former guest an offer for twenty percent off a new booking."

"I'll take care of it," Evan said. "What about lowering prices across the board? We're running about sixty to seventy percent occupancy. Lower prices could bring that up."

I shook my head. "Dad lowered prices two years ago. It hasn't helped."

"Maybe it wasn't enough."

"I don't think we need to lower prices." I leaned forward and folded my arms on the table. "I want to *raise* prices, Evan. Calypso Key Resort used to be one of the premier resorts in the Lower Keys. We've lost that because we've been trying to blend in instead of standing out. We're not Sunset Siesta, for God's sake."

Several years ago, Dad had become worried that the Coleridges' competing resort on Dove Key was stealing business from us. That was what led him to lower prices.

Evan took a long pull. "That sounds pretty risky, Gabe."

"Not if we're able to back up the price hike with an equal rise in guest experience. But that's the problem. I took a hard look at a beach cottage last week. They need to be remodeled. Everything does. We need a large cash infusion, except we're barely hanging on."

"So what are you going to do?"

I raked my hand through my hair. "I don't know yet. Dad already took out a loan at a shitty interest rate, and I hate debt anyway. I'm hardly eager to add more." I was essentially supplementing the resort with my own funds at this point, since I was living off my savings to roll my resort CFO salary back into the business.

"I'm glad you're here, Gabe. I'm sorry I didn't give you the warmest of welcomes."

We stared at each other, two brothers who loved each other but weren't afraid to get in each other's faces. "Don't worry about it. I'd have probably felt the same way if our roles had been reversed."

"Can we start hiring people again? I've got two restaurant workers moving and a landscaper retiring at the end of the month."

"Yeah, go ahead and replace them."

Evan cracked a smile. "I'm sure it's a relief to confirm you won't need to let any divemasters go, huh?"

I kept my poker face on. "I'm glad I don't have to let anyone go."

He took another drink, then laughed. "Oh, don't be all strait-laced and stiff! How was your date with April?"

I rolled my eyes. "How do you know about that?"

"You told Maia, remember?"

A reluctant smile raised my lips. "How could I forget? April and I had a great time, little brother. She's a lovely woman I'm enjoying getting to know."

"In other words, you're not going to tell me a thing."

"Exactly. Except to mind your own damn business."

April and I had just started what sounded like the perfect relationship. We'd be devoted to each other, yet not expect anything more. Even better, I couldn't wait to see her again. None of which I wanted to discuss with my brother. I set my beer on the table and stood. "Come on. Let's jump in the pool."

Evan peeled off his shirt, revealing he still maintained a

regular weight routine. "Excellent. That will give me a chance to show your daughter what an awful arm you have."

We strolled across the patio. As we neared the edge, I shoved Evan in the shoulder. He lost his balance and fell into the water. But not before he grabbed my arm and pulled me in with him. Family might have its complications, but I couldn't deny my attitude regarding moving back here was changing.

And a certain blond divemaster was part of the reason why.

Chapter Eighteen

April

DOVE Key's residential district lay in the northwest portion of the island. As with most islands, parking was at a premium and I finally found a spot nearly a block away from the one-story cottage that was my destination. A lovely, early summer sun warmed the island.

As the weeks had gone by, Gabe and I settled into a routine. Everyone around the resort knew we were a couple, and after the inevitable teasing had run its course, no one remarked on us anymore. We worked well together, and I enjoyed the days he drove the dive boat. From his smiles, he did too. Hot Grumpy Guy still made an appearance now and again, but Gabe was much more approachable now.

Turning to the passenger seat, I grabbed the wine I'd just bought at Dove Market. A bottle of white and another of red would be the perfect accompaniment to our monthly-ish Sips and Pages meeting.

As I stepped onto the sidewalk, a woman with a head of

long, brown, curly hair exited her car in front of me. I quickened my step, a smile rising on my face.

"Liv!"

I'd met Olivia Jacobson at my first book club meeting. She was also new to the area and looking to make friends. About my height and a few years younger, she had round curves and a fun personality that had made me quick to warm to her.

Liv's head whipped around at my call, and she met my smile as she waited on the sidewalk. Her face fell at the bottle I held in each hand. "You brought two bottles? Crap! I only thought to bring a white wine."

As we fell into step together, I nodded with my chin at the pink *Sweet Dreams* box she balanced on one arm. "Don't worry. You'll always be welcome wherever you go."

Liv had recently opened a bakery on Main Street. From the sampler she'd brought to our last get-together, Sweet Dreams would be a giant success.

"Besides," I said. "There will be plenty of wine there, if last time is anything to go by."

Liv's pretty face pulled down in a frown. "Good. I need something to drink to distract me from my disastrous date last night."

"Uh-oh. That doesn't sound promising."

She groaned, then broke into laughter. "I got up and left halfway through dinner. I've never done that! But the guy would *not* stop talking about himself. I just couldn't waste another second. How about you? I don't see a ring, so I'm guessing you're not married."

"No, not married."

A soft, fuzzy warmth rolled through me. Hailey had taken our relationship in stride, and we were careful around her. Which suited me fine—not spending nights with Gabe kept me from getting too close emotionally.

Because physically?

Wow.

I'd never experienced anything like this. That first night with the whisky had only been the beginning. From the start, I'd understood exactly how to give Gabe what he wanted, and God knew he could push my buttons expertly. And if a tiny part of me wanted to snuggle up all night instead of leaving?

That tiny part was what had gotten me in trouble in the past.

Hailey had become a regular visitor to the dive shop area and was intensely interested in diving. I'd taken her into the gear room to show her the individual pieces. I had a feeling Gabe was going to have a junior diver on his hands soon.

As we neared our destination, Liv's laugh brought me back to the present. "Maybe not married, but judging from the look on your face, very happily involved!"

I grinned back at her. "Yes. I got together with a guy fairly recently. So far, we're great together."

After we entered the house, we sat on a couch. A dozen women clustered around a bright living room filled with tropical plants. A liberal selection of wine bottles sat on a coffee table in the middle of the room, and I poured myself a glass of white. An appreciative hum went around the room when Liv set her pink box down, and several women dove for the box.

Soon our conversation turned to this month's book, an instalove romance. I absently thumbed through my paper-back. "I'm just not sure I buy the whole instalove thing. It just doesn't seem real that two people would just magically fall for each other at first sight."

Pam, who hosted most of the meetings, nodded. She was tall and willowy, her soft waves of dark-blond hair pulled into a clip. "I'm more of a slow-burn fan, myself."

Liv giggled. "Are you sure you're not into instalove, April? From what you told me on the way here, you're feeling pretty warm toward your new man."

A round of *ooohs* went around at that, and Pam held out a hand. "Hold on a second, ladies. You two are new, so you might not know this rule. But when real life competes with fictional romance, we always break to discuss it." She turned to me, her eyes sparkling. "You simply must tell us about this man, April."

Laughter rang around the room. I joined it, giving in with grace. "We certainly weren't love at first sight, but I thought he was beyond gorgeous the first time I saw him."

"Excellent start!" Pam exclaimed, slapping her thigh. "I take it he's a local and not a visitor?"

"Yes. In fact, some of you may even know him since he was born around here."

That sent up a round of giggling, making me laugh more. I'd had a regular girls' group when I lived in St. Croix and hadn't realized how much I missed it.

Another club member, Janie, leaned forward and set her glass on the coffee table as she swept light-brown bangs from her forehead. "I'm dying here! Don't keep us in suspense! Who is he?"

A chorus of agreement went around the room.

"I'm seeing Gabriel Markham."

In an instant, the entire room fell silent. The ticking wall clock became deafening. My smile faded as I panned my gaze around the room of stunned faces.

Janie still leaned forward, but now her face was slack. "Did you say Gabe Markham?"

"Yes," I said slowly, my happy, fizzy mood fading. "Why did everyone get so quiet? I admit he can be a little grouchy, but he's a very nice guy once you get to know him."

That made Pam sit back in her chair and laugh. She fanned herself with one hand. "Oh, honey. You have no idea. If the Lower Keys had a most eligible bachelor list, Gabe would be number one on it. Everyone knows he moved back, though hardly anyone has seen him. But apparently *you* have."

A sense of protectiveness fell over me. "Well, we work together."

Janie waved a hand at me. "Oh, don't start feeling awkward because we're a bunch of jealous crones. We're all happy for you. Really. Even if we do want to claw your eyes out just a little."

After that, the meeting got back on track discussing the book over several varieties of wine. I stayed mostly quiet, processing my thoughts. The discussion about Gabe served as a reminder that I needed to be careful. He wasn't just some guy I met. Gabe was the prodigal son returned to a family who *owned their own island.*

Good thing we had that pact. I just needed to keep up my end of it.

And try not to notice that he was also a devoted, full-time parent. And that under that growly exterior lay a sweet, protective heart. And that he could make my body sing like no one ever had.

Sigh.

Liv and I both walked back to our cars empty-handed. Her pastries had been demolished within the first fifteen minutes.

"I'm sorry I brought up your relationship," Liv said, clutching her purse in front of her. "I never meant to make you uncomfortable. Even if you'd mentioned his name, I wouldn't have realized who he was."

"It's fine, but everyone's reaction reinforced that I'm not a local here. At least they were honest about it."

Liv laughed. "That they're happy for you, even though they're insanely jealous?"

"That summed it up pretty well. I'm sure Gabe never intended what happened between us any more than I did. And neither of us is looking for anything serious, so I guess their dreams are still intact."

Liv glanced at the saltwater taffy shop we were passing. "It's kind of weird moving to a small town like this, isn't it? You're welcomed, yet still feel like an outsider."

"With the way you bake, I don't think you'll be an outsider for long. I'm glad we met."

She wrapped an arm around my shoulder and squeezed before letting go. "So am I, April."

"You guys did great!" I said to the couple in front of me. The resort pool sparkled behind them. "Meet me down by the dive shop tomorrow at eight thirty for your first dive in the ocean." The twentysomething couple were in the process of removing their scuba equipment and setting it on the deck. We had an entire section of the pool to ourselves. Once guests realized what we were up to, they gave us plenty of room to operate.

Amber glanced at me as she wrung the water out of her brown ponytail. "We're not going deeper than thirty feet, right?"

Her husband, Dan, laughed as he brushed his hand down her arm. "She already promised that."

"Thirty feet is the maximum depth for Discover Scuba Diving," I replied to her. "You'll have to take the full certification to go deeper. This is just a taste."

"A taste will do for now. See you tomorrow." Amber smiled as Dan draped his arm around her and squeezed her shoulder. They were on their honeymoon, and she'd reluctantly agreed to try diving. Over our pool session, she'd gradually relaxed and enjoyed herself more and more, which was gratifying to both me and her new husband.

"Enjoy the rest of your day." I shrugged out of my own kit and unscrewed the regulator from the tank valve. Corbin, the resort's dive instructor, was between students, which meant he got to lead divers on the boat today. While I got bumped into teaching intro classes.

I didn't mind, especially since I was still the new guy.

"Hi, April."

I looked up as Hailey strolled toward me. She wore a Calypso Key T-shirt and shorts, her long, coltish legs moving easily over the pool deck.

I smiled as she approached. "And how is Hailey doing this afternoon?"

She hunkered down next to me to study a scuba kit. "Good. I was coming down here to bug my dad. Then I saw you and decided to bug you instead."

I laughed. "You're not bugging me at all."

I knew Gabe was working in his dive shop office because we'd had a rather hot, yet short, make-out session in there before my DSD class. Over the past couple of months, Hailey and I had developed a friendly relationship. She was such a gregarious, outgoing child I didn't understand how anyone couldn't love her. Especially her mother. "Are you glad to have school out?"

This was her first full week of summer break, and Gabe had been scrambling to make sure she kept busy and supervised. Nona watched her most afternoons.

Hailey shrugged. "I like school. I made new friends and it's harder to see them during the summer. Dad signed me up for a camp on weekday mornings, and that's been fun. Today we visited the Turtle Hospital in Marathon."

"That does sound fun."

She picked up a regulator second stage and inspected it. "What were you doing with that couple?"

"Teaching an intro scuba class. I'll take them on a dive in the ocean tomorrow."

Hailey raised her eyes to mine. "You told me you weren't an instructor."

"I'm not. Divemasters can teach this class." I hid a smile, pleased at how sharp she was. Then again, her father wasn't lacking in the brains department, either, so that wasn't a surprise.

She played with the Velcro cummerbund on the BCD. "How come you haven't become an instructor? I bet you'd be good at it."

"Thanks. A couple of reasons. One—it's expensive. But most importantly, most instructors spend the majority of their time teaching classes. I love being in the ocean and leading dives."

"Corbin told me once he wishes he led dives more often."

I smiled at her. "Then he should be happy. That's what he's doing right now."

Hailey pressed the purge button on the mouthpiece,

and the regulator issued a hiss. She gave me a measured look. "Can I breathe off this?"

"Sure. The regulator sounds different in air, so you'll hear noise when you exhale. Go ahead."

She placed the black mouthpiece into her mouth and inhaled. A deep hiss issued out of the regulator, followed by a loud honking noise as she exhaled. Hailey spat it out and giggled. "I sounded like Darth Vader! But that got kind of ruined by the loud farting noise when I breathed out."

Joining her laughter, I pressed the purge button, eliciting a long, loud hiss. "In water, this is just a bunch of bubbles escaping. It's not making the farting noise because I'm purging it—expelling the air forcefully. The sound you noticed happens because your exhalation is traveling through air, not water."

Hailey shifted her eyes to the clear water of the pool, then lifted them to meet mine. "Can I breathe off it underwater?"

My heart sank.

Uh-oh. Probably should have seen this coming.

I shook my head and smiled sadly. "Not without your dad's permission."

"Please? Just a breath or two?"

"Sorry, sweetie. I can teach intro classes to adults, but not to kids. Besides, knowing your dad, he'd probably want to be right next to you."

Her shoulders slumped. "Yeah, I know. The last time I brought up diving, he wasn't too happy about the idea." Then her smile reappeared. I loved her sunny disposition. "Can I breathe off it again up here in the air?"

"Absolutely. That's completely safe."

Hailey commenced breathing in Darth Vader hisses and farting exhales, stopping for fits of giggles now and again. I helped her into the BCD, and she sat on the pool deck with her legs sticking straight out, the heavy tank resting on the concrete behind her. I disassembled the other kit, laughing with her.

"Hailey, what are you doing?" Gabe's voice was so unexpected, I jumped.

She took the second stage from her mouth and smiled up at him. "April's letting me breathe off a scuba kit!"

"I see that." His voice was pleasant, but he held his shoulders rigidly. Then he smiled at Hailey. "There are fresh donuts in the break room at the dive shop. Why don't you grab one before they're all gone?"

Hailey had ripped open the BCD and scrambled to her feet before he even finished his sentence. "I'm on my way!"

I smiled as she took off at full speed.

"What the hell do you think you're doing?" Gabe's low voice was harsh and gruff, completely opposite to what he'd used with Hailey.

I stood and faced him, my brow lined. Both hands were parked on his hips, his mouth set in a gash. Hot Grumpy Guy was back.

"Showing Hailey how a scuba regulator works."

His jaw bulged as he ground his teeth together. "So you thought you could take it upon yourself to teach my daughter to dive?"

I stepped forward, surprise turning to anger. Heat sliced through me. "No, Gabe. I let her breathe off the mouthpiece. In air. She asked to use it underwater, and I told her not without your permission. *And* that I'm not qualified to teach her. Do I look stupid to you?"

At least no one else was nearby. Several couples sat around the large free-form pool but in other sections.

Still seething, Gabe hadn't moved. "No. But you should have asked me first."

I hissed an exhale. "We didn't plan this. She lives at a tropical resort! Of course she's curious, and what I showed her was completely safe. Why are you so upset?"

"Because diving is dangerous. Because she's *my* daughter. Because I want to know what's going on with her."

We stared at each other, and my heart was about to leap out of my chest. His eyes were icy, sending a trickle down my spine. She was his daughter, not mine. Finally, I took a step back. "Then I apologize. I was only trying to be friendly. I happen to like Hailey very much." Picking up a BCD and regulator in each hand, I stormed past him and toward the gear room.

"April, wait."

I sped up, nearly trotting as I angled onto the path toward the canal. Opening the door of the gear room, I tossed the two BCDs inside before whirling around to get a second load. As I reached the main path toward the pool, Gabe strode toward me.

His forehead was lined, and his eyes now held concern instead of anger.

I looked past him, focusing on the remaining kit lying on the deck. As I brushed past him, he grasped my upper arm. "Would you stop? I'm sorry I came across as harsh. It was a gut reaction, okay?"

"If you say so." I pulled my arm away, and he let go. "I have work to do. I'm the help, remember?"

I started to turn, but Gabe stepped forward, blocking me. "No, you're not. You're a lot more than that to me."

I snorted. "Yeah. I could tell by the daggers your eyes shot into me."

He breathed a deep sigh. "Damn. I really am sorry."

I turned to face him squarely, lifting my chin as I stared him in the eye. "We're not serious about each other, remember? You don't need to apologize. I'll get over it—I'm used to men treating me like shit."

"April. I don't want you feeling like that!"

"I need to get back to work. And I imagine you want to get back to Hailey. See you later."

After picking up my BCD and reg, I headed back to the gear room without another backward glance. I should be grateful for what just happened. It was a vivid reminder of why I didn't want to get seriously involved with Gabe. Why I needed to keep him at arm's length. He didn't want another serious relationship. And I didn't want to be another *good enough* in someone's life.

I could handle being irritated and pissed off. That would pass. But I couldn't let him crush my heart. And I'd felt him starting to work his way into its beating crevices.

And that wouldn't do at all.

Chapter Nineteen

Gabe

AS I PUSHED through the dive shop door, it was just past 5:00 p.m. I glanced at Carissa, who was putting things away.

"Hailey's in the back room."

I nodded at her. "Thanks. You can take off now. I'll lock up." I headed down the hall. Suggesting donuts this late might not have been the best choice, but I'd just wanted to get Hailey away from that dive gear.

Though considering how badly I'd screwed up the situation, I might have been better off just leaving with her.

April had never been afraid to stand up to me, but I'd never seen her that angry. And it wasn't without justification. I'd seen what Hailey was doing, opened my mouth, and the raging papa bear had roared out.

When I walked into the break room, Hailey was licking her fingers while holding the Sweet Dreams box open with the other hand.

"Do I even want to know how many you've had?"

Instantly, she dropped the lid and rushed her sticky hand behind her back, turning an absolutely angelic look toward me. Which let me know she was completely guilty. "I only had one."

I smiled as I crossed the room, my frustration at the conversation with April slipping away. "Is that right?"

"Well, there were some pieces of others, so I might have had two."

"Now that I believe. I just hope you left room for dinner."

She turned a smile to me. "That's actually why I came down here. Nona wants me to tell you we're expected at dinner tonight."

"We'd better get going then."

I locked up the dive shop and we left via the back door. The gear room was locked up tight. April must have already finished.

Hailey gave the pool a long glance as we ambled up the path. "I like April. She was really nice and let me play with the scuba equipment."

"She is nice."

"But she wouldn't let me get in the water with it. Said I had to get the okay from you first."

I tried not to flinch.

Yeah, I really owe April an apology. And maybe flowers too.

"Well?"

Clueless, I looked down at Hailey. "Well, what?"

She rolled her eyes like only an eight-year-old can. "Can I learn to dive?"

A cold, prickly ball formed in my gut. "You're still too young to get certified." I had no idea if that was true or not, but I wasn't about to let her dive at eight. Then I got another idea. "Why don't we go snorkeling tomorrow?"

Her crestfallen expression at being denied diving turned to excitement at the prospect of snorkeling. "Okay! Do you want to go on *Shark Bait*?"

April was also off tomorrow, so I wouldn't need to worry about us being awkward together on the boat. But I also needed to fix things with her. I studied her apartment as we passed but saw no sign of her. *One thing at a time...* "Let's make a day of it. We can go to Bahia Honda Park and hang out."

"Baya Honda?"

I spelled it for her. "But most people pronounce it like Bay-a."

"That doesn't make sense."

Lots of things don't make sense, baby girl.

"Yeah, but it's fun to listen to the tourists pronounce it wrong. Now you're officially a local."

She giggled as we edged toward our cottage, and I draped an arm over her thin shoulders. "Come on. We've got enough time to change before dinner."

DAD HAD LED a trip on *Reel Deal* that morning and caught two beautiful wahoo. Once word got out he was personally leading trips, the resort's fishing charters had gone from sporadic to a waiting list. Even locals were signing up. And the difference was noticeable in Dad's more relaxed face. He was helping the resort while doing his favorite activity.

Most of the family sat around the huge kitchen table. Pilar sat near the doorway, staring at us with her bright green eyes. She lowered her head to lick her smoke-gray coat.

Hailey had peered suspiciously at her portion of fish. But after some gentle chiding from me, she ate it without protest. Getting a kid to eat fish was easier when it was prepared by a professional chef.

Maia pushed her plate away and leaned back in her chair, rubbing her hand over her broad abdomen. Next to her, Wyatt smiled and tucked a lock of hair behind her ear. After plenty of initial misgivings on my part, I had to admit my brother-in-law wasn't the disaster I'd feared.

He was completely devoted to both Maia and their upcoming daughter, and he gave me no complaints at work. Maia was well into her seventh month now, though her increased girth didn't slow her down. She still led snorkeling trips four or five times a week.

Hailey leaned forward in her seat, her eyes glowing. "Is she kicking?"

Maia glanced at her stomach. "No, she moved a little, but now she's settled down again."

"I can't wait for her to get here!" Hailey flopped back, resting against the wooden back of the chair. "It's taking so long."

Wyatt grinned at her. "Good thing you're right next door. You can pop over anytime you want."

"Thank you. Since I'm never getting a brother or sister, I'm going to be a big sister to your baby."

All eyes turned to me, and heat crept up my neck. That had been a fun conversation with a seven-year-old. When Hailey had asked about babies, I'd simply told her that a man and a woman had to be together in a relationship for a baby to come along, and not to plan on any siblings.

I was trying to come up with a reply when she gasped and whipped her head toward me. "Daddy! You're together with April now. Does that mean she's going to have a baby?"

God, I hope not.

Evan's face morphed into a total shit-eating grin. "Yeah, Daddy. How about it?"

I shot him a look ten times more lethal than the one I'd given April, but he only laughed. Apparently, Pilar had had enough of the conversation because she padded out of the room.

Drawing myself up with dignity, I gave Hailey my attention. "No, angel. It's more than that. We're not even married."

"Oh. You mean sex."

Maia burst out laughing, and I darted a quick glance at Nona, afraid she was about to blow her top. But she was openly grinning, apparently deciding the entertainment value of the conversation outweighed its impropriety.

"Hailey, this isn't the time for this conversation," I said with as much dignity as I could muster.

She went on like she hadn't even heard me. "You have to be married to have sex, right?"

Wyatt choked on his water and Maia quickly lifted a napkin to her mouth, her shoulders shaking.

Hailey turned a censorious frown around the table. "I'm only saying this to let Dad know it's okay with me if he marries April."

Evan made a strangled noise as he choked back a laugh.

"Hailey, you need to stop, all right?" I kept my voice soft, but my heart was pounding.

"Yes, dear," Nona said as she arched a brow from the head of the table opposite Dad. "Perhaps before your father goes ring shopping, he should invite the woman to a family dinner."

I dropped my head into my hands as the whole table erupted into laughter, including Dad.

Nona was the first to get it together and addressed Hailey. "What are your plans tomorrow?"

Hailey lit up, the horribly embarrassing conversation about weddings and babies forgotten. "Dad and I are going to Bahia"—she carefully pronounced the word—"Honda Park tomorrow."

"That sounds fun!" Maia said. "Are you going to snorkel?"

"We are," I said, feeling I ought to get at least a couple of words in during dinner.

"Can April come with us?" Hailey asked me, both hands bunched on her thighs. "She'd be a much better snorkel guide than you."

"She's got you there, Gabe," Maia said with a sly grin. "You can't tell the difference between an angelfish and a blenny."

I had no idea what a blenny was, which prevented any smart comebacks. Plus, Hailey's idea was pretty good. It would give me a chance to repair the damage I'd done this afternoon.

If April would let me.

"She's off tomorrow," I said to my daughter. "But she might already have plans."

"Tell her to cancel them!"

Yeah, that would go over well.

"I'll ask her, but I can't promise anything."

Nona placed her napkin on the table. "Well, if impending births and weddings are all settled, I think I'll head upstairs. My new puzzle arrived."

"The one with the cats?" Hailey asked.

"Exactly. You want to work on it with me?"

Hailey whipped her head to me. "Can I sleep here tonight?"

I placed my hand on her shoulder, already running over the possibilities this gave me with April. "Will you be good for Nona?"

"Of course!"

"All right. You go with Nona to put the puzzle together, and I'll go see if April will go with us tomorrow."

And I'll try to put the pieces together with her.

When I knocked on her door, April answered wearing sweats and fluffy slippers. She wore an oversized sweatshirt, and the neck had shifted to expose one bare shoulder. I tried not to stare at it. No bra. Even in sweats and slippers, I couldn't take my eyes off her.

"I didn't expect you again today," she said as she turned around and padded back to the couch.

I sat next to her, resting one arm over the back of the couch. "I wanted to talk to you. Hailey's spending the night at the Big House."

Her eyes flicked to me, but she didn't reply.

"You're right," I said softly. "I overreacted. I'm sorry."

Her throat moved as she swallowed. "I've been thinking about it all evening. If some random guest's kid had come up to me like that, I would have let them take a puff or two off the reg, but no more. Definitely not put the whole kit on. So you were right too. Hailey's your daughter, and you have the right to call the shots about what she does."

Tension I hadn't realized I'd been holding drained from my sore and stiff shoulders. I stretched them. "I never meant to question your judgment. I know you'd never put Hailey's safety at risk."

Finally, she met my eyes. "I wouldn't, Gabe. I'm pretty damn good at what I do."

"I know you are. You're good at a lot of things."

She smirked but didn't respond, letting me know we

weren't quite back on normal footing yet as she returned her gaze to her hands. And I had something else to say anyway. "You said something this afternoon that really bothered me."

"What?"

"That you're used to men treating you like shit."

She shrugged one shoulder. "That pretty much sums up all the relationships I've had."

I reached out and placed two fingers under her jaw, tilting her head to face me. "If I made you feel like that, I am really, really sorry. I mean that, April. I like the man I am when I'm with you. I've had a rough couple of years, and it's made me... more guarded than I used to be. But I'll try to do better. Because you deserve better."

"You're talking about your wife."

Now it was my turn to swallow over the sudden constriction in my throat. I nodded. "I can't say I ever felt Kora was the love of my life, but I was in it for the long haul. I thought she was too, until she told me she was leaving. She moved across the country and pretty much abandoned Hailey. Our divorce was pretty ugly and contested. It left me bitter. Then, about a year ago, she called me out of the blue wanting to renegotiate our custody arrangement and get partial custody of Hailey."

"She obviously didn't win."

I smiled grimly. "No. I told her if she wanted a legal fight, she hadn't seen anything yet. I was a little surprised at how easily she gave up the idea. Then she went back to whatever rock she's been hiding under. We haven't heard from her since, and I have a feeling it's for good this time. Which is fine with me."

April shook her head. "Poor Hailey."

"Yeah. I've done my best to help her understand her

mother's behavior has nothing to do with her, but that was the main reason I moved from Miami. I wanted Hailey to have a strong, supportive family around her."

April reached over and placed her hand over mine. "You're an amazing father. I hope you know that."

I turned my hand and laced my fingers between hers. "I'm trying as hard as I can. And who knows? Maybe Hailey will be a part of the resort one day."

"Maia told me you came back here to help shore up the bottom line. Have things improved?"

I gave her a lopsided smile. "They have, so you don't need to worry about me handing you a pink slip. Though I've got big ideas for this place. I just need to come up with the funding to make them happen."

"You might try offering packages with lodging, diving, and meals combined. The resort I used to work at had a lot of success with that."

That was already on my list. "Good idea." I slid closer and moved my hand from the back of the couch to stroke her golden strands. "But I didn't really come here to talk business."

She lifted her head, exposing a length of creamy neck. "Did you have something else in mind?"

I moved in and whisked my lips over hers. "Yes. Something completely different."

I grabbed a handful of hair and pulled her head back. I crushed my mouth to hers, finally giving in to the desire that had been building since the first moment I saw her and that bare shoulder. April's lips were soft, and when she opened her mouth, I tasted red wine.

Then I remembered something else.

"Oh, shit," I said, laughing as I pulled away.

She fluttered her lashes, looking slightly dazed. "What?"

"There actually is another reason I came down here. Would you like to join Hailey and me tomorrow at Bahia Honda Park? It's a beach park on Big Pine Key. We're going to hang out for most of the day—snorkel, hike, eat, drink, and just have fun. She informed me that you would make a far better snorkel guide than me and practically forced me to ask you. Though I rather like the idea myself."

April burst into a full smile that warmed my heart. "I'd love to! Does that mean I'm finally going to get you in the water?"

Smiling, I leaned closer. "You can have me any way you want me."

Chapter Twenty

Gabe

THIS TIME, I moved in and kissed her softly, taking a slow, leisurely tour of her mouth. I loved running my fingers through the silky strands of her hair. Breaking the kiss, I stood up and pulled April to her feet. After another soft brush of lips, I wrapped one arm around her upper back and picked her up, sliding my other arm behind her knees.

I carried her up the stairs and to the master bedroom. She wasn't a large woman, so her weight was nearly effortless for me to carry. I couldn't keep my mouth away from hers and lowered my head as I set her on her feet next to the bed.

She smiled against my lips. "That's the first time I've ever been carried like that."

I opened my eyes. "I hope you approve?"

"Oh, yes." She ran her hands over my shoulders. "You're such a strong man. Might as well put those muscles to use."

I kissed her temple. "I'm hoping to put something else to use."

"Mmm. We're in the right room."

Her sweatshirt had slipped off her shoulder again, and I leaned over to run my tongue over her warm skin. Then, in one fast motion, I ripped it off. She wasn't wearing a bra and I cupped her breasts in my hands. They were the perfect size—just like the rest of her. She was a work of art.

How could she ever think she wasn't enough?

I kissed her again, softly touching my tongue to hers. The conversations we'd had about her past lovers made me determined not to be seen in that light.

I wanted to please this woman more than any I'd ever known.

My breath caught as she rushed both hands under my shirt and up my abdomen, fanning her fingers over my chest. Her touch lit me on fire, my blood turning molten as it coursed through my veins. I ripped my shirt off and kissed her deeply, pinning my chest against hers.

She gave a soft moan that made me grip her even tighter.

"Do you have any idea how bad I want you?" I whispered against her mouth.

She opened my shorts and palmed me, and I pushed against her hand. She slid my shorts off, and they fell to my feet. I kicked them off without breaking our kiss.

Our kisses were loud and wet in the silent room. God, this woman turned me on. I wanted to consume her, possess her, make her scream. But that tiny, sad voice she'd used was stuck in my head. I needed to be gentle tonight. I grasped her face in both hands and fluttered a soft kiss across her lips, kissing each corner of her mouth. "I don't have any condoms with me. We need to use yours."

April jerked her head back. "Oh! I knew I forgot something at the store." She swallowed and met my gaze. "I don't have any."

A pang went through me, but I gave her a smile and brushed my index finger over her shoulder. "There are other things we can do, aren't there?" I closed my hand on her shoulder and started to press her backward toward the bed when she held her hand against my chest.

"Wait."

I cocked my head.

"I have an IUD. We don't need condoms... assuming you're safe... I am."

She stared at me, but her eyes were uncertain. I understood her hesitancy. Using condoms was an unacknowledged symbol between us that our relationship was casual. This... was moving to another level.

And we both knew it.

April had just told me she was willing to take the next step and was waiting for my answer. Every cell of my body was throbbing for her, but I wasn't some goddamn caveman using her just for sex. The answer was simple.

"I'm safe."

Her eyes turned sultry, and she let her hand trail down the center of my chest and over my abs. I twitched hard as she brushed my shaft. Then she slipped her shorts off, turned, and folded back the covers. She slipped inside, giving me a gorgeous view of my goal.

I climbed in and stretched out against her warm, welcoming body. April grabbed a handful of my hair, smashing her mouth to mine. I wanted her so bad I could hardly contain myself. But I softened the kiss, still mindful of what she'd said earlier. She grabbed my hand and placed it between her legs. A long, blissful sigh escaped her lips as I stroked her.

I was getting more turned on by the second. She was being more deliberate tonight, being clear about what she wanted.

"Now, Gabe. Come to me."

She opened her legs, and I moved on top of her. I couldn't control the deep groan that issued from my chest as I entered her in one long push.

We had already proven we were great together. But without the condom, the feeling was more intense than I'd ever known. I moved in a slow, stroking rhythm and she grabbed my ass with both hands. She squeezed hard and I grunted against her mouth, trying to stay in control. Trying to stay tender. Opening her lips, she probed her tongue into my mouth. Desire raced through my veins as I touched it softly with mine, then moved my mouth across her delicate jawline.

"Gabe."

"What?" I asked in a whisper.

"I don't want you to be gentle tonight."

My entire body shuddered violently, and I had to grit my teeth.

That was unexpected.

I lifted up and gave her a smile as I thrust hard. "Oh?"

April cried out and arched her stomach against me. "Yes!"

I grabbed her wrists and moved her arms out sideways, lacing my fingers through hers. I pinned her with my body, not allowing her to move. "Is this what you want?"

"I want to lose myself, Gabe. Possess me. Take me hard. Now."

Pushing her hands into the mattress, I slammed into

her. Both of us cried out. I withdrew, then pounded her again. And again.

Deep, guttural growls were coming from the depths of my chest and her cries escalated. A dim part of me worried about hurting her, but most of me was beyond rational thought. And from the sounds April was making, I didn't need to worry about that. I lost myself, giving in to the tide sweeping over me in a way I'd never experienced. It was all-consuming, shattering.

In possessing her fully, I had to give up my own control.

And it was glorious.

AFTER I ROLLED OFF HER, I pulled her tight against my chest and wrapped my arms tightly around her. I pressed my lips to her sweaty temple. "I didn't hurt you, did I?"

She wiggled her hips. "Yeah, a little. I'm not complaining. I enjoyed that, in case you couldn't tell."

I laughed softly. "I could tell. That was... incredible."

A giggle tumbled out of her mouth that made me hold her tighter. "Good thing the Barn is isolated. Otherwise, we might have woken up the whole resort."

"And there wasn't even whisky involved."

Her giggle turned into a full laugh, and I joined her. She lifted up and rested her head in her hand, propped on her elbow. "I'm still surprised every time I hear you laugh. It's so unexpected."

"Is that a bad thing?"

She poked me in the rib. "No! I wish you'd laugh more."

My smile faded as I stared at her. "I feel years younger than I did a few months ago. There's still a lot of pressure with the resort, but it doesn't weigh on me as much. If I'm laughing more, it's because of you, sweetheart."

She brushed a lock of sweaty hair off my forehead. "Does that mean you're not looking to get into fistfights anymore?"

I rubbed my eyes, laughing reluctantly. "Hell, no. I still can't believe that happened. Ben Coleridge and I have never been pals, but I've never gotten in a fight with him about it."

"Did he attack you? Were you defending yourself?"

My grin remained. "Oh, no. I threw the first punch. That's why he threatened to press charges. I was just so pissed off, and he pushed me too far." Then I sobered and reached out to cup her face. "I'm protective and occasionally a little grouchy, but I'm not violent, April. I promise you don't need to be afraid of me."

Her smile remained, which pleased me. "*Occasionally* grouchy?"

I narrowed my eyes. "Yes. Occasionally."

She laughed and swept her lips over mine. "I know I don't need to be afraid of you. That's what tonight was about. I wanted to be overpowered—it kind of surprised me. I felt safe with it because I trust you. You're a towering, masculine guy, Gabe. It's pretty hot."

The soft warmth in my chest spread. "I'm glad you trust me. And I'm even more glad you believe I don't do jail time on a regular basis." I sighed. "Given how small these two islands are, it's amazing no one's nailed my ear to the pillory yet."

She laughed softly. "Yeah, I ran into that at my book club meeting. I've become friends with the woman who owns Sweet Dreams and told her I was seeing someone. During the meeting, she asked who it was, so I opened my big, fat mouth and said your name." She gave me a pointed look. "You could have heard a pin drop in the room, though not because they were incensed about your lockup escapade. Most of the women were nice about it, but I could tell one or two wanted to stick a pin in me for being involved with you."

"Sorry about that. People love to gossip, and the Markham family always seems to be fodder for the grist mill. It's an absolute miracle Hailey hasn't found out about my jail stint, though I guess that proves the townsfolk do have a sense of decency. Hopefully, enough time has gone by now she'll never find out."

"At least until she's forty and you two can laugh about it?"

"That would work for me. Fifty would be better."

Our gazes locked and the smile remained on April's face. "Speaking of Hailey, if she's up at the Big House, does that mean you're spending the night?"

I pulled April back down to my chest, wrapping her up tight. "Just try to pry me out of here."

"It's my bed. Don't sass me or I'll kick you out of it."

I grinned at the ceiling. "It's not your bed. It's mine."

"Oh, that's right! This really is the most amazing bed I've ever been in, Gabe."

"Me too. But only because you're in it with me." I rested my cheek on her hair and stared out the window. Pale, ghostly light shone on the wooden floor.

"I should open the window," April murmured. "I like the fresh air at night."

"You want some fresh air?"

"I love it when it rains overnight. The scent fills the room."

I took in the starry sky through the window. "Doesn't look like it's going to rain anytime soon. But I can take care of the fresh air." I slapped her on the butt. "Come on. Let's go for a walk."

"What? What happened to not prying you out of bed?"

I grinned. "A nighttime walk is much more enticing when I know I get to crawl back in with you afterward."

Soon we were redressed and strolling up the sand path toward the Big House. Her hand was snug within mine, and the night was fragrant and a perfect temperature.

April snuck a glance at the blanket folded over my arm. "Another blanket? You tend to do wild things to me involving blankets."

I rubbed my thumb over the back of her hand. "You'll see."

We passed by the cottages and angled around the side of the Big House. I took the lead, still holding April's hand as we skirted the pool deck. Tall hedges of groomed bougainvillea fringed the area, ensuring we had privacy while using the pool. I led us through a gap and onto another sand path that ran along the bluff.

April slowed, tugging on my hand as she took in the view. "Wow, even with no moon, this is spectacular."

A wide expanse of ocean lay before us. The lights of Dove Key were visible ahead and the more distant ones of Big Pine Key twinkled farther to the north. April craned her head around and studied the Big House. "Which room was yours growing up?"

I pointed to one end. "Third floor end room. It's been remodeled for Hailey now. She loves that she gets to sleep in my old room. The view is incredible from there."

"I'm sure it is." She took a deep breath and met my eyes. "Was your childhood happy here? Without your mother?"

My eyes automatically traveled to the opposite end of the third floor, to the master bedroom my father occupied.

A small smile stretched my lips. "I was happy. Losing my mom was awful, but Dad and Nona did everything they could to make sure we knew we were loved."

"Maia told me about it. I'm so sorry. You were what? Eight?"

I nodded. "Hailey's age, actually. It made me very protective of my siblings." I took her hand and led her forward, leaning close to her as we continued along the path. "And protective of others too." I spared a quick glance at the Big House. "We were happy kids, and all very different. On any given day, you'd find Dad grooming me to take part in resort operations, though we had some big fights about it. Stella was always looking over the chefs' shoulders, and Evan would be practicing one of his sports. Hunter would lie in a hammock half the day with his nose in a book, and Maia was always in the water—either the pool or the ocean."

April laughed softly behind me. "That sounds wonderful."

We came to the edge of the bluff where it curved in, creating a small bay. "Hold tight to my hand," I said over my shoulder. "There are no lights here, but steps are carved into the stone all the way down."

"All the way down where?"

I turned around and gave her a smug grin. "You'll see."

I led the way as we descended the stone staircase cut into the side of the bluff. I had done this so many times I didn't need light.

"How long has this staircase been here?"

"Some ancestor had it carved out of the rock back in the 1800s. I'm not sure exactly when. Dad or Nona would know."

"Wow. There's so much history here."

The path zigzagged and continued down the bluff in the opposite direction. "Yeah. That's one of the reasons I wanted to bring Hailey back here. I want her to understand she's a part of this."

April squeezed my hand. "That's wonderful."

Another hairpin turn appeared and the rock rose on both sides as we descended through the valley between.

"This path was a lot of work to make."

I nodded. "Yep. We're there."

I stepped onto the sand and led April to the left, around a protruding boulder. We emerged at the head of a small bay, the sand making a perfect white crescent as the ocean softly swept upon it, protected by the tall cliffs at the edges.

April gasped. "This is beautiful!"

She joined my side, and we ambled over the powdery sand. Small, scrubby trees and brush grew at the closed head of the bay, with a sheer limestone cliff rising behind them to the bluff overhead.

Stopping, I moved behind her and wrapped my arms around her front, pulling her back against me. "We call this the Cove. It's invisible from the top and the only access is by that path from the Big House. It's always been a special place just for us Markhams."

She stroked her hand up my forearm. "Thank you for sharing it with me."

As soon as she'd said she wanted fresh air, I'd had an irresistible urge to visit the Cove with her. I hadn't been to it since I'd come back. As a familiar sense of serenity washed over me, I wondered why it took me so long. As I concentrated on the soft warmth pressed against me, a smile rose on my face.

Because I wanted to share it with her. I just didn't know it yet.

I spread the blanket out on the sand and helped April lie down on it. The air was warmer here without the breeze. I lowered my head and reached for her soft, yielding lips. After a soft moan, she broke away and swept her gaze over the top of the cliff behind us.

"Don't worry," I whispered. "We're completely hidden here. The beach is invisible from the bluff and the Big House."

She peaked a brow. "Ah. I take it this is where you bring all your girls?"

I gave her a cocky grin. "Hardly. I made out with a few here in my teenage years." As I stared at the pale curve of her cheek, my smile faded. "Making out was all. I brought you here because I wanted to show the Cove to you, but now I'm kind of hoping for round two."

My heart beat faster as she smiled up at me, starlight reflecting in her eyes. "I'm glad you did, and I can't think of a better place. You might need to be a little more gentle this time, though."

I rubbed my nose against hers. "I can do that."

I could be whatever she needed.

The warm night embraced us, and the only sound as we came together again was soft waves washing ashore.

Chapter Twenty-One

April

GABRIEL MARKHAM WAS A CUDDLER. Of the things that had amazed me about Gabe—and the number was legion—this was among the most surprising. We had only spent a handful of full nights together. Most nights we retired to his bedroom after Hailey was safely asleep, and I made sure to stay awake. But on those rare luxurious full nights, I had always woken up in a different position from what I'd fallen asleep in, yet with Gabe wrapped around me somehow.

Smiling, I blinked my eyes open to golden light streaming into my bedroom. Gabe breathed deep and steady next to me. We faced each other and one strong arm lay draped over my waist. Our legs intertwined. I was warm and wonderfully comfortable.

Except I needed to pee.

Slowly raising my arm from his hip, I gently scooched backward. Eyes still closed, Gabe murmured and pulled me tighter to him, our bellies pressing together. As much as I loved his strong arms and legs around me, this wouldn't do. He settled again, so this time I slowly moved my left leg from his, then my right.

Okay, mostly there.

With agonizing slowness, I moved my hand and picked up his arm encircling me. As soon as I started to lift it, his hold tightened. His arm became a steel rod. Immovable.

I frowned, then glanced at his face.

At his smiling face, though his eyes were still closed.

"You asshole. You're awake!"

He burst into laughter, opening his eyes. "Wow. That's a nice greeting. Are you always this warm and fuzzy in the morning?"

I couldn't help smiling back. "When I have good reason to be. If I was wearing pants right now, I'd be about to pee them."

He made a rumbling noise in his throat. "But you're not wearing pants, are you?"

"We really ought to get up. Don't you need to collect your daughter?"

He closed his eyes and snuggled into his pillow. "At some point. What time is it?"

I glanced at the clock on the nightstand behind him. "Seven thirty."

His eyes flew open. "Shit! Really?"

"Did you think we'd be awake at the crack of dawn? We were at the Cove half the night."

"Don't remind me or we'll never get out of bed."

"Is this beach park busy?"

My abrupt subject change caused him to slit his eyes open again. "Yes. It's very popular, but since it's a weekday, we should be able to get a good spot."

I firmly dislodged his arm. "Then let's get going. The

snorkeling will be better before other people get in the water and scare the fish away. We can stop by Sweet Dreams and pick up donuts to take with us."

As I sat up and swung my legs off the bed, Gabe made a final lunge for me, wrapping his arm around me. I swatted him away and scampered to the bathroom, smiling the whole way.

An hour later, we drove down the main road toward Dove Key. Gabe was behind the wheel of a Calypso Key Resort pickup truck, I was buckled into the passenger seat, and Hailey sat in her booster seat behind me in the extended cab. The bed of the truck was filled with snorkeling gear, a large cooler, blankets, and other miscellany we might need for our beach adventure.

Gabe took a left on Main Street and glanced in the rearview mirror. "Settle down back there. I don't want you squirming out of your seat belt."

Hailey laughed. "I won't! But I'm excited about finally getting to see Sweet Dreams in person! Uncle Evan has been bringing their donuts in every week—I'm kind of addicted."

Gabe smirked. "Yeah, I've noticed that. Still not sure why he won't get the pastries our own chef makes."

"Because they aren't as good!" Hailey leaned forward. "Do you really know the owner, April?"

"Yeah. She moved down here to open the shop. I'm glad it's a success."

Gabe parked in a slanted stall near the store and Hailey skipped in front of us as we headed toward the bakery. She darted in the door ahead of us and Gabe caught the glass entry before it closed, waving me ahead.

Delicious aromas of cinnamon, fresh dough, and sweet confections filled the air, and I couldn't resist a deep lungful. Hailey was already at the glass counter, peering at the pastries inside.

"What would you like, honey?" Liv asked her from behind the counter.

"Do you have a chocolate-frosted glazed with peanuts on top?"

"I sure do," the baker replied as she bent down and slid open the door. When she popped back up, I stood next to Hailey with Gabe resting his hands on her narrow shoulders. Liv saw me and smiled. "April!"

"Hi, Liv. We came by for a little treat."

Liv had a mop of long, curly brown hair that was currently wrangled back with a hairband. She was slightly plump, and her friendly personality made her perfect for her chosen line of work. "You're in the right place then!" Her eyes drifted back to Hailey, then widened when she saw Gabe behind her.

"This is Hailey and her father Gabe," I said.

Recovering quickly, Liv nodded at Hailey as she slid the donut into a white paper sack. "Pleased to meet you. And you too," she said to Gabe.

"Can I have two, Dad?"

Gabe frowned. "You don't need two."

Liv arched a brow. "Need has nothing to do with donuts, now does it?"

He smiled. "Okay. I know when I'm beaten."

After a maple bar joined the first donut in the bag, Liv bounced her eyes between Gabe and me. "And what will you two have?"

"Apple fritter," we said in exact unison.

Both of us laughed as Liv slid the tray of apple fritters out and selected two. I guess I shouldn't have been too surprised we liked the same donuts.

"We're spending the day at the beach," Hailey informed her. "April's going to take us snorkeling."

"Well, you should have a great time then. You're in the hands of an expert." Liv folded the top of the bag over and handed it to me.

Gabe took his wallet out of his back pocket. "How much do I owe you?"

"Nothing," Liv said with a smile. "I couldn't charge such a pretty young girl. Or you two, either."

Hailey beamed, and I laughed. "Thank you," I said. "That's very kind of you."

A tip jar sat in front of the cash register and Gabe slid a twenty into it. I was pretty sure Liv couldn't see the bill. I winked at her. "Thanks for your generosity. Have a good day."

"You guys also, but I think you've got it handled."

As Gabe turned, he wrapped an arm around my shoulders. Liv deliberately widened her eyes and gave me a long stare. I gave her a demure smile back over my shoulder as we left the shop.

Bahia Honda State Park was only a few miles up the Overseas Highway from Big Pine Key. Gabe paid the entrance fee, and we were early enough to find parking in front of a beautiful stretch of white sand. Scrubby trees even provided some shade.

We circled to the tailgate. Gabe lowered it and we all loaded up with lawn chairs, blankets, snorkel gear, and anything else we could carry. We set up on the sand in front of the trees, and Gabe strung a tarp to provide consistent shade. After laying down the blanket and making sure plenty of ice remained in the cooler, I stepped onto the beach. Shading my eyes with my hand, I glanced at the remnants of the old overseas railroad trestle visible in the distance.

In front of us lay a calm stretch of aquamarine water. I could see encouraging darker patches, giving a hint of seagrass or reef to investigate. I headed back to our base and organized the three sets of snorkel equipment I'd grabbed from the gear room that morning.

"I'm jumping in the water!" Hailey yelled and took off.

"Hold on there!" Gabe called, and she reluctantly turned around. "You're not going in the water with your hair free like that. It will be a total mess. And what else are you missing?"

"Sunscreen," she said begrudgingly but trudged back to the blanket.

Gabe sat on the blanket with his legs in a V. Hailey returned and sat between them, facing away from him. He pulled an elastic hairband out of his pocket and stuck it between his teeth. A huge smile rose on my face at the sight of Hot Grumpy Guy quickly and expertly braiding her hair into a long tail down her back.

Gabe tapped her shoulder. "Okay, you know the drill."

He grabbed a can of reef safe, spray-on sunscreen and Hailey turned around. He placed his hand over her closed eyes and misted her face. Then she stood and twirled with her arms out as he covered her with the spray.

The ease and familiarity of how they accomplished the procedure touched me deeply. The routine was obviously one they'd completed many times, and my smile softened as I stared at Gabe.

Hailey parked both hands on her slim hips. "*Now* can I go?"

"Now you can go," he said and handed me the can.

As she splashed into the water with her snorkeling

equipment, I sprayed the front of my body. "You want to spray my back?"

"Oh, absolutely."

I shivered as the cold fluid touched my skin, but Gabe's hand was much warmer as he spread the sunscreen around. I did the same to him, slowing to caress his broad, muscular shoulders.

"Hurry up back there," he said. "My board shorts aren't that baggy, you know."

Laughing lightly, I returned the can to our beach bag and picked up two sets of snorkel gear. "Shall we?"

I found a nice patch reef a short distance offshore. I wore a weight belt so I could investigate more closely and discovered a juvenile spotted moray eel. Hailey was eager for a closer look, so I let her hold on to my arm as we dove down to the reef. Gabe dove on my other side. I let Hailey inspect the small creature whose head poked out of a hole in the coral, and she exclaimed through her snorkel as it opened and closed its mouth to breathe.

Not wanting her to stay submerged too long, I rose to the surface, and we inspected the rest of the reef from the top of the water. I discovered a huge green sea turtle snacking on sea grass, and we spent ten minutes above it. The massive animal completely ignored us, chomping on the grass as it moved slowly along.

After snorkeling, we explored the trails in the park and got a good look at the abandoned, decrepit railroad trestle, which Gabe told us had originally stretched from Key Largo to Key West. In the early twentieth century, it had brought guests to Calypso Key Resort.

Gabe brought a lunch of fried chicken, potato salad, and fresh fruit he'd picked up from Dorado, so we ate like kings under our shady tarp. Black frigate birds soared above us, amid the white, soft clouds.

I couldn't imagine a more perfect morning.

After so much activity and with a full stomach, Hailey curled up on the blanket and was asleep in minutes. Gabe sat with his back resting against the trunk of a palm tree and beckoned to me. I eased to the ground in front of him, then leaned back against his solid warmth. I laced my fingers together over my stomach and he rested his on top, his arms around mine.

"Thank you for inviting me," I said. "This has been wonderful."

"I'm glad you're here with us."

"Did you enjoy the snorkeling? You looked plenty comfortable in the water."

He traced his fingers up and down my arm. "Yeah. I love being in the water. It's been so long, I kind of forgot that."

"Does that mean I might get you to dive?"

"I've been thinking about it, even before today."

My heart soared, and I turned around to grin at him. "I happen to know an excellent dive professional who could give you a refresher."

Gabe frowned. "I was thinking about asking Corbin to do it. You've already seen me act idiotically too many times. I don't want to give you any more ammunition. If Corbin helps me first, I can wow you with my diving prowess."

I smiled and folded my hand over his. "I want whatever makes you comfortable, but I deal with nervous, out-of-practice divers just about every day. I'm pretty good at it."

He pressed a kiss against my temple. "Do you promise not to laugh at me?"

"I absolutely do *not* promise that."

A grin burst across his face. "You never let me off the hook easily. I like that about you. Will you at least promise not to humiliate me?"

My smile faded. "I'd never do that. Promise."

Our eyes held, and I had to admit I loved the idea of being the expert. I had the feeling not many women had that experience with Gabe. "Well? Are you in or out?"

He leaned forward and brushed his lips over mine. "In. You can give me a quick refresher in the pool behind the Big House. Then we'll take a boat out by ourselves for a dive. How's that sound?"

"Like my idea of a perfect date."

"Even more than outdoor movies and fine whisky?"

"Maybe we can bring the whisky with us."

He laughed softly and I turned around again, snuggling my back up to his chest. I turned my gaze to Hailey, who looked angelic in sleep. "You two have a wonderful relationship. You should be really proud. Of both of you."

"Thanks. I'm lucky—she's an easy kid... Have you ever been interested in having children?"

I sighed and relaxed my head against his shoulder. "Yes, but life didn't work out like that." This wasn't a fun subject, but Gabe had opened himself by inviting me today. He deserved the same. "I thought I was headed in that direction in my mid-twenties. I'd been with Mark for almost two years—we lived together. I figured marriage was the next step and would happen soon. Until the dive boat broke down as we were leaving the harbor and I got an unexpected day off. I went home and found him in bed with his other girlfriend."

Gabe's arms contracted as he winced behind me. "God, how awful. I'm sorry."

I snorted. "Don't worry. I got tested for everything in the book."

"I wasn't worried. I trust you."

"At least the son of a bitch was careful when he cheated. Anyway, after that I moved to St. Croix and decided I needed a different kind of man—one with integrity. And I found him. Ex-military, honor was the center of his makeup. I fell pretty hard for him, but he wasn't even slightly interested in me. Even after he got together with his girlfriend, I kept hoping it wouldn't work out between them. Once he got engaged to her, I finally gave up. I don't chase after married men, and I like his wife a lot."

I sighed, watching a pelican rocket into the ocean. "And I found someone new last year. We went away for a romantic weekend to St. John. Brian liked it so much he decided to stay there. Without me. So I've never even come close to getting married, let alone starting a family. I'm awful with men. That's why my relationship with you is working—we both want the same thing. Or rather, *don't* want the same thing."

He had started stroking his fingers along my arm during my monologue. "Sounds like you've never met the right man."

I shrugged. "Doesn't matter. I'm happy here. I know I'm an outsider, but... I feel at home here in a way I didn't in St. Croix."

Gabe kissed my hair. "You're not an outsider. And I'm very glad you're here."

A rustling came from the bushes behind us, but I didn't move. If someone was coming to investigate, they'd discover we were here soon enough and leave.

"I love the history your family has at Calypso Key," I

said. "That's something I've never had—roots. I never asked for much from my relationships. I just wanted to be important to someone. I watched my friends find men who couldn't live without them, but I guess that doesn't happen for everyone. I'm sure there are a lot more people like you and me. Those who found nothing but heartbreak with love."

"Kind of a depressing outlook but accurate."

I caught his hand and squeezed. "Thanks for listening."

"Of course."

The soft rustle came again, and Gabe shifted behind me.

"April," he whispered urgently. "Turn around slowly."

With my heart pounding, I expected either a knife-toting crackhead or a wild boar as I slowly turned around. My breath caught, wonder sending chills through my body. A delighted smile cracked my face as three tiny deer stepped out of the brush and onto the sand ten feet away. They looked like normal deer, except they were the size of a Labrador retriever.

"Are those Key deer?" I whispered, afraid to spook them as I slowly sat upright.

Gabe nodded and matched my soft voice. "They're pretty common on Big Pine Key and they even swim across to Dove and Calypso Keys. I've never seen any here before, but Bahia Honda isn't too far away." He reached over and gently shook Hailey's shoulder.

She fluttered her eyes open, and Gabe held a finger to his lips and pointed behind her. She turned around and the nearest deer flicked its ears as it stared at her. The other two froze as they saw us too. They watched us for a long moment that became suspended in time. The trio didn't act skittish, though we did nothing to startle them.

The first deer was slightly larger than the other two. After pawing the sand a time or two, it turned around and reentered the bush. The other two deer followed, and they disappeared as quietly as they'd emerged.

All three of us smiled at each other, remaining silent. I had wanted to see a Key deer since arriving but had never glimpsed one.

Their visit was the perfect cap to a perfect day.

Chapter Twenty-Two

Gabe

I CARRIED a scuba tank on each bare shoulder as I walked along the brick path next to the canal. Balancing carefully, I stepped aboard *Indigo Dreams*, our backup boat kept tied up a short distance from the slips of the two workhorse boats. She was smaller than the others but more than roomy enough for April and me. I slid the two tanks into their plastic holders. The canal was currently empty. *Shark Bait* was on the afternoon dive with Wyatt leading the group, and Dad was leading an all-day fishing charter.

The day after our adventure at Bahia Honda, I'd worked on the dive schedule to give April a couple of afternoons off to give me a dive refresher and go on our private trip. A week later, here we were. I glanced absently at the two tanks, considering their implications.

It had been a very long time since I'd had as much fun as our day at the beach. We'd almost been like a family, though I wasn't quite sure what possessed me to ask April about wanting kids.

Not exactly a question for a casual relationship, is it?

But she'd answered honestly and confirmed our pact, which helped me get my own head screwed back on straight. I felt so damn comfortable around April, it was easy to get lulled into thinking we were something we weren't.

I was a little worried about Hailey getting too attached. As I'd put her to bed that night, she'd wrapped her arms around my neck. "Can we go to the beach again with April? Soon?"

"We had a great day, didn't we?"

She lay down and I pulled the blankets up to her neck. She nodded. "I like April."

"She likes you too, angel. I'm glad you had a terrific day. Sweet dreams." I kissed her forehead and turned off her bedside lamp.

Returning to the living room, I sat on the couch, taking comfort in the fact that April was happy at Calypso Key. I shouldn't need to worry about her moving on and hurting Hailey. Just the idea opened a hollowness in my stomach. I picked up a woodworking magazine, banishing that troubling line of thought.

April convinced me to take my refresher from her. I had misgivings about it. I was rustier than hell and didn't want to admit to being a little nervous too. But she meant what she'd told me on the beach.

She was a confident and encouraging teacher, taking me slowly through the skills and procedures until I refamiliarized myself with them. The experience made me realize how much I'd boxed myself in. It had been years since I'd attempted something I wasn't an expert at, and learning from my girlfriend was definitely a new experience.

One I found I didn't mind at all.

April had a quiet way of instilling confidence and never once gave a hint of superiority. We'd taken over the pool behind the Big House, so I didn't have a resort audience watching me make a fool of myself. And even my nosy family had stayed away. I'd never used scuba in that pool before, so it was a good place to make my new start. Of course, April thought my nerves and hesitation were simply due to the long layoff from diving. Why would she think otherwise?

Maybe it was time to let the old, painful memories go.

If only I could get the guilt to leave as well.

With a sigh, I turned my mind from the subject, not wanting to go down that path when I had an afternoon alone with April to look forward to. Hearing footsteps, I looked up and smiled as she hopped aboard. Dressed in a skin-tight, long-sleeved rash guard and shorts, she looked delectable. She carried a BCD and reg in each hand and set them on the fiberglass deck before sidling up to me.

I inhaled as she ran both hands up my bare torso, a gleam in her eye. "Ready to get wet?"

My smile turned wicked. "You're stealing my line."

With a laugh, she rose onto her toes and touched her lips to mine. "I think we've got everything. Let's get our kits set up."

After several months of driving the dive boat, I was an expert at this and assembled my equipment quickly. April did a final equipment check to make sure we weren't forgetting anything, then turned to me and rubbed her hands together. "All right. We're ready. Any site in particular you want to dive?"

Anything but the goddamn Benson.

But I wouldn't voice that thought out loud. I smiled and

traced my fingers down her cheek. "I've always liked Central Park. How about that?"

"I love that site! Great choice."

April's smile helped dispel the last of the negative thoughts, and I concentrated wholly on the present. And the woman right here in front of me. The past couldn't compete with her.

Central Park was only a ten-minute boat trip from Calypso Key. The site consisted of a long sloping wall that nature had divided into sections—different varieties of coral inhabited distinct areas within the site. As we approached the mooring ball resting on top of the ocean, April used the long hook on the bow to bring a length of attached rope aboard. A metal clip attached to another clip on the end of our line, ensuring the boat would stay firmly attached while we were underwater.

After tugging on our wetsuits, we slid our BCDs on and stood up. I tried to give her a hand with the heavy tank, then grinned when she stood up before I could get to her. After putting on our fins at the stern platform, we pulled our masks down, stuck regulators in our mouths, and jumped into the ocean.

As I floated back up to the surface, butterflies were fluttering steadily in my gut. The seafloor was only twenty feet below, but I was unaccountably flustered.

April turned to me. "Ready?"

I nodded, putting more confidence in the motion than I felt. She held out her fist and gave a thumbs-down, and I deflated my BCD. Immediately, I sank below the surface. I cleared my ears every few feet, trying to remember everything I was supposed to do. April sank next to me. To calm my nerves, I concentrated on her.

She descended like a free-falling parachutist, with her

legs behind her. Completely relaxed, her head moved on a swivel as she took in the site and any animals that might be in the area. Then she turned to me with raised brows and gave me an okay signal.

My heart was beating faster than I was happy with, but I returned her signal and added several blasts of air to my BCD to keep from crashing into the rapidly approaching coral reef. April beckoned me to follow, and I stayed by her hip, letting her choose our course.

Our depth gradually increased. April turned when we hit fifty feet and swam parallel to the slope, holding our depth steady. I was more comfortable now and able to relax as she swam at my side.

That was when I realized I was relaxing *because* she was near. I didn't have to worry about anyone else or be responsible for them. Indeed, I was the one she was watching closely. And that fact gave me confidence—she was an expert, and I only now realized just how good she was underwater. She stopped to show me several lobsters hiding under an overhang. She hung motionless in the water and held my arm so I could use her to steady myself.

Ten minutes later, I spotted half a dozen fish that had always been favorites of mine. I couldn't remember what they were called, though. The yellow, black, and white fish were the size of my hand and vividly colorful. A long, black snout protruded in front of them.

April saw me studying them and unclipped her magnetic dive slate. She wrote on it, then turned it around.

Longnose butterflyfish!

I slapped my head and smiled, then pointed to a different pair of butterfly fish. These were black and white. With white bodies, speckled diagonal lines decorated their sides, and a large round black dot lay near their tails. April wrote for a longer time, and I couldn't help admiring how still she remained in the water. Anytime I stopped moving, I started sinking or rising. She flipped the slate for me to read.

Four-eyed butterfly fish. The large spot at the back looks like an eye and fools predators into chasing the wrong end!

We smiled at each other. April clipped her slate back to her BCD and turned to lead once again. With two powerful kicks, I moved up to her side and took her hand. Turning to me, she made sure I was doing okay before she squeezed back.

I was doing more than okay. A huge school of yellow-tailed snappers appeared as we came around a bend. How could I have forgotten how much I loved this? And all because April had refused to back down when I said I wanted Corbin to teach me. Looking back, my reluctance to let her see me as a fumbling novice seemed stupid.

I'd built some pretty strong walls in the past couple of years.

Good thing April packed a mean sledgehammer.

As soon as we were back on the boat and out of our gear, I swept her into my arms. Kissing her deeply, I smiled at her appreciative hum.

"Thank you," I said, cradling her head against my chest. "I loved that."

"So did I. Diving with you meant a lot to me, Gabe."

"Me too. I feel like I got a monkey off my back today."

"Diving's always awkward after a long layoff. It came back to you really quickly."

I placed a knuckle under her chin and tilted her head up. I whisked my lips over hers, barely touching them. "I'm a lucky man. Not only is my girl incredibly hot, she's also a born teacher. I'm surprised I'm not fighting guys off all the time."

She grinned. "They're probably all scared to death of you. Gabe Markham casts a big shadow."

I tipped my head back and laughed, basking in how good I felt. "If you say so." Then I swatted her gorgeous ass and headed toward the console. "Come on. Let's get back and I'll buy you an after-dive beer."

As I drove back to Calypso Key, April stood at my side. I pulled her in close and kept my arm wrapped around her. The sun was warm but not punishing, and sunlight sparkled on the ocean surface all around. Right now, I couldn't imagine life being any better.

Chapter Twenty-Three

April

THE NEXT MORNING, I ambled past Maia's butterfly bush as I headed toward the dive shop. She had explained the plant was a representation of the bond between her and her mother. Warren had planted it the day his wife died and Maia had been born—with no idea it carried a mutation causing two different colors to bloom. I studied the plant. A new explosion of lavender and dark-purple blossoms had just burst forth, and butterflies danced all over the tall bush. The sight brought a smile to my face, not that I needed any extra cheering up.

The dive yesterday with Gabe had been everything I'd hoped for.

When I entered the dive shop, I made my way down the hall and into the break room. Evan and Maia stood around the employee table, and I greeted them as I placed my backpack in a locker. Santiago padded across the floor and sat at my feet, meowing up at me.

"Well, good morning to you too." I scratched the six-toed cat behind his ears. He slitted his eyes and purred, maneuvering his head so I could scratch under his chin. Standing upright, I moved across the room and joined the siblings.

"I'm surprised to see you here this early," I said to Maia. Our first dive site was the *Benson*, which wasn't suitable for snorkeling, so she wasn't scheduled to take a group until the second trip. We would come back to the resort after diving the wreck to pick up the snorkelers.

Maia swallowed the bite of donut she was eating. "Carissa has an appointment this morning, so I'm covering the shop for a couple of hours."

I dropped my gaze to the Sweet Dreams box on the counter and widened my eyes at the apple fritter still inside. "Yum. Anyone got dibs on that apple fritter?"

"Nope," Evan said. "Take it."

The pastry was still slightly warm, and as I took a bite, the flavors of apple and cinnamon exploded in my mouth. I had no idea what Liv did to make these so good. She was a genius. "What brings you by?" I asked Evan.

"Keeping tabs on my big brother and making sure he's not ruining the place." Evan grinned and took a sip of coffee.

Since turning over the dive shop management to Gabe, I hadn't seen Evan as much. Which was a shame. He was friendly and always had a kind word. But he wasn't the Markham who could make my heart stop just by walking into a room.

"Congratulations," Maia said to me. "Gabe said your dive was a huge success. I've been trying to get him in the water for the last five years. All I ever got for the effort was a surly refusal."

I laughed, delighted I got such a different response. "He did great and said he'd forgotten how much he enjoyed diving."

"I'm glad he did it," Evan said, his face serious. "Thanks. He should have gone back to diving a long time ago."

There was an undercurrent between him and Maia, and I had the feeling I was missing something. "He said life just got in the way and he didn't have time. That happens a lot."

Evan blinked several times, then smiled. "Yeah. He was pretty busy in Miami." He walked to a locker and opened it to take out a leather toolbelt. He buckled it around his trim hips. "The other reason I came down here was to work on the air compressor."

"Oh, thank you!" That was music to my ears. The machine was essential and had started wheezing several days prior when I'd been filling tanks.

"Evan's our resident Mr. Fix-It," Maia added. "He's one of those guys who can repair anything."

"I wouldn't go that far, but it sounds like the compressor needs a tune-up," the general manager said. "I'd better get started before the room is a hundred degrees. See you guys later." He walked out of the room, his right leg slightly hitching. I still didn't know why he had a limp. I got the feeling it was a traumatic story, so I didn't want to pry.

When I turned back, Maia had both hands pressed to the small of her back, stretching.

"How long now?" I asked.

"Six weeks or so. At my ultrasound last week, they said she's really starting to grow, so it might not be that long."

Maia had been terrified when she first learned she was

pregnant. She and Wyatt hadn't been in a relationship long, but life seemed to be going much better for her now.

"Looks like married life agrees with you."

She smiled. "It does. Wyatt's a terrific husband and I know he'll be a great father. His dad ran out on him and his mom, and that made him determined to be the best dad and hubby possible. I'm not complaining!"

We both shared a laugh, but mine faded. "And your pregnancy is going well? No signs of trouble?"

Her smile remained, no traces of unease on her face. "Textbook. My blood pressure has remained normal, and my doctor has assured me over and over that what happened to my mother wasn't something I needed to worry about."

I moved in and gave her a hug. Her large belly pressed against me, and I rubbed my hands in circles over her back. "I'm so glad to hear that, Maia. You're going to be a great mom."

"Thanks, April. Early on, you really helped talk me off some ledges. And you were right—everything is turning out okay. I love how you can always see the positive in situations."

"I try," I said, pulling back and smiling at her. "I feel like living here has brought that back some. I was in such a funk in St. Croix. I needed a shift in attitude, not just location."

Her gaze turned speculative. "You're happy with Gabe?"

"Very. Things are working out well. Both of us are in agreement about our relationship—exclusive but no long-term commitments."

"How do you do that? Keep from wanting more? What if one of you changes your mind?"

I do that by building stone walls around my heart, and

not concentrating on the fact that Gabe is an incredible man and father doing everything he can to save his family legacy. A man any woman would be proud of.

A man any woman would want more from.

More with.

I shrugged one shoulder. "We each have our reasons for not wanting deeper involvement. I respect his thoughts on the subject, and he feels the same way about mine. We're great together, so there's no reason to want more."

"If you say so."

"I do. I just said it, Maia. We're *great* together."

She pulled a face. "First of all—Yuck. This is my brother we're talking about! Which is kind of weird. Normally, I'd want all the details of what was going on between you two. But with Gabe? Gross."

I laughed. "I couldn't feel more differently. Your brother is anything but gross."

"Oh, I'm not blind. It's kind of funny. You two are opposites personality-wise. You've been good for him. He's noticeably less grouchy these days and has even been known to crack a smile now and again."

"Your brother is a good man, Maia."

"Yeah, I know. He's a pain in the ass, but I love him anyway. Kind of like the other two. Just spare me the details, okay? All my brothers are hotties, but that doesn't mean I want to know about their sex lives."

"I'm sure they feel the same way."

Maia laughed out loud. "To an extent. When Gabe first came back, he loomed all over Wyatt about me getting pregnant. But Wyatt and I had worked out our problems and were happily married by then. Wyatt stood up to him and basically told Gabe to piss off. I'm pretty sure that actually impressed my brother."

"I could see that. Gabe can certainly be intimidating, but I've never been afraid of him. He's outright told me he likes it when I stand up to him."

Maia wrinkled her nose. "I don't want to hear how much he likes it, okay?"

"Deal." I laughed and finished my donut. "Speaking of Wyatt, I'd better get to work. I'm sure he's wondering where I am."

<hr>

Gabe

My hair was still damp from my shower as I strolled down the hill toward the dive shop. I'd gotten up early to get in a thorough weight session in the gym at the Big House. Dad had installed a state-of-the-art gym years ago when Evan needed his rehab, and he'd continued to use it. Now I was a regular visitor too. After driving Hailey to her summer camp, I'd gone for a run on the path that circled the perimeter of the island. The sandy trail wound its way through the mangrove wetlands, and we hadn't had rain lately, so it was completely dry.

I bent around the end of the canal. *Indigo Dreams* sat where we'd tied it up yesterday, but the other two boats had already left for the morning. April was probably in the water right now.

When I walked into the dive shop, Carissa stood behind the counter.

"I thought Maia was filling in for you?" I asked.

"She did. She's in the break room, I think."

I strolled down the hallway and entered the employee lounge. Maia stood by a round table, picking through a pink donut box. I smiled. "Okay, I guess you're allowed to eat all the donuts you want."

She startled, then lifted her eyes and grinned. "Well, I'm glad I have your permission. The worry has been keeping me awake at night."

I joined her and glanced in the box, but frowned to see the apple fritters were all taken. Before I could even think about it, my fingers moved to pick up a maple bar. I took a bite and mumbled, "Why are these Sweet Dreams pastries always in here?"

"Don't talk with your mouth full, you caveman." Then she shrugged. "I guess Evan likes them too. He brings them in a lot."

Just then, he walked in, cleaning his hands with a rag.

I nodded a hello. "You working on the air compressor?" Evan's magical ability to fix anything made him worth his weight in gold.

"Yeah. Just needed a tune-up. She's running fine now." He crossed the room and picked up a Boston cream.

"What's with the pastries every morning?" I asked.

He scowled, his bushy beard moving lower. "It's not every morning. Besides, people like it when you do nice things for them, Gabe. You should try it sometime."

I rolled my eyes. "Yeah. Sure. We're not paying good money to give shit away, you know."

Maia held her donut up. "I'm not complaining. These are better than ours."

I still didn't get it. "So what? Evan, why would you get up at the crack of dawn and make the trek to Dove Key just to get donuts? We have plenty at Dorado. Every damn morning."

Evan dropped his eyes and turned scarlet.

His reaction surprised me so much I took a step back.

Maia met my eyes and sucked her bottom lip into her mouth, trying not to smile. "Maybe it's not the donuts he's interested in," she drawled.

"Oh, shut up, you two," Evan muttered, still blushing. "No good deed goes unpunished. I pay for these out of my own pocket—I never expense them off. I need to get back to my office." Spinning on his heel, he stalked out of the room.

Maia and I turned back to each other and grinned. She burst into laughter, trying to keep the volume down.

"I didn't expect that," I said.

Maia shot me an appraising look. "I seem to recall someone's girlfriend knows the owner of Sweet Dreams rather well. Maybe we should introduce the baker to our dear brother?"

I'd already lost interest. "You talk to April. I have zero desire to play matchmaker." My gaze dropped to her round belly, stretching the staff T-shirt she wore. "Do you have a few minutes? I came down here to show you something."

A short time later, I slid the twin doors of the Barn open several feet, ushering Maia into the shop before me. I flipped on the bank of overhead lights, and we moved to my workshop area.

"You're being very mysterious," she said, peering at projects I had in various stages of development.

"Not for much longer." I slid between two headboards I was working on and stopped next to an object draped under a sheet.

Maia stopped in front of it, eyeing the mystery speculatively "Hmmm. About four feet tall and rectangular. I know! A fish tank?"

I scowled. "A fish tank? That's the best you could come up with?"

"Sorry, I suck at guessing games. Is it something for April?"

I barked a laugh. "Most definitely not. Here." I grabbed the sheet in the middle and yanked it off.

Maia's hands flew to her mouth as the crib was revealed. I ran my fingers over the top rail, enjoying the smooth warmth of the wood.

"Oh, Gabe! This is stunning."

"Thanks. I made it out of teak I sourced in Big Pine Key."

The crib had been my main project for the past month, and April was the only other person who knew about it. Working on it had allowed my mind to wander and develop solutions for the resort's financial issues. I was close to my solution—I just needed a little more time before bringing it up with Dad.

Maia hunkered down, balancing carefully as she lovingly ran her fingers down the vertical rails of the crib. "I can't believe you did this. Didn't you make something similar when Hailey was born?"

I smiled, though the memory was bittersweet. "Yeah. But when she outgrew it and it became clear Kora wasn't interested in any more kids, I gave it away."

Maia stood up and grasped my arm, resting her head on my shoulder. "I won't do that. This will be a family heirloom. I promise."

I planted a kiss on the top of her head. "It's yours, so do whatever you want with it. No strings." I ran my fingers over the top rail, enjoying the smooth warmth of the wood.

I wrapped her in a hug as she slipped an arm around my waist and melted against my side. As the summer had progressed, so had her girth.

"I'm so glad you're home."

"So am I." I smiled at the realization I wasn't just humoring her. It was true.

"I know you've been shielding me from the financial changes you've been making. But the resort's doing okay?"

"It is. I'm still working things out, and hopefully, I'll have some ideas for remodeling soon. Now that the initial stress is past, I'm enjoying the challenge."

She laughed softly. "That's not the only thing you're enjoying. I'm happy April is here to keep you out of jail. You can call her next time to bail you out."

I grinned as we pulled apart. "Trust me. There won't be a next time. No matter how many Coleridges cross my path."

"I'm very glad to hear that." She returned to inspecting the crib. "I can't wait to show this to Wyatt! He'll love it."

"He and I can move it into your cottage tonight if you want."

She nodded rapidly. "I want."

I smiled and stepped forward to place my hands on her shoulders. "Get ready for your whole life to change, little sister. In the best way possible."

"I'm a little scared. Not the birth so much anymore—I've done everything possible to prevent any complications. But the responsibility of raising a kid and not screwing it up."

"You don't need to worry about that. You'll do a great job. I admit I was suspicious of Wyatt to start, but he's a good man. You two will be fine."

She patted my chest. "At least I don't have to do this alone. You've done such an amazing job with Hailey."

"Thanks. It hasn't been easy."

She pulled away and stroked the crib again, then looked at me from under her lashes. "You're happy with April?"

"I am. She's helped me to remember that life can be fun and not just responsibilities."

"I'm glad to hear you say that. As long as you two are happy, I'm happy."

I cocked my head. "What do you mean by that?"

She walked around the crib, trailing her hand along the top rail as she circled. "I don't know. It's just that Wyatt and I are so... fulfilled, after working out all our shit. I just want the same for you and April."

I raised a brow. "Not everyone wants the same thing, Maia."

"I understand that. And I understand why you didn't want to fall in love after your divorce. But maybe being with April might help you see things differently?"

"No. We're both happy the way things are right now." And I didn't want to let a woman have that kind of power over me again. April wasn't going anywhere, and neither was I. "There's absolutely no reason to rock the boat."

Maia stopped and stared at me. "But that's the problem. Sometimes the boat gets rocked without you having anything to do with it. What then?"

I smiled. "My little sister, the relationship expert. I don't see any reason things should change between me and April. And I don't believe in going looking for trouble. Things are great right now, and I'm not about to risk that."

After tossing the sheet over the crib again, I draped an arm across Maia's shoulder and steered her toward the double doors. "Let's get back to work, mama. You need to get ready for the snorkel trip when they get back from the *Benson.*"

I twitched the side of my mouth, still finding it hard to believe my baby sister was about to become a mother. But I was very pleased she was more at ease about the prospect. I knew from experience those early weeks could be very overwhelming. But at least Maia and Wyatt would have all the help they could want.

Probably more than they want.

My faint smile became a full grin as we emerged into the sunshine. We headed down the hill, ready to face the rest of the day.

Chapter Twenty-Four

April

I FOLDED FORWARD and relaxed onto Gabe's chest, both of us breathing heavily. We were in his bed and Hailey was sound asleep in her room. His room was darker than mine, though by now I could recognize every inch of his body by touch alone.

Still, I didn't mind looking at him either.

I traced my fingers down his pec, smoothing the hair and enjoying the feel of his sweaty skin. Encircling his arms around me, Gabe held me tight. I closed my eyes. Under my ear, his heart slowed to its usual steady thud, and my body relaxed against him.

Then I blinked my eyes open. I needed to stay awake, as tempting as it was to fall asleep like this.

That was part of the pact. No overnights while Hailey was in the cottage.

Nearly two weeks had passed since I'd talked to Maia about her impending motherhood. Tonight, I'd had dinner at the Big House. I'd been nervous about it, but instead of a formal affair with a disapproving family, we'd eaten at the kitchen table where I'd had lunch previously. Everyone was at ease and joking, and I felt right at home.

"Thanks for inviting me to dinner," I murmured.

"I should have done it sooner. I swear time slips—you plan to do something, then look up and a month has passed. Nona let me know in no uncertain terms I was slacking."

I laughed quietly. "Your grandmother is a hoot."

He smiled. "She's not boring, that's for sure. And she's as much a mother to us as a grandmother."

"I've noticed she always calls you by your full name, never Gabe."

"Yeah, unless she's mad. Then it's my first and middle ones."

"Gabriel Michael," I said, remembering her words when Gabe had invaded the kitchen sweaty after his run. "You have the archangels covered, don't you?"

He smiled. "Guess my parents thought I might have need of some serious protection."

"Or they were covering their bases."

He tickled my side, making me squirm as I laughed. Then I sighed. "I'd better get going. I'm leading the advanced group on the *Benson* tomorrow. I'm excited, but I want to get a good night's sleep."

Gabe squeezed his arms tighter around me, making it hard for me to breathe. When he let go, I patted his chest as I sat up. I redressed as he got out of the opposite side and pulled on a pair of shorts. We stepped out his front door and he cupped my face in his hands, tilting my chin up. A soft warmth spread through me as he pressed a feathery kiss against my lips.

"I'll see you tomorrow," he whispered.

I nodded. "Good night."

A blanket of stars covered the sky as I strolled down the hill, and the warm air caressed my skin. An expanse of meadow separated the cottages from the Barn, but it wasn't a long walk. As I turned onto the short path leading to my apartment, I glanced back.

Gabe hadn't moved, watching as I walked home.

I raised my arm and waved. He returned the gesture but still didn't move. He wouldn't until I was through my front door. We went through this every time. He didn't like to leave Hailey alone in the cottage, but he made sure I made it back to my apartment safely.

A smile raised my lips as I opened the front door. "Gabriel Markham, you might like to hide behind that growly exterior, but I'm on to you now."

And if a part of me wanted to stay wrapped in his arms all night long and feel him snuggle back every time I changed positions? That was why we had the pact. To keep me from falling.

Because Gabe was exactly the type of man I could fall for.

My group was five advanced divers plus Rick, their own divemaster, all diving their way down the Keys on what was known as the Wreck Trek. Shipwrecks were strewn throughout the area from Key Largo down to Key West. Some had been intentionally sunk to become artificial reefs, and others were the result of natural or man-made disasters.

We descended to 110 feet, and I led the divers single file into a covered deck running along the side, like a promenade deck on a cruise ship. At this depth, the ambient light was dim, and the colors of the spectrum had faded except for blues. I turned right and entered a large chamber, turning on my dive light for extra illumination.

With a group of advanced divers, I was comfortable leading them through the ship. The route I used was safe for recreational divers—easy outlets from the structure were never far away.

As long as they followed me, anyway.

Which everyone in the group should know to do, including their divemaster who was unfamiliar with the *Benson*. I'd given everyone thorough instructions to keep the diver ahead in sight at all times. My dive plan was far removed from a full wreck dive and needed no guidelines or extra tanks.

A staircase lay at the end of the hall, and I finned the fifteen feet up it, emerging onto an open deck. A smile rose on my face as I encountered Clarence, an enormous goliath grouper who called the wreck home. I moved away to keep from startling him and enjoyed the divers' reactions when they ascended the staircase and saw him.

Clarence was mottled gray in color and nearly seven feet long. The divers fanned out so everyone could see him and take any photos or video they wanted. I glanced at the dive computer on my wrist, ever mindful of the time. Divers used substantially more air at this depth.

After a quick air check to confirm no one was sucking through their tank, I proceeded with my dive plan. We left Clarence behind and swam through the ship from the port side to the starboard. I loved this section. I descended through a large hole cut in the floor and finned through a chamber. Gears, pipes, and other nautical mysteries surrounded us and beams bounced all over the room from the divers behind me. I exited into a hallway and proceeded a short distance before turning into another room.

This was an old cabin, and a bedframe was still welded to the steel hull. A metal desk sat across from it. I continued through another hole cut into the wall and entered yet another hallway. After ten feet, I proceeded into an expansive chamber, swimming across it to the exit cut in the side of the ship's hull.

Back in the open ocean, I hovered nearby, counting silently as my divers exited the *Benson* in single file. Rick, their divemaster, was third in line and we exchanged nods. He gave me an enthusiastic okay signal, making me smile. Then he was out, and I waited for the final two divers. After several seconds, number five exited, her eyes enormous behind her mask and her smile obvious around her regulator.

I applauded her and she swam off to join the others.

Turning back to the exit hole, I waited for Ted, the final diver.

And waited.

I counted to ten in my head, and when he still hadn't appeared, I marked the time on my dive computer. I signaled the group to wait.

After thirty seconds, he still hadn't appeared.

Shit. Where is this guy?

My heartbeat accelerating rapidly, I beckoned to Rick. He swam over as I wrote on my dive slate:

I'm going back in to find Ted. Take the group to the surface and do a safety stop.

Rick nodded and gave me the okay signal. I exhaled a line of bubbles, relieved I had a qualified divemaster to hand the rest of the group off to.

At a hundred feet, Ted would be using air rapidly, especially if he was lost and beginning to panic. I swam back into the steel hull and retraced my path. I kept my light off so I could see the lost diver's beam easier.

I reached the area where we had traversed the hull of the ship with no sign of Ted. A sense of dread crept over me as I stared at Clarence. This was the last place I had seen the diver.

He'd taken a wrong turn somewhere.

Turning around, I retraced my path yet again, peering into every room and chamber I could. I kept my breathing regular to conserve my own air supply. This time I turned on my light, so I'd be more visible to Ted. I shined it into every chamber, and all were empty.

I almost missed it.

Just as I was ducking out of a room, I saw a flash of light in the distance. Surging forward, I entered an empty chamber, but I could see a light frantically bouncing around outside an open door. My training and experience kicked in. As I finned across the chamber, I made mental notes of where I was and how to get out.

I emerged out of the doorway into another long hallway I had never explored. Ted was at the far end, frantic bursts of exhaled bubbles illuminated in his light as he slashed it around the narrow area.

Unclipping my metal pointer, I banged my tank loudly with it. Ted spun at the noise and motored toward me. I stopped immediately and tipped upward, placing my fins slightly in front of me. If he lunged for me in panic, I needed to be ready to move backward or kick him off me if necessary. The first rule of rescue was making sure the person being saved didn't kill the rescuer in the process.

Ted's eyes were huge round discs behind his mask. He breathed rapidly but not explosively, and his shoulders relaxed at seeing me. I held out both hands in an *easy, easy* gesture, and he slowed as he approached.

I formed two okay signals with my thumbs and forefingers, and Ted slowed further, placing a hand against the metal wall to stop himself.

I breathed a long sigh, deeply relieved he was calming down and not spiraling into panic. I took hold of his hand to provide contact and gave him an okay sign again. This time he nodded back.

Letting go, I tapped my palm with two fingers of my other hand, the signal for an air check.

He fumbled with his computer, and his throat worked in a swallow when he read the result. He raised his eyes to me and held up the five fingers of his right hand.

Shit! Five hundred psi?

But I schooled my face, giving nothing away, and nodded gently, beckoning him to come with me. The submerged hall was wide enough for us to swim side by side. I kept a reassuring grip on his hand the whole way and easily remembered my route. As soon as we emerged from the large cut in the side of the ship into open ocean, I unclipped my slate.

You're doing just fine, okay? But I'm going to share my air with you on the way up. Just to be safe.

Ted jerked a shaky nod, his brown hair floating in the water around his head. I removed my octopus backup regulator from my side and held the bright yellow mouthpiece out to him. Replacing a regulator underwater was a basic open-water skill, but I still crossed my fingers as Ted transitioned from his regulator to my spare.

Practicing the skill in a pool was one thing. Doing it for real at one hundred feet after becoming lost inside a shipwreck was something else altogether.

But Ted made the transfer flawlessly, remembering to purge the water out of the mouthpiece before inhaling.

I looped my arm around his and gave him a thumbs-up, followed by another slow, easy signal. We weren't in an emergency here, and I didn't want him to get any more nervous. As both a professional diver and a woman with smaller lungs, I had great air consumption. So I had plenty of air for both of us.

Unless we needed to stop on the way up.

My stomach clenched as I surreptitiously glanced at my dive computer. The flashing display confirmed what I had already suspected.

I was in deco.

Frequent diving causes nitrogen to accumulate in the body. And few people dove more often than divemasters. If I didn't follow my computer's instructions and stop for several minutes on the way up to exhale the excess nitrogen, I was in serious danger of developing decompression sickness—the bends.

Since Ted had been on many deep dives over the past few days, he was at risk too. I studied my computer, discovering I needed to make a three-minute stop at eighty feet.

I pulled out my slate and wrote. There was no way I could communicate this via hand signals. When I explained the situation, Ted's eyes got huge again. He whipped his computer up and examined it.

His breathing increased, bubbles flying out.

Dammit, Ted! Calm down, or you'll run us both out of air.

I gently but firmly grasped his shoulder, providing a comforting touch to ground him. But he hardly noticed as he turned the computer around to show me the display.

He was in deco too.

Chapter Twenty-Five

Gabe

I SAT in the padded chair behind the console, alone on the boat as *Shark Bait* gently bobbed in the waves. I crossed my arms, still pissed off I was here. As much as I loved being out on the water—not to mention my reintroduction to diving—I did not want to be anywhere near this goddamn wreck.

Too many bad memories.

I carefully arranged my schedule with Miguel, so he always captained on *Benson* day. Until he called me this morning at 6:00 a.m., saying he was puking nonstop.

I glared at the placid ocean surface. "It's just a dive site, like any other. April and Wyatt are both pros. Nothing will go wrong."

For the umpteenth time since the divers descended, I got up and moved to the side of the boat, shading my eyes with my hand. A few minutes ago, two distinct groups of bubbles had been visible.

Now only one group was.

I rolled my head around on my neck, reminding myself that this was expected. Wyatt had the less experienced group who were staying outside the wreck. Of course April's group's bubbles would disappear as they entered the ship.

I exhaled sharply, more a growl than a sigh. April was a professional.

And she's not doing anything advanced divers aren't fully capable of. She'll be fine.

Shark Bait was moored to one of several buoys attached to the wreck, this one midway down the three-hundred-foot ship. I watched the bubbles as Wyatt's group moved along the hull, traveling at a measured, slow pace. I tried to concentrate on the tropical morning. The sun was out, soft, fluffy clouds bounded across the sky, and a soft breeze caressed my face. The morning was perfect, but I couldn't appreciate it.

When I crossed to the starboard side and searched the surface, this time I saw a second group of bubbles. We were the only boat diving the wreck this morning, so I relaxed at last. Several minutes passed before the first divers popped to the surface, but they were still earlier than usual. Though with a deep dive, that wasn't unusual—air didn't last as long at depth.

I did a quick head count. Five divers. The group was seven total.

I worried my bottom lip between my teeth as I searched for April's blond head and didn't see it. She often stayed down with divers who had better air consumption and sent the heavy breathers up first. So I wasn't too worried. Yet.

The group's divemaster, Rick, swam to the stern platform and I moved to meet him.

"We might have a problem," he called.

Those were the last words I wanted to hear right now, and my stomach clenched tight. "What kind of problem?"

"Ted didn't come out of the wreck. April went in after him and had me bring the rest of the group to the surface."

"Shit!"

I ran to one of the side benches and grabbed a lead scuba weight before returning and kneeling on the platform. Rick was gesturing for the other divers to get back on the boat.

"Can you get everybody on board?" I hollered to him. "I'm going to recall the other group."

Rick nodded as I leaned over the side with the weight in my right hand. Ducking it beneath the surface, I rhythmically pounded it against the boat's hull. Sound traveled much farther through water than air, and I had no doubt Wyatt would hear the recall message.

I kept up a steady rhythm and Rick was the last to board. Standing on the platform, he frowned at the surface. "I'm worried. I was thinking about jumping back in to check on them."

Still pounding, I made eye contact with him and shook my head. "I'll send Wyatt down when he gets here."

Rick eyed me, then nodded before stepping fully onto the boat. He might be a dive professional, but he was a guest here. And he knew that. I didn't want anyone but Calypso Key people in the water if we had to perform a rescue.

A rescue of April.

Hot bile rose from my stomach at the thought, and I swallowed hard.

A few minutes later, Wyatt's group's bubbles returned. One diver separated from the rest and headed toward me, and I stopped banging.

A moment later, Wyatt popped up. "What's up? I left my group doing their safety stop."

"April had to go after someone inside the wreck. Can you go down and see if you can find them?"

Wyatt licked his lips and nodded. "Sure. I'll send my group up on the way down."

He disappeared, and soon I was busy getting his group back on board. Several divers clustered toward the stern, asking what was going on. I had to resist the urge to rip their heads off.

Instead, I took a long breath. "We've got one diver unaccounted for. We're just initiating our standard procedures—there's no emergency." *God, I hope not.* "Help yourself to some soft drinks and snacks."

And get the hell out of my hair, I thought as I spun back around.

Definitely not the way to think about guests who kept the resort in business, but I was beyond caring. I resisted the urge to pace, sweat breaking out on my palms.

Seeing something in the gentle waves, I lifted my sunglasses. But that made the glare worse, so I replaced them. Bubbles were headed back to the boat, but my heart sank. I couldn't tell exactly how many were in a group by the amount of bubbles, but I could tell the difference between a lone diver and a group of three. Someone was coming back.

Alone.

Soon Wyatt popped up. "I descended to fifty feet, but I couldn't go any lower without violating my computer and going into deco."

"Did you see them?" I shouted, wanting to jump in the water myself.

"Yeah. They are both out of the wreck and at around eighty feet."

A cheer went up from the divers and they dispersed, now apparently taking my advice to get something to eat and drink.

Wyatt swam over to me and lowered his voice. "I'm pretty sure they were doing a deco stop. I can't be sure, but I think I saw them sharing air. I'm going to stay in the water and watch. If they need help coming up, I'll be ready."

Our eyes held for a long moment, then I nodded. "Thanks, Wyatt."

The next ten minutes took hours to pass. Giving in to my anxiety, I paced back and forth on the platform as acid tried to eat through my stomach. No one on board bothered me.

Wyatt called out the divers' progress as they ascended, mentioning they stopped again at fifty feet, then at fifteen. He put his face back in the water but stayed on the surface. That calmed me. If there was an emergency, he would immediately submerge to help.

Finally, he lifted his head. "They're coming up now!"

Another cheer went up and the divers returned to stand around me. I couldn't really tell them to piss off—Ted was their friend. They had every right to be there. But I didn't have to be happy about it.

My pulse roared in my ears, and adrenaline surged through my body. Two heads surfaced and tension drained from my stiff shoulders when I saw April's face break the surface. Our eyes met immediately, and I couldn't look away as she made a fist and tapped the top of her head twice.

The signal for okay.

She and Ted embraced, and she linked arms with him,

helping him swim back to the boat as Wyatt shadowed his other side.

I turned around to search for Rick and found him right behind me. "Can you help Ted? I need to make sure April's okay."

"Absolutely." He turned to the other divers, both his group and Wyatt's. "All right, guys! Stand back and let these folks have some room to come back on board." He stood at the head of the ladder as Ted handed his fins up. "Felt like some extra exploring?"

Ted shook his head, his face pale. "I turned to look at a gear assembly and guess I lost track of time. When I finished, everyone was gone. I got completely lost. If April hadn't come back, I don't think I could have made it out of there."

"You're okay, man," Rick said softly. "That's what counts. Welcome aboard."

I clapped Ted on the back as he passed by, even though I felt like punching him.

You got lost, asshole? You almost got her killed.

Turning back, I bent down and hardly noticed when Wyatt moved past me. I searched April's face as she removed her fins and climbed the ladder, but there was no sign of injury. She didn't even look scared or tired.

Instead, she beamed at me. "Hello again!"

I wanted to crush her to me, wrap her in my arms, and convince myself she was okay. But I just stood there, my feet planted to the deck. My throat was parched, and I had to clear my throat. "Are you all right?"

She waved a hand casually at me. "Fine. It didn't take me long to find him, then we had to do a couple of deep stops on the way up. Normal day at the office." She laughed and patted my chest as she walked by.

My lungs hardly seemed to work, like I couldn't take in enough oxygen. I just stared at her as she slid down onto the bench and unhooked her BCD. Ted sat by her, and her mouth widened in her trademark sunny smile.

I almost jumped when Wyatt placed a hand on my shoulder. "Everything came out fine," he said quietly but firmly. Reassuring me. "Every*one* came out fine. Including April, okay?"

I jerked a nod, then wrenched my eyes away from April to stare at Wyatt. "Can you get on the radio and call this into the dive shop? We need to cancel the second dive. Neither April nor Ted can dive again today."

With a reassuring smile, my brother-in-law nodded. "Sure thing."

With my head spinning, I hurried to the console and started the engine. My hands were clenched tight as I spun the wheel and headed toward home.

Chapter Twenty-Six

April

SHORTLY AFTER WE started the trip back to Calypso Key, Wyatt pulled me aside. "You all right? Any signs of DCS?"

I'd been running over the symptoms of decompression sickness, so I was confident when I shook my head. "I'm fine. Ted's computer cleared after the first decompression stop. The second one was for my benefit. We should both be safe."

Behind the console, Gabe's shoulders became rigid. They stayed like that the entire way back.

Is he mad at me?

I spent most of the trip next to Ted, pleased his blue eyes were sharp and focused. I smiled at him. "Still feeling okay? No tingling or pain in your joints?"

He shook his head and smiled sheepishly. "My ego is the only thing bothering me. What I did was really stupid. I'm sorry."

And I'll bet you never do it again.

"Everything turned out all right, and that's what matters."

Gabe throttled down and idled into the canal. Several people stood on the brick path by the dive shop, including Warren and Evan. I was pleased to see such a serious response, though I thought it was a bit over the top. Ted and I needed to stay out of the water for the rest of the day to ensure the nitrogen was cleared from our bodies, but neither of us needed medical attention.

Guess it never hurts to be too careful.

I stood as Gabe slid the boat sideways toward the edge of the canal, his face tight and drawn. I nodded to Ted. "You should be fine, but if you feel anything unusual today or tonight—numbness, pain, difficulty breathing—contact the front desk immediately. DCS symptoms can be delayed sometimes."

"I will. That was my first decompression dive. Can't say I'm eager to do another."

I laughed, trying to put him at ease. "It's better all-around when they're planned in advance."

Warren and Evan came aboard as the other divers filed off, and we explained everything again to them, reassuring them we were both fine. Gabe moved stiffly and quietly around the boat, cleaning up but not meeting my gaze.

Ted clapped me on the shoulder as he faced Warren and Evan. "You have a real top-notch divemaster in April. I'm pretty sure she just saved my life." Then he turned to me. "Thanks again, and I'm sorry I screwed up."

"Stop apologizing! You're welcome. Enjoy a nice, lazy afternoon. And no booze!" I added with a smile. With an answering wave, Ted joined Rick and the rest of his group as they headed back to their cottages.

"Good work, April," Warren said. "That could have been a disaster."

"Once I found him, everything was fine."

"You need a lazy, relaxing afternoon too, okay?" Evan asked, tapping the fingers of his right hand against his hip rhythmically.

"No problem there. I just got the new book for my book club. I'll sit on my patio and read this afternoon."

After the two men stepped off the boat and headed back toward the resort, Wyatt approached me. "Go ahead and take off. I'll take care of the gear. You were great out there, April."

"Thanks." I peered behind him. Gabe stood coiling a regulator, his shoulders still rigid. "Gabe, I'm heading into the dive shop."

He nodded, pressing his lips tightly together, but didn't turn around. He hadn't said much since I came on board after the dive. Then again, he wasn't exactly Mr. Happy Go Lucky on the best of days.

Stepping off the boat, I ambled down the brick path. I was proud of myself. Certainly not a novice to emergencies or rescues, I was very pleased with the boat's and my response. And the outcome. I entered the dive shop and stopped, taking a deep breath of cold air.

I heard the door open behind me and Gabe marched right by.

He called out over his shoulder. "April, I need to see you in my office."

Carissa stared at me blankly as I passed by the check-in counter. Gabe was already entering his office as I walked down the hall. I had just cleared the doorway when he whirled around in front of me. Reaching behind me, he slammed the door shut. Then he marched me backward until my back bumped into the door.

Hard.

An involuntary squeak issued from my lungs. Gabe grabbed my face with both hands. He kissed me savagely, raking his mouth over mine.

I could hardly breathe as he pushed me against the door. He pressed his entire body against me, deepening the kiss as he plunged his tongue into my mouth. I was so shocked by his ferocity I hardly knew how to react. I ran my hands over his tight shoulders before sliding them down to grip his biceps.

Finally, he broke the kiss and leaned his forehead against mine. His entire torso, from his stomach, to his shoulders, to the arms I gripped, heaved with the force of his breathing. "Are you sure you're okay?"

My alarm morphed into a soft warmth I hardly dared name. He was worried about me!

I spoke softly, "I'm one hundred percent fine, Gabe. There was no emergency. I knew exactly what to do and followed procedures to the letter."

With a deep, growling sound, Gabe pushed away from me. He paced back and forth in front of his desk. "That goddamn shipwreck. I'm taking it off our schedule. It's too dangerous."

My jaw dropped. "You can't do that! The *Benson* is one of the best things about this area! It's an integral part of the Wreck Trek. Gabe, it's not that dangerous of a wreck. Conditions at the ships near Key Largo are far more unpredictable."

He shot me a glare but continued pacing. "Let those dive shops take the risks, then. That guy could have died today! And you could have died going after him."

I wanted to hold him—calm him down. But I was afraid to interrupt his agitated pacing. My confusion grew by the second. "But we didn't! We're both fine. I don't understand why you're so upset."

"Of course you don't!" Then he halted in the middle of the room and pushed his palms against his eyes. "How could you?"

"You're not making any sense."

He didn't reply, his frown growing deeper.

My stomach did summersaults. "Gabe, please talk to me."

And like a balloon, he deflated. His arms fell from his eyes to rest at his sides. A couch was pushed against one wall, and he flopped onto it with a giant sigh. "Come sit down."

I lowered myself gingerly, putting some distance between us.

He rested with his eyes closed, his head leaning back against the wall. "Have you noticed that Evan has a limp?"

I blinked. I didn't know what I expected to come out of his mouth, but that wasn't it. "Yes..."

Opening his eyes, Gabe rolled his head and looked at me. His eyes held sadness and grief. "That injury is due to the *Benson*. All of us kids got dive certified as teenagers. We all loved diving, but Evan and Hunter were practically obsessed. They were best friends growing up—Evan's less than a year older."

He took my hand, holding it gently. His agitation was gone, now replaced by a despondency that was much worse. I held back tightly.

"Early one summer when Evan was nineteen, he and Hunter went to dive the *Benson*. They'd been talking about diving that deep room at the stern to look for treasure, but I told them absolutely not. I had just graduated from college and was at home until I started my job in Miami. The three of us made plans to dive the *Benson* together, but I had just started seeing Kora. She lived in Miami but wanted to meet me in Key Largo for the day."

He stared at me, his handsome face bleak. "My two little brothers were no match for my new girlfriend. I ditched them to spend the day with her, but not after giving them strict instructions to go no lower than a hundred feet."

A deep roiling disturbed my stomach. I had a feeling I knew where this was going. I squeezed his hand. "What happened?"

"Hunter loved that ship. He'd been over every square inch of it above 120 feet, but always with someone more experienced. They took *Indigo Dreams* out there and he talked Evan into diving the stern. They entered that room, which of course had no gold. Then a hallway beckoned, so Hunter continued with Evan following. They got lost, and Evan panicked. Hunter tried to help him—but they were 150 feet down, and their air was going fast. Finally, Hunter saw blue through one of the doorways and was able to lead Evan out. Their tanks were nearly empty by then."

My skin crawled, invisible creatures prickling up and down my arms. What I'd just experienced had been a few minutes of worry. Gabe was describing every diver's worst nightmare.

He dropped his head against the wall again, staring blankly at the far wall. "As soon as Evan was back in open water again, he bolted for the surface."

I winced, picturing the damage that could be done from all that nitrogen coming out of solution and damaging his tissues. "He got bent?"

Gabe nodded slowly. "Hunter tried to hold on to him

but couldn't. Evan was punching and kicking him. But Hunter refused to let Evan go up alone, so he followed. Both of them went straight for the surface. From 150 feet. After they climbed back on board, Evan was furious with him. Then his legs started tingling. Hunter started the engine and drove back at full speed. He radioed in what happened and that Evan was having symptoms."

Gabe exhaled a long, deep breath. "By the time they reached the canal, Evan couldn't move his legs and was throwing up."

"Oh my God," I whispered. I pressed my shaking hands into my thighs, trying to steady them.

"An ambulance was waiting and took him straight to Tavernier where the recompression chamber is. Evan needed treatments over several days, each lasting for *hours*, to prevent any further damage. When he was discharged, he was paralyzed from the waist down. He was nineteen! He had his whole life ahead of him, and everything changed because of one goddamn dive. He needed two years of physical therapy and a solid workout schedule at the Big House to walk again. Now he's barely got a limp, but it was a long, brutal road to get there."

I brought Gabe's cool hand onto my lap and wrapped it between both of my own. "And what about Hunter?"

He shook his head. "He was perfectly fine. Absolutely no effects, even though he rose nearly as fast as Evan. He actually ran out of air on the way up."

"Decompression sickness is unpredictable. Sometimes it strikes people doing very safe dives, then it spares others like Hunter. I'm so sorry, Gabe. I can understand why you don't want to be near that wreck."

"The whole thing was my fault, and I almost let another disaster happen again today."

I wrinkled my brow. "What do you mean? You weren't even there when Evan and Hunter dove. How could it be your fault?"

He stared at me, his face growing grim. "Because I abandoned them to be with my girlfriend! If I'd been there that day, the accident would have never happened. I would have never let them do that dive, no matter how much they wanted to. They weren't qualified—none of us were."

"That doesn't make it your fault. They made that dive out of their own free will. Yes, it was stupid, and Evan paid a terrible price. Have you been blaming yourself all these years?"

Gabe let go of my hand to rake it through his short hair. "Not really blame, but how much might be different right now if I'd told Kora to get lost and gone diving with my brothers?"

I closed the distance between us and placed my hand on his thigh. "For one thing, you might not have Hailey."

My heart warmed when a smile rose on his lips. "That's what I tell myself. It helps."

"And the accident is why Evan and Hunter don't speak?"

His smile plummeted off his face. "Yeah. Evan's an easygoing, kind guy. But he can't forgive Hunter for that dive. When Evan got out of the hospital and came home, he said some pretty awful things. Hunter was eighteen and had just graduated high school. He immediately joined the Marines. He spent ten years in the Corps, trying to make up for his mistake by helping others. Dad thought it was a good idea to put some distance between them, but he never envisioned them being permanently estranged and our family being split apart."

My body was numb, but it had nothing to do with the dive. "What an awful story. I'm so sorry. For all of you."

Gabe twitched another smile, then drew me against him. "Thanks. Hunter lives in Miami now. I've kept in touch with him, and so have Maia and Stella especially, but he doesn't come home. Ever."

"You said he works as a security guard or something?"

He barked a single, humorless laugh. "Or something. He was in Special Forces in the Marines. I don't know what the hell he did. Or what he's doing now. Not sure I want to."

That sounded ominous, but Gabe had also said his brother joined the military to help people. That didn't sound like someone who would become an assassin or something. "Thank you for telling me. When I first got here, Maia mentioned that Evan and Hunter weren't on speaking terms, but she didn't want to talk about it. Now I understand why you were so tense on the boat. I thought maybe you were mad at me for what happened."

He tightened his arms around me and rested his cheek against my head. "Never. I just felt like the whole thing was happening all over again."

"I understand now. I'm not injured—really. I've done decompression dives before, and I knew how to handle every part of that dive, Gabe."

He kissed my temple. "And that's the difference between you and my brothers. I hate that you went through that, but I'm really proud of you at the same time."

I sat up and kissed him softly, glad we'd had the conversation, but needing to get one point out in the open. "Diving will never be completely safe. I do my best to mitigate the risks. And maybe today was a good reminder that I need to be more alert, even when I'm leading advanced divers with their own divemaster. But I love what I do. And I love diving that wreck. It's one of our most popular dives—we can't stop it because something bad *might* happen."

He swallowed. "I know. I said that in the heat of the moment, but I feel a little better after getting the story out in the open. Look, I'm not real great with words, but I care about you. And I admire you—how you approach everything you do."

"Thanks. That means a lot."

He rested his head against the wall again and shut his eyes. "But I really don't want to drive the boat on that dive again, okay?"

"I don't blame you. Can I say one more thing?"

He cracked open an eye to look at me.

"The *Benson* is no different than any other site. Accidents can happen on any of them."

"Thanks," he said dryly. "Now I feel much better."

I laughed, bringing an answering smile to his face.

"Okay," I continued. "I didn't put that well. What I'm trying to say is that the *Benson* isn't some malevolent being out to get your family. It's just a shipwreck. Stop giving it so much power. Maia doesn't mind diving it."

"Maia wasn't involved in Evan and Hunter's disaster."

I leaned forward until our faces were inches apart. I poked him in the chest to emphasize my words. "Neither. Were. You. So stop holding yourself responsible for an *accident*."

Chapter Twenty-Seven

Gabe

THE SUN WAS WELL above the eastern horizon as I strolled toward the Big House, in a much better frame of mind than yesterday. Miguel was back at work, and I intentionally left my day unscheduled in an effort to make up for the stress of yesterday.

I raised my head and smiled as the warm air bathed my face. Last night, I'd put Hailey to bed and was lying in my bedroom thinking over the day for the thousandth time.

And worrying whether April was still okay. What if delayed symptoms had set in? What if something was wrong *right this second*?

I needed to see her. To touch her. I texted her and asked if she would come up the hill. Relief poured off me in waves at her quick reply. Minutes later, April was at my door, and I practically dragged her to my bedroom. I couldn't think of a better way to make sure she was safe and healthy than by inspecting every square inch of her.

Which I had. Twice.

I shook my head. April brought out a tenderness in me I still didn't understand. Yeah, I was protective, but this was something different. Something new. And together, what we shared was completely unfamiliar. No matter how many times we had sex, I wanted more.

I wanted *her* to want more.

The side of my mouth twitched up as I rubbed my upper chest. Judging from the mark she'd made on my skin trying to keep quiet last night, I was succeeding.

When I entered the kitchen, Nona sat at the table eating a bowl of oatmeal. She wore a cream-colored vest with a turquoise long-sleeved shirt underneath, her white hair braided down her back. "Good morning, Gabriel. Alone for breakfast?"

I sat across from her and nodded. "I dropped off Hailey at a friend's house for the day. Now that Maia's crib is done, I want to work on the headboards for the beach cottages today."

"I'm sure they'll be beautiful." Nona's sharp eyes moved over my face. "How are you feeling today?"

I had an errant thought that she was asking about my tryst with April last night, then realized she was referencing the incident on the *Benson*. "I'm okay. April handled the whole situation perfectly."

Nona picked up her coffee cup and held it between both hands. "We're lucky she moved here."

Our eyes locked, and the force of my grandmother's presence kept me from looking away. "We are. I am."

A smile creased her face. "Any woman involved with you is lucky too. It makes me happy that you're not ruminating over the incident yesterday. I think our new dive-master has had a good effect on you."

"Thank you, Nona," I said mildly as the chef set a plate

of eggs, bacon, and hash browns in front of me. I nodded my thanks to him and poured a cup of coffee before meeting her eyes. "Don't go getting your fishing pole out just yet."

She batted her eyes. "When am I ever nosy?"

"Never! But you've got a new grandchild coming soon, so that must make you happy."

"Very. Though I wouldn't mind more, you know."

I just smiled and snapped a bite of bacon in my mouth. "If you want to play matchmaker, do it with Evan."

She pursed her lips. "He's well aware of my feelings. The man needs to stop living like a hermit."

I remembered his reaction when I called him out on the Sweet Dreams donuts and rubbed my lips to hide a smile. "He has his reasons. When he finds the right woman, he'll make a move."

She dotted her mouth with her napkin and set it on the table. "I'd better get moving. Lucille got a new shipment of clothing in, and I need to get to the boutique before the best stuff is gone."

"Maybe she has a metal star to go on your vest," I said with a grin. "Or some chaps."

Nona narrowed her eyes as she stood from the table. "Don't mock one of the few joys an old woman still has."

Laughing, I pushed back and rose to take her in my arms. "I would never do that. I love your piss and vinegar. You know that."

She patted my back. "I know, dear boy. Just keeping you on your toes."

I glanced at her turquoise cowboy boots. "Buy yourself a fancy new pair of boots and tell Lucille to send me the bill, okay?"

Nona smiled gleefully. "Absolutely! She's had a pair of handmade snakeskin boots I've had my eye on." Her stare turned appraising, but my smile didn't falter. She was worth every penny.

"Get them, unless she got something better in. I insist."

"Well, I have to make my grandson happy, don't I?"

With a wave, she swept out of the room, moving with a firm stride that belied her age. My smile lingered as I sat down to finish my breakfast.

My next stop was Evan. I was eager to discuss my idea with him and headed down the hill. Entering the lobby building, I swept my gaze around the large, open-air room. It was clean, though it hardly shouted the modern tropical vibe I wanted to imbue the resort with.

One step at a time...

The check-in desk stretched the length of the far side of the room, but my destination lay to the right. I walked down a hallway, passing doors on either side until I knocked on the frame at the end of the hall.

Evan glanced up. "Hey. Come on in."

I sat in a chair in front of his desk. His office was painted white and had a large window overlooking the grounds. Garden cottages could be seen a distance away. "How's today going?"

"A damn sight calmer than yesterday. I've kept pretty close tabs on Ted. He's fine—no signs of the bends." Then Evan smirked. "I figured you could handle the job of making sure April was all right."

I kept my face expressionless. "And she is. She's back diving this morning." I shook my head. "It was pretty bad yesterday. For a while, I felt like it was all happening again."

Evan's smile was sympathetic. "But it wasn't. Very different circumstances. And outcome."

"I told April everything yesterday."

His expression changed, and it took me a moment to

figure out who it reminded me of. Evan's calculating eye was the same Nona had used on me earlier. "That's not a story you throw around often. You two getting serious? You've been together a while now."

I scowled. "No—nothing's changed. I still don't believe in love. April's not a fan, either."

Evan burst into laughter.

My frown deepened. "What the hell's so funny?"

"I can't speak for April, but for a guy who doesn't believe in love, you sure seem taken with her."

"I like the woman. That's all."

Evan's eyes grew warmer. "I saw you yesterday when you guys got back, Gabe. Your expression wasn't that of a guy only interested in getting laid."

"I never said I was!"

He held out a hand, but his smile remained. "Calm down. Do you realize your eyes follow her every time she enters a room?"

I stared at him, a hot flush creeping up my neck. Then I leaned forward. "I'm not in love with her. End of story." Slouching back in my chair, I ignored my hammering heart. "Let's change the goddamn subject. Are you okay after yesterday?"

My brother stared at me, then let the subject drop. "I'm fine. The debacle with Hunter was over a decade ago, and I've learned to handle dive emergencies. They crop up now and again—sometimes divers aren't as advanced as they say they are. I've got personal experience with that, remember?" He frowned and leaned forward to rest his elbows on the desk. "You're not still feeling that weird big-brother guilt thing about my accident, are you?"

I shrugged uncomfortably. "I have occasional what-if moments."

"Well, stop. Gabe, only one person is responsible for what happened to me that day. Our bastard of a brother. He was hell-bent on looking for that goddamn imaginary gold, and I couldn't let him go down there alone. At least I learned my lesson and won't have anything to do with the son of a bitch."

I kept my voice soft. "That son of a bitch is still your brother. And his name is Hunter."

"He stopped being my brother a long time ago. The second we got lost inside that wreck."

This was old territory, and it was clear Evan's thoughts hadn't changed on the matter. As much as I wanted Evan and Hunter to reconcile, I had no idea what it would take to make that happen. "I actually had a reason for coming down here this morning. I want to talk about my idea for upgrading the beach cottages."

Evan's brows shot up. "Can we afford that?"

"With some changes, yes. The last payment on that loan Dad took out is in two weeks, thank God. So that will free up some cash."

"Not enough to renovate ten cottages."

"No. You're right." I eyed him steadily. "How would you feel if I took a portion of Dad's share of the resort? I'm thinking about investing some of my own money."

Dad was fifty-one percent owner of the island and resort. Us five kids plus Nona split the other forty-nine percent evenly. Years ago, all of us had stopped taking profit shares to help the bottom line for the resort. But I had plans to improve profit and change that.

Evan shrugged. "I don't mind. If you're risking your money, you ought to get more shares."

I picked up the old baseball Evan kept on a wooden stand on his desk, rolling it between my hands. "It's not just me I have to think about. Every move I make affects Hailey too. I'm thinking about asking Dad to stake me twenty percent out of his shares. We need to upgrade this place, Evan." My mind flashed back to the drab lobby and nondescript cottages. "My God, presidents have stayed here!"

"Not since the early twentieth century."

I gripped the baseball, wanting to throw it against the wall. Though Evan would kill me if I did that. "That's exactly my point! This resort goes back over 150 years, yet right now it looks like a low budget, mid-century mom-and-pop resort. It's time to stop trying to compete with Sunset Siesta and remember *no one* can compete with us."

Evan smiled. "If you pitch it like that, Dad might give you thirty percent."

Smiling, I put the baseball back on its stand. "It's just hard to ask him. He feels terrible about how the place has slipped financially, and it's hard for me to watch."

"Me too."

I shrugged. "All of us. But Calypso Key has to move in a new direction, or we won't make it. And that's going to take some cash."

"Good thing you're Daddy Warbucks."

I shot him a look from under my brows. "Not exactly, but I can funnel most of the profits from my Miami business into the resort. Jake and I talked recently, and the company is doing fine. I think it could make a big difference."

"Sounds like a great idea. You told anyone else?"

"I'll mention it to Maia, but in general terms. She hates the money stuff as much as you do."

"At least she can get out of hearing about it."

"Yeah, cry me a river, Mr. General Manager. I'll call Stella and Hunter later. I'm sure they won't mind." Stella was two years younger than me and a rising chef at Blue

Nirvana, one of Key West's most storied restaurants. She'd only dropped by once in the months since Hailey and I had returned, which I wasn't happy about.

"Then it's only Dad you'll need to convince."

"Yeah. That should be fun. He's guiding today, so I'll catch up with him tomorrow or the next day."

I went to the Barn and lost myself to the soothing, familiar motions of creating something lasting from my own two hands. The headboards I'd been making were constructed from solid mahogany, and all with live edges along the top. They were the essence of the modern, beachy design I had in mind. As I ran my belt sander over the rough wood, my troubles with finances and the resort gradually faded away. Occasionally, April's face flashed before me, and a small smile would come over my face. I might not believe in love, but as long as she was near me, she made it easier for me to do whatever I had to.

Chapter Twenty-Eight

Gabe

IT WAS several days before my schedule and Dad's meshed to discuss my idea. I waited for him in his office, sitting in his leather executive chair. I'd gone back and forth on whether to take a folding chair and let him have the big one. But in the end, I decided if I was going to present an offer to become a prominent stakeholder, I ought to look the part and project confidence.

But it made me feel like an asshole, even though this was how we usually sat when going over numbers.

He was still my dad.

I sat back and let my head rest against the leather. I placed my elbows on the armrests, tenting my fingers and letting my mind wander. April had come over again last evening after dinner. We'd sat around the table and played Monopoly, quickly settling into a game of friendly competition. Hailey and April ganged up against me, but I still won. When it was Hailey's bedtime, we'd both sat in her room, and she'd asked April to read her bedtime story. I sat there watching the two of them, and the sheer *happiness* of the evening had brought a lump to my throat.

Hailey fell asleep quickly, so we left her room, and I made sure the seahorse nightlight was glowing softly. I opened a bottle of red wine, and April and I sat on my back porch. A meteor shower streaked over the sky as I held her wrapped in my arms. We didn't even need to talk. She stroked my arm, and I rested my chin on top of her head. We finished the bottle, and I pulled her to her feet. A powerful wave of desire rose in me when we kissed. Her mouth was wet, and her lips were soft and welcoming. The wave strengthened when she grabbed my hand and led me to my bedroom. After sex that had left me breathless and utterly sated, I cocooned myself around her and we both fell asleep.

When I woke at 3:00 a.m., April was gone, her side of the bed empty and cold. A hollowness twisted in my stomach as I brushed my hand over the cool sheet.

A deep, soft laugh made me look up as Dad entered the room and sat next to me. "That was quite a succession of expressions on your face. And if I know anything, I'd bet you were thinking about April."

I blinked, not realizing I'd been so transparent. "Guess that dad radar is still going strong. I hope some of that wears off on me when Hailey's a few years older."

Smiling, he clapped me on the back. "I'm sure it will. Things are going well with April? I was really impressed with how she handled that incident on the *Benson*."

I hesitated, trying to figure out how to answer. Things were going very well with her, but not in the direction I'd intended. And that frightened me. I didn't want to ever feel the way I did after Kora left. It made me wonder how Dad felt after Mom died. "We're doing great together... Can I ask you something, Dad? It's damn personal, so you can refuse."

He peaked a dark brow at me. "Go ahead."

"How come you've never remarried? You've never even been in a serious relationship that I know of."

He smiled, but sadness lined the corners of his eyes. "There are several answers to that. But the bottom line is that I've never found another woman who made me feel like your mother did. She's the example I compare all women to, and none have been able to match her."

"It's not because you never want to feel the way you did after her death?"

"Grief never leaves, Gabe. Your mother will always be with me. But it fades, and eventually, you realize you still have a life to live. That looks different for everyone. If I found another woman who measured up to your mother, I'd be happy to get involved again—love is one of the best things in life. But are we talking about me now? Or is this about how you felt after your divorce?"

I picked up a pen and twirled it in my hands. "Both, I guess. For years now, I've kept my heart locked up tight. Somehow, April's managed to get hold of the key, and I'm not sure how I feel about that."

Dad smiled. "A day will come when you *will* know. Then you'll have your answer." Then he breathed a long sigh. "But I'm glad you wanted to get together to talk finances. We've got some things we need to get settled. One in particular."

Isn't that the truth...

"I don't mean to interrupt, but I have a business proposition for you," I blurted out, nervous now that we were onto the subject I'd called him here for.

Dad's face went blank. "Oh?"

"I saw that the loan is paid off, which is going to free up some cash flow." His jaw tightened and his shoulders tensed, but I soldiered on. "I want to funnel profits from my Miami business to pay for upgrading the guest cottages. Then we can move on to the main facilities. What would you say to giving up some of your ownership shares to make me a twenty percent stakeholder?"

I'd done a complete 180 since arriving, going from not wanting to be here to doing my best to ensure the success of the resort. And this was a good idea, one I believed in. My heart pounded against my ribs as I waited for his reaction.

But Dad didn't say anything, instead rising and moving over to the small liquor display he kept on a bookcase. I'd inherited my love of fine scotch from him, though he preferred Glenlivet to Macallan. He picked up a bottle of Glenlivet 18 and poured two healthy measures.

I slumped in my chair, my heart beating even faster. "Dad, it's ten a.m."

Returning to the desk, he set one of the glasses in front of me and took his seat again, holding his whisky in one hand. "You might want that in a few minutes."

"Great. You hate the idea that much, huh?" I stared at the amber liquid and contemplated downing the entire thing.

"On the contrary, I think it's a fantastic plan. And I can't tell you how proud I am that you want to invest in the resort. And that you're in a financial position to do so."

I drew my brows down. "Then what's the problem?"

He sighed and took a long drink. His throat worked as he swallowed, staring at the glass. "It's the loan you were just talking about."

"What do you mean? There are no more monthly payments scheduled."

"No more monthly ones, yes. But there's another payment due next month. A balloon payment." Dad's voice was flat, emotionless.

His last three words sent my stomach plummeting. Goose bumps raised the hair on my forearms. As a man who hated debt, few things got my back up more than balloon loans. "How much, Dad?"

Closing his eyes, he tipped his head back. "Two million dollars."

The air exploded from my lungs in a rush. How was that even possible? "My God. Can't you refinance the balloon?"

"I've tried, but my credit has gotten worse over the years. That's how I got stuck with this loan in the first place. It was the only one I could get to keep the lights on."

A deep sense of numbness overcame me, and I downed the shot of scotch. "Why didn't you tell me?"

He drank the rest of his glass and got up to refill both, setting the bottle on the desk. "Because I was ashamed, Gabe. I've been trying to get hold of another loan, but no bank will give me one. That's why I'm talking to you now."

I took another drink. "What do you mean?"

Dad's words came out in a rush. "I'm hoping you can refinance it in your name. Use the profits you were talking about to make the loan payments. I'll trade my shares with yours, so you'll become the fifty-one percent majority shareholder."

Hailey's face flashed in my mind. There was no way I was taking on two million dollars in debt and risking her future like that. "Dad, I can't take out a loan like that. I'll never sleep again."

"I know—you hate debt. You always have. Could you pay off the loan outright?"

I stared at the Glenlivet and set the glass down with a thump. "I don't have two million dollars just sitting around."

Dad's voice was hollow, forlorn. "Gabe, if we don't find a way to pay that balloon off, the bank will foreclose on the entire island."

A wracking shiver took over my body as the consequences flashed in my brain, and I picked up my glass again. I knew what would happen, which was why I despised balloon loans so much. They were designed to be difficult to pay off. After foreclosing, the bank would put Calypso Key —all of it—up for auction. Some sleazy developer would buy it, raze everything, and build shitty condos to sell for top dollar. All this history—wiped out. We'd become homeless. All our employees would lose their jobs.

My breath froze in my lungs, and I dropped the glass. It tipped back and forth on the blotter but settled upright. I hardly noticed.

April would lose her job.

Nausea roiled my stomach as I sat forward and buried my hands in my hair. A deep groan issued from my chest.

I would lose April.

Forever.

She could get another job anywhere. She *would* get another job anywhere.

A yawning hole opened inside my chest as a succession of memories flashed through my mind. Of interactions April and I had had since she'd arrived. How could I not have seen it? Everything I'd done since moving back here had been to make sure April stayed. At first it had been to cut finances as well, but I didn't have to keep driving the boat now.

I wanted to. So I could work side by side with her.

I tried to imagine life without her, the board game and bedtime story flashing through my mind. I couldn't do it, and the wound gaped open more.

I couldn't let this happen.

"I'm so sorry, Gabe. I know you don't deserve this." Dad's face was ashen. He looked ten years older than when he'd entered the room mere minutes ago.

"Neither do you, Dad." My voice came out quiet and shaky.

"Is there anything you can do?"

Slowly sitting upright, I drummed my fingers on the desk. The lassitude filling my body drained away, replaced with resolute purpose. I knew exactly what I had to do. "Yeah. There is." I looked at him. "I need to go to Miami. I may need to stay a couple nights, so can you and Nona watch Hailey while I'm gone?"

"Of course. Whatever you need."

Whatever I need... I need April.

Even if she didn't need me.

That was the other thing that was now obvious—that I'd avoided seeing. Every time we were together, I did everything possible to be different than those bastards she had dated. To show her I was faithful, caring.

That I'd be there when she needed me.

April might not want more from me, but I had just been hit full force with the fact that I couldn't say the same anymore. And I'd been blind and in denial that I'd felt this way for a while.

Even if she refused me, I had to try.

I had to find a way to show her I was different.

I turned to Dad. "Thanks. I need to drive to Miami. I'll

set up a meeting with Jake on the way. Don't worry, Dad—we'll figure this out. Calypso Key's been part of the Markham family for 150 years. There's no way in hell that's changing now."

Chapter Twenty-Nine

April

"SO YOU'RE gonna be all book nerdy this afternoon, huh?" Wyatt asked with a laugh as we disassembled scuba kits. We were returning after the second dive, and he was on his own for the afternoon trip. I glanced up at the building clouds in the sky. A low-pressure system was moving in. We'd had sunny skies when we left, but rain was forecast this afternoon and tonight.

"Yep," I replied, coiling a regulator in my hands. "Sorry to leave you alone on such a lovely tropical day. We get together and chat about romance books and drink wine."

I was glad to have book club to distract me. A tiny hint of uneasiness in my gut had blossomed into a slithering creature eating my insides. Yesterday afternoon, I'd texted Gabe. Just a little hello asking how his day was going, since he'd planned on working in the Big House all day.

He never answered.

One of the unspoken rules of our pact was not to be clingy. If I wasn't looking for a long-term relationship, I had no right to expect Gabe to jump to every message and request I made. But he was an extremely straightforward man who didn't play games. He always answered texts in a reasonable amount of time.

I sent a second one last night before bed, just to say good night. When I checked this morning, that one was unanswered too. The most likely scenario was that he took off with Hailey on a spontaneous escape since summer would be ending soon.

I kept telling myself there had to be a good explanation for him not answering. We might have some clear boundaries in our relationship, but surely by now I meant enough to him that he wouldn't just ignore me. No, he had to be with Hailey somewhere.

As we approached the canal, a few small patters of rain began falling. Since *Shark Bait* would be going out again shortly, Miguel had us tie up the boat near the canal entrance. I grabbed my backpack and slapped Wyatt on the back. "Hope the weather holds off until after you guys are back. See you later."

"You're off tomorrow, right?"

I nodded. "Corbin's taking my group."

"Enjoy your ladies' afternoon and don't get too hammered." Wyatt tossed me a cocky grin, which increased in size after I rolled my eyes.

As I stepped off the boat and walked down the brick pathway, Hailey's laughter drifted to me. I'd spent enough time with her over the summer to recognize the sound anywhere. As I passed the gear room, two forms holding fishing poles over the canal were revealed, one tall and one small.

My eyes glanced over Hailey, immediately moving to the tall man next to her. Though the build was similar to

Gabe's, Warren's salt-and-pepper hair caused my shoulders to drop.

If Hailey's here, where the hell is Gabe? And why won't he answer me?

She caught sight of me, and a grin nearly split her face. "April! We saw a manatee earlier. And I've caught *three* fish!"

Her excitement was irresistible, and an answering smile rose on my face as I joined the duo. "Wow, sounds like you've had quite the morning! I imagine your grandfather has probably forgotten more about fishing than most people have ever known."

Warren shook his head, but a smile crept through. "I seriously doubt that."

"I never catch this many fish with Dad," Hailey said, grinning at him. "He says he doesn't have the patience for it."

"You must take after your grandfather then," I said, trying to be polite and ignoring the disquiet rising inside me. "Since you've caught three already. And Manny paid a visit too?" Several manatees lived in the area, especially in the mangrove wetlands in the northwest of the island. One in particular liked to pay a visit to the canal if the boat motors weren't running. None of us could resist turning on the hose and lowering it over the side so Manny could have a drink of fresh water.

Warren recast his line. "I haven't seen him in quite a while. Nice to know he's still healthy."

"He does a good job of staying away from propellers," I added. Then I took a deep breath to ask the question that had been eating away at me. "What's Gabe up to? I haven't seen him today."

"Dad went to Miami," Hailey said matter-of-factly. "I'm

staying with Grandpa and Nona until he gets back tonight or tomorrow."

"Oh," I said, the word coming out small and quiet.

"Gabe had some business to attend to," Warren added.

I pasted a smile on my face, acting like I hadn't just been punched in the gut. A physical pain twisted my insides. "I'll let you two get back to fishing. You might not have much longer."

Warren nodded and glanced at the dark spots on his shirt. "Yeah, we've gotten splashed by a few raindrops. A couple more minutes, sunshine, then we'll head up to lunch."

I said my goodbyes to the pair and walked woodenly toward the main path. Gabe wasn't on a last-minute trip with Hailey. He'd gone on a *business* trip. Yet he couldn't even be bothered to let me know. Or answer any of my texts.

Tears sprang to my eyes, and I dashed them away, angry. Not at Gabe—at myself. How had I let this happen? A quick business trip shouldn't be an issue for a casual boyfriend I didn't care deeply for.

And that was the problem.

Despite my best intentions and our pact, I had fallen for him. I only now realized how much—when I was faced with the obvious truth that he hadn't. Otherwise, why wouldn't he let me know he was leaving? Or answer my texts?

Because we had an agreement. Exclusive but not serious.

And once again, I'd fallen in love with the wrong man. Even though Gabe had been crystal clear about what he was after. I couldn't blame him for this.

It was all on me.

. . .

I TRIED to participate in the book discussion, but I couldn't concentrate. Liv sat next to me and fortunately made up for my quietness. The book was a rom-com about a fake relationship, and she loved it. All I could think about was how I should find a tattoo parlor and have a giant L tattooed on my forehead.

In my pocket, my phone buzzed silently. My heart pounded, and I couldn't resist sneaking it out for a quick peek. The text bubble on the lock screen said it was from Gabe. I swallowed hard and opened the app.

> Gabe: I'm in Miami. We'll talk when I get home.

I stared bleakly at his words. What was I expecting, a declaration of love? That he missed me and couldn't wait to get home? An apology for waiting almost twenty-four hours to answer?

Any of the above.

Which made me nothing but a fool.

With a deep sigh, I shoved my phone back into my pocket and took a healthy swig of white wine.

When the meeting ended, I got up and headed toward the door, smiling mechanically as I said my goodbyes. I moved down the cement walkway, my steps halting.

"April! Wait up!" Liv hurried behind me, her curvy figure enhanced by a flowing purple top and black capris.

I halted and waited for her to catch up.

Her eyes bounced over my face. "Are you okay? You hardly said a word in there."

We walked side by side, the leafy green trees keeping most of the light rain off. "I'll be all right. Just some real-life romantic problems."

Liv slid an arm around my shoulders. "Come on. You sound like you could use someone to talk to. I know just the place."

A few minutes later, we sat down in a booth at Conch Republic Brewpub. The bar and grill sat at the southeastern edge of Dove Key, with a wide view of the ocean. The bluff of Calypso Key was visible too, the Big House obscured by hedges. The section of the restaurant we sat in was open to the air, with an aluminum covered roof. The fresh scent of rain blew toward us occasionally. Both of us ordered one of their Queen Conch IPAs brewed on site.

Liv stared at me after our pint glasses were delivered. "Things aren't going well with Gabe anymore? When I saw you with his daughter in the store, you looked like the perfect family."

"I just got a rude awakening today. I screwed up—Gabe and I had a pact not to get serious. He went to Miami on business yesterday and didn't let me know. Which would be fine if we were in a casual relationship."

Compassion filled Liv's eyes, and she reached across the wooden table to squeeze my hand. "And things aren't so casual on your side anymore?"

I barked a laugh that wanted to be a sob. But I refused to let it. "Yeah. I thought I was doing so great this time. Keeping myself from falling in love with him. You met Hailey—she's incredible. And Gabe is absolutely amazing with her. The last couple months have been so great between us, I think my feelings just kind of snuck up on me. Now I don't know what to do."

"But you're hurt because he took off without saying anything?"

"Yeah, I am. He can be grouchy and serious, but he's

also protective and dependable."

"Maybe he has a good reason."

I stared at her and forced my fist to unclench. "To just up and disappear? Letting his family know all about it, but not his girlfriend?"

"I agree—that's pretty thoughtless. So is Hailey staying with his dad?"

I nodded.

"Well, that explains why Gabe let him know. He had to make sure Hailey was taken care of."

Tears welled in my eyes. I blinked rapidly, but one rolled down my face. "But what if I want to be taken care of? I'm so goddamn tired of being an afterthought, Liv! I'm not even important enough to inform when he leaves town suddenly. We see each other every day! We work together!"

"I know, honey."

I wiped my cheek. "I've been fooling myself for a while now. I only realized that the last couple of days. Physically... I've never felt like this. Gabe brings out a confidence in me that's completely new. I thought it was because of our strict boundaries."

"But it's not?"

I took a drink of beer. "No. It's because I love him. Because I feel *safe* with him. Safe enough to let my walls come down. Now look at me."

"What are you going to do?"

I propped my elbow on the table and rested my chin in my palm. "Hell if I know. I can't exactly complain. This is why we have the pact. If I can't handle this, I'm going to have to find a new job. Leave Calypso Key."

Liv's eyes grew round. "Well, at least hear his side of things before you make any drastic moves. Maybe take a step back while you're at it. That might bring some perspective."

"That sounds like good advice. Thanks, Liv." I smiled and made an effort to be positive. "Enough about my life. How are things with you? No more disastrous dates, I hope."

"No dates period. The bakery is taking a lot of my time. I hired a kid to help me, but so far she seems more interested in scrolling on her phone than working. I bought the equipment second-hand, and it's finicky. So is the building. I've had a repairman out twice in the last couple of weeks to fix the oven."

I smiled. "Love in the bakery with the repair guy?"

Liv laughed. "Hardly. He's a little old and a little married for my taste. The only guy I've noticed is my mystery man."

"That sounds interesting! Tell me more."

"Oh, there's this sweet guy who comes into the store at least once a week. He's shy and always has a smile. I just think he's cute."

"You don't know any more about him?"

"No. I enjoy making up stories about who he is. He kind of looks like a lumberjack, so I imagine him chopping wood and sawing down trees."

We both laughed and I was grateful to find my mood lightened. "Well, let me know if you need me to go on a recon mission. Maybe I can figure out who your lumberjack is."

"He's not even my type! I like my men neat and clean, not with a bushy beard. But he has the most beautiful eyes."

Like a switch being thrown, the misty rain started falling in a heavy sheet, drumming on the metal roof above us and obscuring everything past the bluff.

The bluff that led to Driftwood Beach, where Gabe and

I had watched that movie on our first date.

Then left before it ended because we were so hot for each other.

Liv glanced out the open window, wincing at the deluge. "Oh, wow. Look at that. We probably ought to get out of here now."

I nodded and scooted out of the booth. "Yeah. Night's going to come fast now. I'll let you know what happens with Gabe. Thanks for listening."

With a heavy heart, I ran to my car, holding my purse over my head to ward off the worst of the deluge. I started the engine as my mind tortured me with images from two nights ago. Images of falling asleep in Gabe's arms, warm and secure. Then waking up later and leaving—even though it was the last thing I'd wanted to do. But I had because it was important to him.

Rain drummed against the windshield as I drove home. Back to my apartment.

Alone.

Chapter Thirty

Gabe

I STARED at my phone as I leaned against the wall outside the boardroom. Our business office was on the twenty-fifth floor of the Miami building, and I had been camped out here since arriving the previous afternoon. After my arrival, Jake and I had negotiated my final severance package. A faint smile crossed my face as another vision eclipsed what I'd been staring at on my phone—the memory of Jake's sweaty forehead during our back and forth yesterday. There was a reason he'd been the schmoozer and I'd been the negotiator in our partnership.

Unraveling my half of the company hadn't been easy or quick, but I was pleased with the end result. My only escape from the boardroom had been crashing for the night at a nearby hotel, where I'd fallen into bed, exhausted after the drive and negotiation. We'd been back first thing this morning to hammer out the final details and draw up the contract.

"Hi there, Gabe. Nice to see you again."

I snapped my head up and managed a smile as Abigail, an executive assistant, walked by. She gave me a long, assessing look that I didn't return. "Thanks."

As soon as she passed, my eyes dropped to the phone again. To April's messages. Which I still hadn't answered, like an asshole.

But I had no idea what to say.

I had so much to tell her—things that terrified me. And none of it was appropriate for a text message. I was nearing the final stretch now and needed to get this deal signed. I could tell her everything in person when I got back to Calypso Key. Hopefully tonight. But I had to say *something*. I flinched, imagining her thinking I was ignoring her.

Or worse, that I didn't care.

My feelings hadn't changed overnight. In fact, they'd solidified even more. I had to make this happen, proving to her in the process that I wasn't a lazy bastard just using her until someone else came along. Like those other pricks she'd been with.

My mind kept returning to that conversation with Dad. *Before* he'd dropped the bomb about the balloon payment. When he'd said I'd know when I'd met the woman who would change my mind about love. About sharing my life.

I knew it, all right.

A flash of stunning clarity had swept over me in his office, unlike anything I'd ever experienced. When I was with April, I felt *free*. And utterly terrified she didn't feel the same way about me.

My thumbs were frozen over the screen, and I needed to get back in the room with Jake.

Finally, I typed out something stupid about being in Miami and talking when I got home.

There. At least I answered, and she isn't just hanging. I'll make it up to her.

An ice-cold knife twisted in my gut. Yeah, I'd make it up to her if she still wanted me. I was in love with a woman who had told me she didn't want a deep relationship. I was flying blind here, trying to prove my intentions. I had no idea how April would take my news. She'd managed her side of our pact to a tee, even leaving my bed the other night after I'd fallen asleep.

Shit, that doesn't sound like someone head over heels in love with me.

Time to focus. I was in Miami for a reason, and it was time to finish the job. Shutting my phone completely off, I tucked it into the inside pocket of my gray suit jacket. I adjusted my red tie, frowning at the constriction. After months of not wearing one, I didn't miss the damn thing in the slightest.

A heavyset, middle-aged woman marched down the hall toward me, a stack of manila file folders cradled against her ample bosom. We nodded to each other, then I turned around and opened the wooden door to the boardroom.

A wall of windows overlooked downtown Miami, but the display was nothing but skyscrapers and a dull, afternoon sky spitting rain. Not turquoise water and white sand. How had I ever thought this was what I wanted?

Jake Tolling sat across the huge rectangular table. A lock of brown hair had fallen across his forehead, and he swept it back. He leaned back in the black leather chair, his legs on the table and crossed at the ankles.

"Mona is coming now with the files," I said, taking a seat across from him.

"Oh, shit!" Jake jerked his feet off the table and sat up, smoothing his tie.

I smirked. Even though we were the two executive officers, Mona was a legend in the office, and everyone treated her with wary respect. After two firm raps, the door opened again, and she entered. She placed the stack of folders in front of me.

"The bottom is your copy, Gabe. I've flagged where you need to sign on the top copy in blue, then Jake needs to sign the green flags." She stopped and cleared her throat. "I wish you the very best. You'll be missed."

"Thank you." I pushed to my feet and took her into my embrace, ignoring the way her eyes became shiny in the overhead lights. To be honest, I was a little surprised. Mona and I had always gotten along well. I treated her with unfailing politeness and courtesy, and in return she never once took a sharp tone with me. But it wasn't a close relationship. At least, I hadn't thought so. Maybe I'd misjudged her. "Take care, Mona. If you ever need some downtime, give me a call. I know a pretty nice resort you might enjoy."

The right side of her mouth twitched. "Be careful with that, young man. I might take you up on it."

"I hope you do."

She patted my upper arms, then turned and walked out the door, closing it softly behind her. My mind turned back to home and April. And what I still had to do after I got back. Whether this risk would pay off.

I sat again and stared at the folders.

"You sure about this?" Jake asked. "I know it's the family business, but do you want out completely?"

I raised my eyes to meet his blue ones. "Yeah. I'm sure. It's time to commit myself." By selling outright to Jake, I'd have enough cash to pay off the balloon note and finance the resort improvements. But this was the only way—a reduced ownership percentage wouldn't be enough.

I picked up a black fountain pen and opened the folder, signing my name where indicated.

A few minutes later, Jake signed his own name as I stared around the boardroom I'd helped create. But it wasn't home anymore. Home was a 150-year-old legacy for my daughter. A legacy I had the means and the ability to save. Right now.

Home was the woman I loved. Even if I was too blind to see it until yesterday. Even if she didn't feel the same way.

I hadn't given Jake any of the specifics as to why I needed to cash out my half of the business. Though he knew something was up since I was in such a hurry.

Across from me, he closed the folder. "We'll mail you a copy of the final, notarized contract."

"Thanks, Jake."

He watched me steadily. Jake and I had been friends for over a decade, and he was no dummy. "You've had a lot of changes over the last few months. Over the last couple of years, really. Is wanting out of our partnership all about family? Or is there something else? Someone else?"

I narrowed my eyes, keeping my face impassive. "Why would you ask that?"

He shrugged. "You were pissed off when you moved at the start of the year and not sure you wanted to go. Your family's the same, so something else must have changed."

"My family isn't the same. My sister's having a baby in a couple of weeks."

"So that's the difference?"

I sighed. "No. You're right. I'm involved with someone. For the first time since Kora. And April is everything she... wasn't."

"Well, thank God for that!"

Though I was hardly being fair comparing April to

Kora. I'd never felt this way before, and now my marriage looked like a farce. But could I convince April of that? "I never wanted to fall in love again. I even told April that. Yet somehow, I have. I'm still not sure how it happened."

Jake grinned, the change of expression startling. "That's what usually happens, isn't it? You think you know exactly what's going on, then something comes along that rips the wool from your eyes."

Behind Jake, rain sheeted against the glass, making a steady tapping sound. "Thanks for getting this together so fast. You really pulled out the stops to make this happen, and I want you to know I appreciate it."

"You're welcome, man. The money should settle in your bank account within a week. I get the feeling the resort might be a little worse off than you'd expected."

"Yeah. Dad took out a shitty loan with a balloon payment. And we need to upgrade everything. This was the most obvious solution."

Jake's eyes softened. "All you had to give up was everything you've worked your entire adult life for."

I sat back in my chair. "Maybe. But I'm looking at it as an investment, one that will pay off even better than this business has."

The financial side, anyway. But what will it mean if April backs away from me? From us?

Jake got up and came around the table. "If anyone can do it, you can, Gabe. Let me know if you need anything."

I stood and gave him a hug. "Thanks. I will. I'd better get going. I drove up here and would like to get started before the weather gets worse."

I can use the trip home to figure out what to say to April.

Jake put his hands in his pants pockets. "You going to celebrate? You just became a very rich man, Gabe. I can't imagine that loan is anywhere near as much as you just wrangled out of me."

I smiled. "No, it isn't. I've got plenty left over to play with. And to make sure Hailey is taken care of."

He returned my smile. "Get yourself one of those ridiculously expensive bottles of whisky you like so much."

"I might do that. I know just how to celebrate with it."

And with that, I turned and walked out of my business for the last time.

I drove home in a steady rain, the sky gradually darkening above me. At least the crappy weather kept the tourists off the highway. I stopped and grabbed dinner on the way, but it still took me nearly four hours to drive back to Calypso Key. I parked my car in front of the dark cottage and stared down the hill. At the Barn.

Hailey was taken care of for the night. I'd never get a better opportunity to talk to April. Except I still hadn't figured out how to phrase what I wanted to say. I didn't want to knock on her door and blurt out that I loved her. And I'd be lying through my teeth if I said I wasn't scared to death of what her response was going to be. After all, I was the one who had fallen in love. Not her.

Heedless of the rain, I exited my car and trudged toward the bluff behind the cottages. I stuck my hands in my pockets, letting the rain sheet over me. I turned to the right and slowly walked down the hill, staying well away from the edge.

In the distance, the lights of the Barn beckoned through the downpour.

Chapter Thirty-One

April

THE RAIN DRUMMED STEADILY on the roof, but the storm wasn't accompanied by wind, which made it more relaxing than worrisome. Too bad I couldn't relax. An occasional bolt of lightning lit up the night, but I hadn't heard any thunder. I sat on my living room couch with my legs tucked next to me. Next month's book club selection lay open on my lap, but I hadn't been able to concentrate on reading.

It was after 8:00 p.m., and I'd had exactly zero word from Gabe. I sure as hell wasn't going to call or text him after that terse, two-sentence reply he'd sent earlier. He could have come home hours ago or be in Miami for another week. I had no idea.

Because I wasn't important enough to talk to. To inform.

I shut the book and rose to my feet with a groan. "I've lost my mind. Isn't that the definition? Doing the same thing over and over and expecting a different result?"

Hemingway lifted his head from the armchair he was

curled up in and meowed, but it didn't clarify the situation with Gabe much.

I ran my hand over his soft gray-and-white fur, and he purred under my touch. "What am I going to do? He was crystal clear about what he wanted. I can't take another relationship with a guy who doesn't feel the same way!" The cat butted my hand, which I took as a sign of sympathy. "I'm not going to be Gabe's doormat, to wipe his shoes on. I don't want to leave, either. But what if I have no choice?"

I moaned loudly.

"Maybe a cup of tea will help me settle down." Padding to the kitchen, I grabbed the kettle from the stovetop. I stared out the window behind the sink as it filled.

Lightning flashed and I gasped, my heart nearly stopping. A dark-haired man stood on the bluff, facing away. He wore a suit, of all things, and was completely soaked.

I didn't know whether to be concerned for him or call the resort front desk to send someone to chase him away. Calypso Key didn't have a regular security detail, having never needed one. But a stranger standing in the pouring rain was rather alarming, and several burly staff members could be counted on to take care of the guy.

My decision was made in the next burst of lightning. The man had turned his head, and his profile was illuminated in the flash. My mouth dropped open, a gasp escaping.

It was Gabe.

Why on earth is he standing outside in the rain?

I hardly noticed when I shut off the faucet. Before I knew what was happening, I had opened the back door and trotted across my patio. Wearing only a T-shirt and pajama bottoms, I ran into the nighttime rain barefoot. The wetness was cool and pelted my face, drenching my hair as I crossed the short grass to where he stood, still facing away.

I slowed when I was a few feet behind him, my pulse racing. "Gabe?"

I hadn't spoken loudly, but with no wind, the word carried easily to him. He didn't startle. Instead, his shoulders tightened. He slowly turned around. The color of his drenched suit was hard to judge with the lack of moonlight, but it was dark, and he wore a red tie. His hair was plastered to his head, and rain beaded down his face and over his scruff, all illuminated from the lights inside my apartment.

He didn't reply, just stared at me.

The look in his eyes was something I'd never seen before.

Hesitation and... fear.

My heart rate, which had already been elevated, ratcheted up even further, and my stomach clenched. I hardly knew what to make of the apparition standing before me. "Gabe, are you all right? What are you doing out here in the rain?"

A ghost of a smile flitted across his face. "Trying to work up the courage to talk to you."

I had taken a step toward him, but his answer stopped me cold.

Oh, God. He's breaking up with me.

"Why do you need courage to speak to me?" I hated the fear coming through in my voice, but I couldn't help it.

Gabe briefly squeezed his eyes shut, then swiped his hand over them, washing away the rain. Not that it mattered. More just replaced it, dripping down his face. I was as soaked as he was, but I hardly felt it.

"I'm sorry I just took off without saying anything. I hardly had time to make arrangements for Hailey, then I couldn't figure out how to answer your texts. Dad made a disastrous financial move, and to keep the resort, I had to go to Miami. I cashed out my half of the business. That's what I've been doing the last couple days."

My stomach unfurled slightly, but I was completely confused why this news had anything to do with me. I struggled for something to say. "That sounds like a lot of stress. I can understand why you didn't have time for chitchat."

He watched me intently as rain poured down all around us. "If I don't pay off a two-million-dollar loan, the bank will auction off Calypso Key to the highest bidder. The resort will be gone."

Lightning flashed across the sky as I inhaled sharply. "My God. Your family would lose the resort? The island?"

He nodded, his handsome face bleak. "I'll have the money soon, then I'll pay off the loan immediately. But when Dad told me, that wasn't the only thing that hit me like a freight train." He paused, his mouth opening and closing. "Another realization was just as devastating. It changed everything."

I could hardly speak. My mouth was as dry as a desert. "What?"

This is it. Here comes the breakup speech.

"A developer would raze everything here. You would lose your job, along with everyone else. Then you'd move away, and I'd lose *you*. Forever. I couldn't let that happen."

A small ember flickered to life inside me, and I swallowed hard.

"As much as losing the island frightened me, the thought of losing you scared me more." Gabe stopped and rubbed his face with both hands. When he dropped them, his face was drawn, haggard. "I screwed up, April."

My heart stuttered again as I drew my brows together. "What do you mean?"

He stood still as a statue, arms at his sides as water dripped from the sleeves of his suit jacket. "Our pact. Our agreement. I broke it. I'm in love with you, and I'm afraid that's the last thing in the world you want."

I tried to blink the rain out of my eyes as I stared at him. My hands were shaking wildly, but it wasn't from the cold. A surge of emotion barreled through me, so strong I could hardly control it.

What did he just say?

Droplets flew from my hair as I shook my head. "I thought you didn't call because you thought it wasn't important." Pressing my trembling hands against my hips, I forced myself to say it. "That *I* wasn't important."

Fear rose in his eyes again. "It was just the opposite. When I realized I might lose you, I jumped in my car and drove to Miami. I called my partner Jake on the way and told him to clear his calendar. When you texted me, I couldn't figure out what to say. I only knew I had to say it to you in person. I'm sorry."

He whipped his head back and forth, water flying into the night. His words came more quickly now, tumbling out of his mouth. "I couldn't stop thinking about what you said. About the guys you'd dated and how they treated you as an afterthought. As if you didn't matter. I wanted to show you I was different. That I *am* different. That's why I went to Miami. Yes, to save the resort, but also to prove to you how much you mean to me. That there isn't anything I wouldn't do for you."

I stared at him, at the water zigzagging through his stubbly beard.

He was saying the words I'd longed to hear. *Dreamed* of

hearing. But he'd put me through a lot in the past two days, and I needed him to know that. "Gabe, you really hurt me. You *knew* this was an issue for me—of being made to feel unimportant. I was thinking about moving earlier. Now, I don't know what to think. What to believe."

His face was bleak as he stared at me. "I know. Too much hit me all at once and I couldn't think straight. I only knew one thing—I need you in my life. I'm tired of you leaving after we make love. I want to hold you all night long and wake up next to you every morning. I want to spend evenings with you and Hailey, playing games and watching TV. To be a *family*." His shoulders moved up and down with the force of his breathing, and deep lines creased his forehead. Dread rippled through his eyes. "April, please tell me what you're thinking because I'm about to lose it here."

Jubilant tears sprang free as I launched myself into his arms.

Chapter Thirty-Two

April

GABE PULLED me against his wet chest, clutching me so hard I could barely breathe. I didn't care—I only held him tighter. "I've spent all day angry at myself for doing it again. For falling in love with someone who doesn't want me. Are you saying I'm wrong about that?"

He tipped my chin up. Rain sheeted over both of us, but I didn't think he cared any more than I did.

"You couldn't be more wrong," he said, a genuine, beautiful smile stretching across his face. "April, you're everything to me, but it took almost losing you for me to see that. I love you."

"I love you too, Gabe."

He clenched his eyes closed as he drew me against him again. I wrapped my arms around his waist, squeezing hard.

He kissed the top of my head and murmured against my hair. "Oh, my April. I couldn't take it if you left me."

My eyes snapped open as his words hit me full force, only now realizing this was why he'd shied away from relationships. Why he was so shattered right now. So afraid of my reaction.

Every woman he'd ever loved had left him.

First his mother, then his wife.

"Gabe... I'm not going anywhere."

His arms tightened around me. "When Dad told me about the loan, my head was so screwed up, and my thoughts were jumbled. I worried about the resort. The island. Hailey. The rest of my family. And most of all, you. You're right, I should have realized how not answering would make you feel. I'm so sorry. Please forgive me."

Adrenaline coursed through my veins, and the sound of my pulse roared in my ears. Gabe Markham loved me? Could I really trust this was real? I was dizzy from the mood swings today had wrought. A white light formed in my gut, then spread throughout my body. Pushing out the fear. The dread. "Of course I do."

Gabe clutched my face between his hands. Lowering his head, he touched his lips to mine.

They were shockingly cold.

I increased the pressure, determined to warm him up, to banish the shock that had caused him to stand in the rain like this. Our lips melted together, rain entering our mouths when we changed our angle. I ran my hands across his back, over the sodden material of his jacket. "All I've ever wanted... was to *matter* to someone." I mouthed the words against his lips.

"I can't live without you. We belong together." He kissed me harder, raking his mouth over mine.

"You're right. We do." Kissing him back, I met him measure for measure.

Eventually, I raised a hand to his cheek, which was also chilled under my fingers. I pulled back, brought to my senses. And the fact that we stood outside in the pouring rain. "You're freezing! Come inside."

He nodded, water flying from his hair.

Taking Gabe's hand, I led him back to my apartment. The room was warm and cozy after standing in the cold rain. We both dripped all over the wood floor. In the light, his face was still drawn, the strain of the past two days written all over him. He stood still and his eyes were dazed, as if he was hardly aware he was sopping wet.

"Stay here," I said. "You've got a pair of shorts upstairs and I have a sweatshirt that might fit you. I'll be right back."

I ran up the steps and ripped my sodden T-shirt and pajama bottoms off. I toweled off before pulling on a long-sleeved shirt and yoga pants, then grabbed Gabe's shorts out of a drawer. An electric current ran through me, and incoherent thoughts raced through my mind. I riffled through my closet until I found the largest sweatshirt I owned, a fuzzy blue one with Half Moon Bay Resort screen printed across the front. It was an XL, so hopefully that would be big enough. Scooping up my wet clothes, I hurried down the stairs.

When I returned to the living room, Gabe had draped his sodden suit jacket over a kitchen chair and was pulling his tie over his head. I relaxed a little at seeing him in motion again. His eyes were more focused now. I handed him the shorts and sweatshirt, setting my wet clothes on the table. "There's a towel in the bathroom you can use."

"Thanks." He dropped his eyes from mine and headed to the bathroom to change.

I crossed the room and removed the kettle from the sink, amazed at all that had happened since I'd stood here just minutes ago. My elation had passed, and now nerves fluttered back and forth through my abdomen. I could hardly process what he'd said.

What would happen now?

I set the kettle down on the counter and leaned back against the granite surface. My head was buzzing. The only man who had ever told me he loved me was the cheating bastard I'd lived with. But hearing those words from Gabe wasn't at all the same.

Because now I could appreciate the difference.

I understood instinctively that Gabe didn't use those words often. In fact, he'd told me he never wanted to say them again. For some reason, that knowledge made me feel fragile, like I might break at any moment.

Or worse, wake up to find this was all a dream.

Footsteps sounded as Gabe crossed the room, and I lifted my eyes from the floor. He stopped at the edge of the kitchen. My sweatshirt was a bit small. The sleeves ended above his wrists, and it was tight over his wide shoulders. But his posture was assured again, and confidence once more radiated from his eyes. Something else was there too —happiness.

He smiled at me. "Thanks for the clothes. This is much better."

A fine tremor ran through my body, and my foot bounced up and down on the floor. "You're welcome."

He crossed to the table and laid his wet pants and shirt over the jacket. That spurred me into action, and I padded over the floor. I swept the wet clothes into my arms. "I'll put these in the dryer. Be right back."

My washer and dryer were in a separate room off the kitchen. I tossed our clothes in the dryer, then frowned. I didn't want to ruin his suit by overheating it. Then I reconsidered. If Gabe had stood in the pouring rain, I didn't think he was overly concerned about the garment. I chose low temperature and pressed start. The purposeful motion settled my nerves somewhat.

Why am I so skittish? He just told me he loved me!

What if he didn't mean it? What if the stress of the past two days confused him?

Men like Gabriel Markham didn't fall in love with me.

I straightened, then turned around and ran right into a mountain of hard flesh. Gabe wrapped his arms around me, cradling the back of my head gently against his chest. I melted against his warmth, powerless to resist him.

He ran a hand over my wet hair. "Don't worry about the suit. If it's wrecked, I've got others. I don't wear them much anymore." His voice was even and sounded like the usual, confident Gabe, but his heart pounded under my ear. Taking a step back, he caught my face between his hands. "You haven't stopped moving since we came in here. Are you okay?"

I opened my mouth to answer, but nothing came out.

His gaze sharpened. "April?"

I cleared my throat. "Yes. No. I'm not sure. I'm afraid this isn't real. What you said to me."

"That I love you?"

I nodded, moving his hands on my face slightly.

Amusement glinted in his eyes. "You said the same thing back to me, you know."

My heart was ready to pound out of my chest. "And I meant it, Gabe."

"And I meant every word of what I said to you. Today, tomorrow, and always."

My insides melted as he bent down and pressed his lips to mine. They were much warmer now, firm and in command. The dam broke and tears spilled from my eyes, happy tears filled with hope.

Gabe broke the kiss and stared at me, a line forming between his brows. I gave him a weepy laugh. "Don't mind me. I might be crying, but I'm very happy right now. I'm just having a hard time believing this happened. That it's real."

The line disappeared and his eyes softened. "Believe it. And we have all night for me to prove that to you."

By the time Gabe led me upstairs, and we slipped naked between the sheets, my mood had cycled again. The range of emotions this man could invoke in me was stunning. Doubt and uncertainty had circled around again as I ran my trembling hands over his perfect, chiseled chest. His skin was still cool from the deluge. He rolled me onto my back, stopping halfway on top of me.

As his lips met mine, my head buzzed. I was breathing in rapid bursts, but another emotion was pushing in front of desire.

Fear.

Fear that this would all be gone come morning.

Gabe placed one large hand in the center of my chest, between my breasts. I winced, sure he could feel my hammering heart. Leaving my lips, he brushed two soft, gentle kisses over my closed eyes. "What are you afraid of?"

"I'm sorry. I'm just afraid you'll come to your senses and realize you can do so much better than me."

He rose up on one elbow, a small smile appearing. "Better than you? Better than the woman who spends her day saving people? You certainly saved me. Better than the woman my daughter adores? Better than the woman who's helped me realize what I want in life? What's important? It took the risk of losing you to finally rip my blindfold off, April. What I'm staring at now is the most important thing in the world to me."

My frantic heart finally calmed as he spoke, and he moved his hand to my breast, stroking with his fingers. My lips parted and his eyes dropped to them.

"What you and I are together is... different," he whispered. "I don't understand exactly what it is, except that I can't stand to be apart from you."

"I can't either. I've been doing everything possible to deny how I felt about you."

"Stop denying it. This is the most real thing I've ever felt in my life."

"I love you, Gabe." Warmth radiated through me in slow pulses.

"I love you too. Let me show you how much."

He kissed me again and gently parted my lips with his tongue. A soft, breathy sound escaped my throat, and I pressed my breast harder against his hand. I relaxed and let myself go, surrendering to the sensations only this man could bring out in me.

Gabe crawled down my body, taking my other breast in his mouth as he stroked and circled the other with his hand. My toes curled, desire rolling through me from my feet to my head. I ran my hands, no longer trembling, over those broad, strong shoulders.

And at last, I believed.

When he settled his head between my legs, I was more than ready for him. Gabe was completely attuned to my body, giving me exactly what I needed. As the rolling waves within me became larger and stronger, my hesitation became a distant memory. I arched my back, clenching both hands in his hair. Pushing him closer, tight against me as I called out into the room.

He left me in shuddering gasps, working his way up my body again. One of my hands was still clutching his head as the other moved in a broad sweep over his shoulders, now fiery hot. When we met eye to eye, I moved both hands to his shoulders and pushed him off, rolling on top.

"Now it's my turn to show you."

Before he could answer, I smashed my mouth to his. Rolling my hips back and forth, I trapped the hard length of him between us. A deep, wrenching groan issued from his chest and I smiled against his lips. I quickly moved downward, whisking my lips and tongue over his muscular chest and over his ridged abdomen. He hissed through his teeth as I took him into my mouth, sliding his feet up the bed. He caught my shoulders between his legs and grasped my head with both hands, guiding my movement.

I listened to every gasp, every sharp inhale. His entire body was moving in concert with me, and it gave me a tremendous sense of confidence to know what I was doing to him.

"Get up here. Now," he commanded, and I smiled as I scrambled back up. I sat up and straddled him. Holding his eyes with mine, I slowly lowered, taking him deep inside me. Gabe made another sound partway between a sigh and a moan, then closed his eyes as I moved up and down.

I watched him, studying every change of expression. It was incredibly erotic. His hands grasped my hips, moving me faster and faster.

I folded over him. "You like me on top?"

A shudder wracked his body, and he slid his knees up to trap me in place. "Yes. Don't stop."

With a light laugh, I moved my mouth to his ear. "I have

no intention of stopping." I flicked my tongue in his ear as I slammed him hard within me. He cried my name, which brought heat coursing through me again, radiating outward from my center.

I grabbed his arms and thrust them out sideways from his body, interlacing my fingers with his. Gabe tried to lift his arms, but I pushed back hard, preventing him. A slow smile came across his face as he complied, relaxing and holding on to my hands. He was more than strong enough to overpower me, but he was enjoying every moment of what I did to him. Enjoying doing my bidding. As I pressed the side of my cheek to his, his stubble rubbed my tender skin.

The rough burning lit me even more aflame.

We moved together, our fingers interlaced and holding tight. As rain poured onto the roof above, I gave him every last inch of me, and he did the same.

We both believed.

Chapter Thirty-Three

Gabe

A BEAM of golden morning August sunlight slanted into the kitchen of the Big House as Hailey tore out the door, eager to prepare for our day's adventure. She slammed it behind her, and I winced. "Sorry about that."

Nona smiled at me over the rim of her coffee cup. "No need to apologize. She's exactly what's been missing from this place."

Two weeks had passed since that momentous night on the bluff. Weeks that had brought changes. Happy changes. April and I had settled into our new, deeper relationship. She'd had no repeats of the disbelieving hesitancy she'd shown after I told her I loved her. I intended to make sure she never had reason to doubt me again.

With a smile, I reached out next to me and cradled my hand over the back of April's neck, luxuriating in the soft strands of hair under my fingers. Only the three of us were left from breakfast.

"You need anything before we go?" I asked her.

She shrugged one shoulder. "I can grab the gear when we head down to the dock."

Nona, wearing her fancy new black snakeskin boots, alternated her gaze between the two of us. "I'm very happy to see you two. You make a lovely couple. Opposites in many ways but meant to be together."

One side of my mouth lifted. "Thank you for not pestering me about it too much. You showed remarkable restraint."

Nona's eyes sparkled. "I helped raise you, so I'm no stranger to how you respond to situations. If I'd pushed you, you would have only buried yourself deeper in the sand. April was the one with the shovel, not me."

I laughed, squeezing my hand on April's neck as we shared a long look. "She sure was." I turned back to my grandmother. "I was so afraid to let someone have that kind of power over me. To lose control."

Nona's smile disappeared, and she regarded me seriously. "Control is an illusion, Gabriel. None of us is in control. The best we can hope for is to find another person to make the journey more... enjoyable? You two look like you enjoy yourselves."

All three of us laughed at that. I tipped back the last of my coffee and pushed to my feet. "We'd better collect Hailey. By now, she's probably packed enough for a one-week cruise."

As April and I walked down the hill, I pulled her close to kiss her temple. "I was so afraid to give up my power. But instead, you set me free completely."

She reached up to clasp the hand of the arm I'd draped across her shoulder. "Same here. When I moved to Calypso Key, I was hoping for a new start. I had no idea I'd find a completely new family."

. . .

"Come on! I want to see them again!" Hailey breathed hard as she dog-paddled in front of April and me, bouncing her gaze between us.

"Calm down, angel," I said with a laugh. "We will. You can do better than dog paddling, you know."

She cocked her head, then relaxed, moving her arms in sweeping strokes as she tipped upright and treaded water.

April laughed beside me. "Much better."

"What are they called again?" Hailey asked her.

"They're baby French angelfish. It's unusual to see half a dozen like this together. Let's dive down again."

After placing our snorkels in our mouths, Hailey grabbed onto my arm, and we followed April down four feet. We were at one of the regular resort snorkeling sites, and *Indigo Dreams* sat moored a short distance away. An isolated bommie lay several feet below, the bottom of it at fifteen feet. Ripples of pure white sand surrounded the multicolored coral explosion.

The round fish were striking, and I located them right away. About three inches long, they were coal black with vivid electric-yellow bars. And very different from the adult version, whose yellow accents were limited to its pectoral fins and the margins of its scales. April hovered, hardly moving at all in her weight belt.

Beside me, Hailey gripped my arm as she gave an excited squeak. The school of fish milled about, nipping at the coral outcropping. After we surfaced for air, I glanced at the sun high overhead. We'd been in the water for nearly an hour, and I was waterlogged.

"Let's head to the beach and have lunch," I said. "You

two go on ahead and I'll get the backpack with the supplies."

I swam back to the boat as they headed to a gorgeous stretch of deserted sand a short distance away. We were snorkeling just off a deserted key whose small beach was a dream for picnics. Climbing back aboard, I shrugged into a watertight backpack and hopped back in. I felt the extra weight immediately and put my feet down to walk as soon as I was able to.

April and Hailey found a nice shady spot and I pulled a blanket from the backpack before spreading it out. After handing out sandwiches and sodas, we settled in to eat. I was struck by how happy I was. Just the three of us out on a family outing.

Family.

I was an incredibly lucky man. Because, even though I'd hurt April by taking off to Miami without notice, she loved me back. Hailey and I had moved back into the Barn apartment a week ago, bringing Hailey's seahorse bedding ensemble we'd purchased just after moving back to Calypso Key.

I was pleased to have my daughter's room on the opposite side of the second-story landing, which gave April and me plenty of privacy. Spending every night with April was heaven-sent, and waking up next to her every morning was every bit as fulfilling as I'd hoped.

I was now the majority owner of Calypso Key, both the island and the resort. Two days ago, I'd gone to the bank in Key West and paid off Dad's loan.

In full.

I had plenty of cash available to start the renovations I had in mind, beginning with the beach cottages. The day I'd made the full balloon payment had been full of ups and downs for me. I'd felt tremendous relief knowing the island, resort, and Markham legacy were all intact. Hopefully forever.

But signing the new paperwork at our lawyer's office that afternoon with Dad had been terribly uncomfortable. I'd felt like I was stealing his birthright.

He'd just stared at me. "It's your birthright too, Gabe. And Hailey's."

And that was what finally made me sign my name. I was securing my daughter's future. And whatever future April and I would have together. And in a flash of a pen, I became the fifty-one percent majority shareholder.

I was further comforted by the obvious change in Dad. In just one week, he looked years younger. He was out on *Reel Deal* nearly every day, either guiding or fishing for himself.

Hailey carefully wrapped up her empty sandwich paper and put it in the backpack. "Can we go by Maia's when we get home?"

April grinned at me, and I held back a sigh. Hailey had already asked—and been denied—three times today.

"Skye was just born yesterday," I said as patiently as possible. "Give them a chance to settle in, okay? We'll go see them tomorrow. I promise."

"Meeting your cousin yesterday at the hospital wasn't enough, huh?" April asked her with a grin.

Hailey shrugged, then smiled. "I didn't realize she'd be so small!"

I grunted. "Not sure Maia feels that way." Skye Taylor had been born early yesterday. She had been average size and the birth had gone well for both mother and child. All of us had given thanks for that.

Hailey pursed her lips together and alternated her gaze

between us. "I just want to repeat that if you two want to give me a brother or sister, I'm okay with that."

I stared at her. She just stared back, finally giving me a sweet, innocent smile that didn't fool me for a second. "If we do, you'll be the first to know," I said dryly as April laughed. "Let's take things one step at a time, all right?"

"I had to try, didn't I?" She batted her lashes, then grabbed her mask and snorkel. "I'm going back in!" She stood up and ran toward the shoreline.

"Wait!" April shouted, sliding across the blanket to grab the sunscreen. "You need more sunblock on your back."

With an impatient sigh, Hailey dutifully returned. I leaned back on my hands and watched as April sprayed her down with sunscreen, then patted her on the rear end. "Go. Have fun and don't go too deep."

With a shout, Hailey bounded into the ocean. April turned to me and caught me staring. She raised her brows. "What?"

"I love watching you two together. It makes me very happy."

"Me too. She's easy to love." April crawled toward me and brushed her lips over mine. "And you deserve to be happy."

She turned around and I pulled her back to rest against my chest. We watched Hailey splash around in the shallows.

"I was thinking about taking *Indigo Dreams* out for another private dive," I said, resting my cheek against her head. We'd dived together recently, and I wanted to make it a regular thing.

"You don't have to ask me twice. That new site Maia and Wyatt discovered is fantastic. You want to dive that?"

"I had something else in mind."

"Okay. What?"

"The *Benson.*"

April sat up and partially turned to stare at me. "Really? Are you sure?"

I shrugged, a smile playing at my lips. Those bright blue eyes drew me in. I was lost in them—willingly. "It's not like it's out to get me. Or my family. And someone told me it's a great dive and one of her favorites. Plus, I'll be with an expert, won't I?"

"I'd love to, Gabe. Thank you for putting your trust in me."

I thought about commenting on putting other things in her, but we were in a serious moment. I brushed an errant lock of hair off her face. "That day I drove when you had the incident with Ted was a real turning point. I was so scared something would happen to you. I was just too stubborn and blind to see it. I had to come face to face with losing you to finally admit I loved you."

"And I had to finally surrender my heart and trust you with it."

"Trust isn't easy for either of us. You trust me with your heart, and I'll trust you with my life. Let's dive that wreck."

Her smile lit her from within. I wanted to see it every day of my life.

"We'll stay shallow and on the outside of the wreck," she said. "There will still be plenty to explore."

I made a rumbling noise deep in my chest and leaned forward until our faces were inches apart. Two openings like that couldn't be ignored. "Explore, huh? Now you've got my full attention. What kind of exploring did you have in mind?"

She grinned. "Diving's not the only thing, is it? We could break out the whisky. There's still some left."

April and I had shared a glass of the Macallan 30 the night Hailey and I moved in. Only a single glass, but it had given me an idea. An amazing idea.

I smiled back at her. "Not sure there's enough for that. There are barely a couple of glasses left. But I've got plenty of Macallan 18 if you're interested."

"Mmm. Might want to wait until Hailey is sleeping in the Big House or at a friend's."

I'd had a talk with Hailey that she was free to come to our room during the night if she needed to, but she had to knock first. And what April was suggesting was something I absolutely didn't want to be interrupted. "Excellent idea. Now that I've got my bed back, I've got a lot of time to make up for."

"I slept in it first. It's my bed."

I grinned. "Never."

"All right. I'll concede the bed if you bring the whisky. Are you in or out?"

My smile widened. "Oh, I'm in, baby."

Chapter Thirty-Four

Gabe

WHEN WE WALKED into Maia and Wyatt's cottage the following afternoon, we joined the throng of family. At least it seemed like a throng. Evan stood in one corner with Dad, and our sister Stella had driven up from Key West. She held Skye in her arms, swinging her lightly. Two years younger than me, Stella had the dark Markham hair and eyes. As she rocked the baby, her hair swung, just touching her shoulders.

"Uh-oh," I said with a smile as we crossed the room. "Look who's getting baby fever."

Stella gave me a deadpan look. "Hardly. But she is very sweet." Then a smile lit her face as her attention shifted to Hailey. "And now I have not one, but two beautiful nieces!"

I took Skye as Stella wrapped Hailey up in a tight hug.

"Hi, Aunt Stella," Hailey said, grinning as she returned the embrace.

I balanced the baby along my forearm, the movement completely familiar and comforting. Glancing at my daughter, I was amazed she'd been the same size once. Happiness spread through me at the baby's warm weight. Skye had a mop of straight, medium-brown hair and dark eyes.

With my other arm, I pulled April tight against my side. "Stel, I'd like you to meet April. About time you came home so I could introduce you two."

The two women shook hands, but Stella refused to be baited. "Very nice to meet you, April." Then she turned to me. "And get that scowl off your face. You should be happy to see me, not all grouchy."

My frown deepened. "Why does everyone think I'm grouchy?"

April and Stella burst into laughter simultaneously.

"I know, right?" April said, getting hold of herself.

Stella patted my shoulder. "I might just have to come home more often. Things are picking up a lot around the old homestead."

"Good," I replied. "You should come home more often."

"I'm going to talk to Evan now. He's much nicer than you." Stella pointed a finger at me as she turned her attention back to April. "Keep this guy in line. He's all ferocious on the outside, but he's a creampuff once he knows who's boss."

April continued to laugh as I closed my eyes. "Stella, go away."

My sister whisked her hand around Hailey's elbow. "Come on, niece number one. Let's catch up with Uncle Evan." The two strolled off arm in arm. Skye mewed, so I tipped her up against my shoulder and rubbed her back.

When I turned back to April, she was watching me with a private smile on her face.

"What's that look about?"

She stepped closer and brushed a finger down Skye's cheek. "You're a real natural at this baby thing."

I shrugged. "I'm the only other person here besides Dad who's had a kid until now. I sure hope I know what I'm doing. You want to hold her?"

April nodded and took her, settling the baby in her arms. As she did, a deep, powerful warmth settled into my gut. I immediately searched out Hailey, confirming she was safe. This was my family today. Who knew what the future might bring?

Half an hour later, I stood on the back porch, nursing a Conch Republic beer. The kitchen door opened, and Wyatt grabbed a bottle of beer from a cooler sitting on the flagstone floor. He crossed the patio to lean on the railing next to me, tipping the bottle up to his mouth. A strong easterly breeze had picked up, and it wasn't forecasted to let up any time soon. Which meant I'd need to bide my time. I needed a calm, perfect tropical day for what I had in mind.

I turned to my brother-in-law. "Congratulations. Your life's about to completely change."

I expected him to smile, but Wyatt remained straight-faced as he stared at the horizon. "That's for sure. Maia made it through the birth without a hitch. I was so relieved I couldn't stop crying."

I knew well enough how becoming a father put things in perspective. "Maia is as strong as they come. You two will make great parents."

"Thanks." Then he paused, darting his eyes to mine before returning them to the water. "How do you deal with the fear, Gabe? That something could go horribly wrong?"

I followed his gaze, staring out at an ocean that had torn my family apart. But it had brought us partially back together again too. "By acknowledging that you can't always control what happens. And mostly, by appreciating every single day you get to spend with her. Every one is a miracle."

Wyatt smiled. "Are we talking about daughters or women?"

"Both."

We were silent as we stared out at the timeless sea, each occasionally taking a sip of beer.

The door opened once more, and Evan stepped out. He cracked a smile, his teeth glimmering behind his beard. "Oh, I guess I can't come out here, huh? Is this the dad zone?"

"Shut up and get over here," I said, gesturing to my other side with my head.

Grinning, Evan grabbed a beer from the cooler before leaning down on the railing too. "I was just talking to April. She knows a lot about DCS and has a way of letting me know she feels bad about what happened without making a big deal of it."

I smiled, nodding. April understood exactly how to talk to Evan, and I loved her all the more for it. I turned my head to look at him. "So, should we take bets that you're the next one to get involved?"

"Hell no! Stella's here too. Bet on her."

Evan's injury had turned him from a confident, athletic phenom into a bashful, near recluse. He didn't deserve that, and I hoped it would change.

Maybe he just hasn't met the right woman yet.

I straightened as I realized the two men I needed to talk to were standing right here.

And we had privacy.

"I need some help with a project. Can you two help me? I don't know exactly when, but it won't take long."

They both nodded.

"Sure," Evan said. "Something to do with your headboards?"

"No, but I've got several of those made now. This is something else. I need help carrying a generator and several strings of lights. And I need your know-how-to-do-everything acumen to put everything together, Evan."

He snorted and took a pull. "If you're complimenting me, it must be important."

I told them what I had in mind. My brother just stared at me for a long moment. Then he groaned, scrunching his eyes shut. When he opened them, his face fell into a deep scowl. "Great, Gabe. You do realize Nona is going to make my life hell, don't you?"

Wyatt just laughed and clapped me on the shoulder.

I broke into a full, shit-eating grin, patting Evan on the back. "Not my problem, little brother."

The kitchen door opened, and the rest of the entourage filed out.

"There you guys are!" Dad said, helping himself to a beer. Maia held Skye, and I left the rail to wrap an arm around her. Hailey and April stood on my other side. I pulled my daughter in front of me and drew April tightly against my side.

"We were just three guys watching the ocean," I said. "And it was getting a little lonely. But now that you've all arrived, we've got everything we need. Right here."

As I stared at the Big House in the distance, I swallowed the qualm that Hunter wasn't here with us. I wanted desperately for him and Evan to reconcile, but after a decade of hatred—mostly on Evan's side—I was doubtful that would ever happen.

Maia grinned up at me. "Look at you. Getting all sappy. Must be the beer."

Smiling, I met her eyes. "Congratulations, little sister."

She leaned her head against my shoulder until Skye started fussing. She rearranged the baby in her arms. Skye blinked as she stuffed her tiny fist in her mouth.

Removing my arm from Maia, I placed it on Hailey's shoulder and kissed April's head. Remembering what I'd said earlier. That every day was a miracle and always to be appreciated.

Even after I thought I no longer believed in love, someone came along to show me what a miracle truly was.

Epilogue

April

TWO WEEKS LATER

THE SKY TWINKLED with a million stars, and the Milky Way was vivid above as Gabe led me by the hand across the pool deck behind the Big House. We'd just finished dinner at Orchid, the resort's fine dining restaurant. I'd loved my grilled snapper entrée, though Gabe had frowned at his own, mumbling that Alfonso, the chef, was resting on his laurels.

Earlier today, I'd been surprised when Gabe snuck up on me. I'd been in the compressor room, adding tanks to be refilled when he came up behind me and pulled me tight against his chest.

He nibbled my earlobe. "Let's go out for dinner tonight at Orchid. After all the family time we've had the past few days, I want you all to myself for a while."

That sounded like heaven to me. After the get-together

at Maia and Wyatt's yesterday, I could do with a date night. I made an appreciative hum as I turned around in his arms and laced my fingers behind his neck. "That sounds fantastic. I imagine you can get us a table on short notice?"

"I know the owner. I can pull some strings." He tugged slightly on my bikini tie behind my neck but didn't actually untie the knot.

I laughed. "Hold onto that thought, buster."

As we approached the bluff, Gabe let go of my hand and pulled out his phone, activating the flashlight. As we were walking home after dinner, he'd asked if I wanted to go for a walk. I couldn't imagine a more beautiful night or setting, so of course I said yes. Hailey was having dinner at the Big House, so we didn't need to worry about her just yet. I glanced at the three-story structure in the background.

We can pick her up on our way back.

Gabe led me down the stone staircase, and a smile stretched my lips. "Ah. A little walk on the beach?"

"It's a perfect night to visit the Cove."

We hadn't been there since the night we made love on the beach, so I wasn't about to argue with him. I wore a form-fitting black dress with spaghetti straps, which hampered my movement slightly. Gabe kept the flashlight aimed at the stairs, so I had plenty of illumination, and he kept a tight hold on my hand to steady me.

I'd thought about asking him to dress in a suit, since the only other time I'd seen him in one he'd been soaking wet. But after I removed his suit from the dryer the morning following that momentous night, he'd tossed his tie in the trash, grumbling how much he hated wearing them. So I kept silent and had to admit there was plenty to admire with him wearing gray slacks and a long-sleeved white shirt, open at the neck.

We reached the bottom of the staircase and stepped around the rocks and onto the soft sand. I slipped off my sandals and left them at the base of the stairs. The night was very calm, and the ocean hardly made a sound as it swept ashore. A three-quarter moon rose in the east and lit the water with a ghostly hue.

I breathed a dreamy sigh. "Look at that ocean."

Gabe laughed softly. "If I know you, you want to get your feet wet. Go ahead."

I tossed a grin over my shoulder as I trotted to the shore ten feet away. With a deep inhale of the bracing air, I closed my eyes as the warm water washed over my bare feet. I soaked it all in.

Everything.

My new home. My new man. My new *life*.

I reopened my eyes to memorize the magical setting. The air was nearly silent around us, undisturbed by anything but nature.

Until a low rumble sounded behind me, accompanied by a soft glow.

I spun around and my breath froze in my lungs. The magical night had just amplified a thousand-fold.

Two strands of party lights crisscrossed ten feet above the white sand, anchored on top of four tall poles pounded into the ground. The hum was a portable generator Gabe was rising from. He tapped an icon on his phone and set it on top of the generator before holding a hand toward me.

As I ran back toward him, crossing the sand under the lights, "Fields of Gold"—the original version—began playing all around me. I reached out and clasped his hand as he pulled me against his chest.

A gentle smile lit his face. "Dance with me, beautiful woman?"

I laughed, completely awestruck, as we fell into a swaying rhythm. The overhead lights danced in his dark eyes as he clasped my waist. I circled my arms around his neck, the warm air caressing my shoulders. We fell into an easy motion—no fancy moves this time. We just swayed together to the music.

I was torn between staring into Gabe's eyes and taking in the magical setting around us. "I can't believe you did this!"

His smile faded somewhat as he raised a hand to brush my arm. "Are you cold? You've got goose bumps."

I rose onto my toes to kiss him. "I'm not cold in the slightest. I'm just stunned."

He pulled me tighter, wrapping both arms around my waist. "I wanted to do something special to celebrate what we've become."

"A family."

He nodded. "I've always thought of this as our song, even if the sand we're on is white, not gold."

"It's a good choice."

He rested his forehead against mine and we moved together. We slowly swayed in the balmy air, listening to the words of the song.

Gabe exhaled a long sigh. "I take promises pretty seriously too. And I never want you to doubt me. Or us. You and I are forever, April."

I brushed my fingers over his short hair. "I feel the same way. It took me a little while, but I believe now."

He pulled me tight again, and I rested my head against his chest for the rest of the song. The sound was coming from all around us, but I couldn't see any speakers. The generator hummed quietly, allowing the song to be easily heard.

When "Fields of Gold" ended, Gabe caught my face gently between his hands and brushed a kiss over my lips. With a smile, he broke away and headed back toward the generator. But he veered off and stopped before a small circular table I hadn't noticed.

I grinned as he lifted the bottle of Macallan 30 and poured the remainder of it into two crystal tumblers. There wasn't much more than a couple of swallows for each of us. Returning to me in the center of our lights, he handed me the glass and we clinked them together.

"There's not enough here to sip, so bottoms up, okay?" He raised a brow.

I hadn't done shots in years, but the scotch was so smooth I wasn't worried about choking and coughing on it. "I'll drink to that."

We raised our glasses together, eyes locked. The warm liquid flooded my mouth, smoky and mysterious. I swallowed quickly just to make sure I didn't try to take too much. As I tipped the glass up to get the last drips, something clinked up the side of the glass and touched my lips.

Startled, I lowered the glass and dropped my eyes.

To the diamond ring lying inside the crystal tumbler.

I gasped, my heart taking flight as I snapped my head up to stare at Gabe.

He was smiling, his eyes completely focused on me. "When I say forever, I mean it. So I just have one question. Are you in or out?"

I burst into laughter, tears springing to my eyes at a dream finally realized. "In!"

My shout echoed off the stone walls around us.

Gabe's smile widened as he took the tumbler from me and fished the ring out. He bent and set the two glasses in the sand. After rising upright again, he took my left hand and slid the ring on my third finger.

My shaking fingers made the large diamond sparkle and glitter in the overhead lights. Gabe folded my hand within his and tipped my face up with the other one. "Will you marry me?"

"Yes." This time my answer was little more than a whisper, and my eyes overflowed. I launched myself at him, and he burst into laughter as he staggered back a step before catching me.

"I love you, Gabe."

"Love you too."

"Will you play the song again?"

"Of course."

He moved back to the generator and tapped his phone. When he returned, we slipped into each other's arms again.

Except this time everything was different.

The magical night had become even more enchanted, captured by the weight resting solidly around my finger. Our shadows stretched out on the white sand, two figures dancing in each other's arms.

"How did you do all this?" I asked.

"Evan and Wyatt helped me. This generator was Evan's idea. I thought we'd have to use one of the huge, loud ones. They helped me bring everything down here, and we set it up earlier when you were on the afternoon dive."

I laughed and shook my head. "Where's the music coming from?"

His grin was huge. "Four Bluetooth speakers we buried in the sand."

Both of us broke into laughter. Gabe laughed more these days, though his grouchy exterior wasn't usually hidden too deep.

"Does Hailey know about this?"

He shook his head, still smiling. "No way. She can't keep a secret to save her life. We'll tell her tomorrow together."

"Tomorrow?"

His smile faded. "She's spending the night at the Big House. I told you—I want you to myself tonight."

Heat spread from my stomach that had nothing to do with the whisky. "Too bad we drank all the Macallan."

"We did. Good thing I have a brand-new bottle back at the Barn."

I tipped my head back and laughed, dizzy at the fact that I was Gabe's fiancée. "Oh. You took my idea to heart then?"

He pulled me tight, kissing me hard. "You have excellent ideas."

I glanced at my ring, then met those clear, dark eyes. "So do you. Fine whisky obviously mixes well with diamonds. We already know what else it mixes with... But I think I need a refresher. So I just have one question. Are you in or out?"

Gabe linked his wrists under my butt and boosted me up to eye level. His smile went straight to me. "What do you think?"

THANK you for reading VISIONS OF YOU! April and Gabe were such a fun couple to write about, and I hope you enjoyed them as much as I did. The Calypso Key series continues with BECAUSE OF YOU, Evan and Liv's story.

BECAUSE OF YOU: A Small Town Fake Relationship Romance
CALYPSO KEY SERIES

Our fake romance was born from flames. But when real feelings spark, will my real wounds destroy us?

EVAN:

I've been managing Calypso Key Resort, our family beachside retreat in the Florida Keys, for so long I can do it in my sleep—which isn't what keeps me up at night. That honor goes to Liv Jacobson, the gorgeous, curvy bakery owner I'm too shy to approach. Past wounds cut deep and I'm a shadow of the man I once was.

But when fate engulfs her bakery, I offer her a refuge, both for her and her business. After all, what are friends for? When I spin a panicked tale of needing a fake relationship, Liv shocks me by playing along.

Every shared secret, every pretend kiss, kindles a blaze that becomes dangerously real. But when my unresolved past explodes, I push everyone away, including Liv. How could a fake relationship have turned so real?

Because now, it's no longer a game—it's our shot at forever.

Grab your copy:

BECAUSE OF YOU: A Small Town Fake Relationship Romance
CALYPSO KEY SERIES

IF YOU'RE NOT QUITE ready to say goodbye to April and Gabe yet, have I got an offer for you! Sign up for my Beach Read Update to receive a glimpse of the happy couple's near future.

As a thank you for subscribing, **I'll send you a bonus scene** that peeks into Gabe and April's lives as they discuss their wedding plans. Click below to sign up:

Beach Read Update
(www.erinbrockus.com/visions)

My Beach Read Update subscribers hear about all my free content, plus exclusive offers and sales. I'd love to have you along! Plus, you'll stay up to date with cover reveals, sneak peeks, and exclusive content about *Visions of You* and other Calypso Key books!

If you're already on my list, I've got you covered! At the bottom of each newsletter is a link to all my free content for subscribers. Just find your last email from me to read this bonus, as well as any others you might have missed. Or you can simply sign up again—you'll have your bonus in a flash.

CALYPSO KEY SERIES:

MAIN NOVELS:

Visions of You: A Small Town Single Dad Romance

Because of You: A Small Town Fake Relationship Romance

Memories of You: A Small Town Second Chance Romance

Shades of You: A Small Town Forbidden Romance

ASSOCIATED SHORT STORIES AND NOVELLAS:

Traces of You: A Small Town Rivals to Lovers Romance*

* Subscriber exclusive

HALF MOON BAY SERIES:

Dive into steamy small-town romance, where passion meets paradise!

Erin Brockus writes steamy small town romances that transport readers to exotic, tropical destinations, and provide a perfect beachy getaway from everyday life. Her mature, relatable characters are impossible not to root for, and she weaves breezy romantic adventure into her stories, emphasizing scuba diving and the ocean.

Drawing on her twin passions for diving and travel, Erin infuses her characters and narratives with a sense of excitement and passion. Her idea of the perfect day involves sipping a cocktail on the beach after exploring the ocean depths.

Erin lives in Washington wine country with her husband, who is also a scuba instructor. She is currently hard at work on her next island adventure. When she's not writing, you might find her out for a run or cycling through the countryside on the next quest for adventure.